Jaci Burton is a *New York Times* bestselling author who lives in Oklahoma with her husband and dogs. She has three grown children who are all scattered around the co lover of sports, Jaci can often tell being played. She watches entirely unhealthy amount of reality TV. When she isn't on deadline, Jaci can be found at her local casino, trying to become a millionaire (so far, no luck). She's a total romantic and loves a story with a happily ever after, which you'll find in all her books.

Find the latest news on Jaci's books at www.jaciburton.com, and connect with her online at www.facebook.com/AuthorJaciBurton via Twitter @jaciburton.

Praise for Jaci Burton:

'A wild ride' Lora Leigh, No. 1 *New York Times* bestselling author

'It's the perfect combination of heat and romance that makes this series a must-read' *Heroes and Heartbreakers*

'Plenty of emotion and conflict in a memorable relationship-driv story' *USA Today*

'Strong characters, an exhilarating plot, and scorching sex . . . You'll be drawn so fully into her characters' world that you won want to return to your own' *Romantic Times*

'A beautiful romance that is smooth as silk . . . leaves us beggin for more' *Joyfully Reviewed*

'A strong plot, complex characters, sexy athletes, and non-stop passion make this book a must-read' *Fresh Fiction*

'Hot, hot, hot! . . . Romance at its best! Highly recommended!' *Coffee Table Reviews*

'Ms Burton has a way of writing intense scenes that are both sensual and raw . . . Plenty of romance, sexy men, hot steamy loving and humor' *Smexy Books*

'A wonderf[...]d!' *The Roman[...]*

'Spy the name Jaci Burton on the spine of a novel, and you're guaranteed not just a sexy, get-the-body-humming read, but also one that melds the sensual with the all-important building of intimacy and relational dynamics between partners'
Romance: B(u)y the Book

'The characters are incredible. They are human and complex and real and perfect' *Night Owl Reviews*

'As usual, Jaci Burton delivers flawed but endearing characters, a strong romance and an engaging plot all wrapped up in one sexy package' *Romance Novel News*

By Jaci Burton

Hope Series
Hope Smoulders (e-novella)
Hope Flames
Hope Ignites
Hope Burns
Love After All
Make Me Stay
Don't Let Go
Love Me Again
One Perfect Kiss

Play-by-Play Series
The Perfect Play
Changing The Game
Taking A Shot
Playing To Win
Thrown By A Curve
One Sweet Ride
Holiday Games (e-novella)
Melting The Ice
Straddling The Line
Holiday On Ice (e-novella)
Quarterback Draw
All Wound Up
Unexpected Rush
Rules of Contact
The Final Score
Shot On Gold

One
Perfect Kiss

Jaci BURTON

HEADLINE
ETERNAL

Published by arrangement with Berkley,
a member of Penguin Group (USA) LLC.
A Penguin Random House Company.

First published in Great Britain in 2018
by HEADLINE ETERNAL
An imprint of HEADLINE PUBLISHING GROUP

1

Cataloguing in Publication Data is available from the British Library

ISBN 978 1 4722 4790 2

Offset in 11.6/12.2 pt Times LT Std by Jouve (UK), Milton Keynes

Printed and bound in Great Britain by CPI Group (UK) Ltd, Croydon, CR0 4YY

Headline's policy is to use papers that are natural, renewable and recyclable
products and made from wood grown in well-managed forests and other
controlled sources. The logging and manufacturing processes are expected
to conform to the environmental regulations of the country of origin.

HEADLINE PUBLISHING GROUP
An Hachette UK Company
Carmelite House
50 Victoria Embankment
London EC4Y 0DZ

www.headlineeternal.com
www.headline.co.uk
www.hachette.co.uk

*To every amazing, hardworking teacher,
I appreciate every one of you for infusing a love
of learning in your kids. What you do matters.*

One
Perfect Kiss

Chapter 1

ZACH POWERS READ over the list of grades, then scanned down to his two football players who had been placed on academic probation. His gaze narrowed when he saw which teacher had been the one to put them there.

Josie Barnes.

"Dammit, Josie." He clenched the paper in his fist and left his classroom in search of the woman who was trying to ruin Hope High School's football season.

He found her in her classroom, looking work-like and gorgeous in her long skirt and white short-sleeved button-down shirt, so unlike the outfits she wore outside the class-room. Here at school, she was buttoned up and professional, always nodding in greeting in the halls but never giving away anything other than polite teacher-to-teacher glances.

When they were out with their friends, though, she flirted with him. Nothing had happened between them yet, but Zach knew she liked him.

He liked her, too. Or he had, until now.

He knocked on her classroom door. She looked over and waved him in. She always wore her hair cut short, which did nothing to detract from her stunning face. In fact, it brought out the amazing sea blue of her eyes and her generous mouth, which today was painted a pale, shimmering pink. Which he shouldn't be noticing while they were at school, but whatever. Classes were out for the day, so her room was empty.

If she'd been his teacher, he would have never been able to concentrate. Like right now, when he was supposed to be pissed off about those grades.

He opened the door and closed it behind him, then walked toward her desk and stopped to hover over it.

"What's this all about?" he asked, shaking the paper at her.

She looked at his hand, then raised her gaze to his face. "What's what all about?"

"You put Paul Fine and Chase Satterfield on probation."

She leaned back in her chair and gave him a confused look. "I have no idea what you're talking about."

He dropped the paper on her desk. She opened it up, read it, then lifted her gaze to his. "Oh. Football."

She said the word *football* as if she had no idea what the word meant. That word meant everything to him.

"Yeah, football. You know, the thing that's my life here."

"Huh. I thought teaching history was your life here." She finished her statement with an arched brow.

He narrowed his gaze at her. "Don't play games with me, Josie. Paul's my best wide receiver, and Chase is my center."

"Uh-huh. Whatever. We're four weeks into the semester, and Paul's missing four assignments. Chase is missing five. Which means neither of them is passing my class. I'm just doing what the school board requires by submitting progress reports."

Zach clenched his jaw. Bureaucracy always got in the way of his players doing what they did best—playing football. Some of the other teachers understood this and were more . . . lenient with grades for his players, giving them a sliding scale to work with so they could catch up. But those instances were typically for players who were on the cusp.

Five assignments? Jeez.

He took another glance at Paul's and Chase's grades in the class. They were both Fs.

It wasn't like you could "sliding scale" your way up to a passing grade when you were already so far down the hole that the fires of hell were licking at your ass.

Damn kids.

"How bad is it?" he asked.

"Take a look."

She took out her grade book and showed him. "Chase has only turned in one assignment. Paul two. And the two Paul turned in—" She looked up at him. "I tried to give him the benefit of the doubt, Zach, but honestly? They were bad. I couldn't even say he was phoning it in. He hasn't even picked up the phone."

This was where he needed to remind himself these were high school students. High school students who had potential college careers ahead of them, which meant they'd have to be able to do the academic work.

He unclenched his jaw. "Fine. Tell me what they need to get done, and I'll make sure it's turned in before you submit this week's grade report."

Probation was one thing. If his players were suspended, they'd be off the team for God only knew how long. Bad for them, very bad for Hope High's Eagles.

"Sure." She got out a piece of paper, opened her laptop, and jotted down the list of assignments. When she handed it to Zach, she looked up at him. "And, Zach, make sure they're the ones doing the assignments, okay?"

"What the hell does that mean?"

"It means not bullying any of my stellar students to do the work for them. Or, even worse, buying the work online. Because I'll know it if they do."

"Christ, Josie. What kind of guy do you think I am? What kind of guys do you think my athletes are?"

She sighed. "Let's just say I've seen students like this before. They get in a jam and they're desperate, and more than willing to do anything—and I mean anything—to turn in passing work."

He laid his hands on her desk and leaned in. "My guys aren't like that. And if they are, they won't play for me for long."

She didn't flinch. She held his gaze. "I guess you should make sure you know your players well, then."

"I intend to, because these two will be sitting with me every day after school this week doing these assignments while their teammates are on the practice field. So I can guarantee you, Ms. Barnes, that when this work is turned in, it'll be work that both Paul and Chase have done themselves."

Her lips lifted. "I'm glad to hear that. And I'm sorry about all that classwork you'll have to do this week. If you need any research assistance, feel free to give me a call."

"I think I can handle it. After all, I've been to school myself, ya know."

She laughed. "Yes, I'm sure you're great and all. But that was a long time ago. And I require a lot of my students."

"How hard can it be?" He scanned the assignments and bit back a curse.

"Poetry? A journal of thoughts and feelings? Aww, hell, Josie."

She smiled. "You did say you were going to help them, right?"

He pushed off the desk and pivoted, already halfway to the door. "Yeah, yeah."

Once out the door, he stopped and read the assignments again.

Poetry. Journals. Ugh.

A small part of him understood why Paul and Chase were blowing off the homework. He'd hated poetry in English class. All that evaluation of shit that had never made sense to him. But he'd sucked it up and done it. And had maybe learned a few things in the process. He might not have enjoyed it, but he'd done the work. Because not doing the work would have meant he couldn't play football. And he'd have done anything to play football.

High school football had gotten him into college so he

could play football there. And college football had paved the way for him to play pro football. All of which had taken a hell of a lot of sweat and hard work. Some of that work had been schoolwork. And some of that schoolwork hadn't been fun, but it had been necessary to get him where he'd wanted to be, which was the pros.

He needed to remind his kids of the long-term goal. Plus, not doing the work was lazy, and he wouldn't accept that from any of his players.

He headed toward the field.

Time to kick a couple of asses from here to next week.

JOSIE PONDERED HER conversation with Zach all the way home, then ended up gravitating toward the library, where she hoped Jillian Reynolds would be working this afternoon.

She'd made friends with so many wonderful women in the time she'd been here in Hope, Oklahoma. And friendship was a new thing to her. She hadn't had much of that in her lifetime. Or any friendship, really.

But she and Jillian had grown closer in the past few months, likely because out of their group of women friends, they were the two single ones. Everyone else was either coupled up or married, and several of their friends had kids or were expecting. So Josie and Jillian had started hanging out more and more lately.

Plus, it didn't hurt that they had a lot of things in common. Jillian was the head librarian, and she had an appreciation for all forms of literature. A language arts teacher, Josie had loved books and reading from the time she was a kid. She had started hanging out in her local library as a means of escape from family drama, but her refuge had turned into a love of reading that had developed into a voracious appetite.

She could still remember Elda, the librarian at her small-town library, who'd introduced her to countless books when she was a kid. She'd fallen in love with classic literature and poetry and mysteries and romances and science fiction and fantasy. She'd returned day after day to turn one book in and check out another. She'd also spent hours at the back of the library reading and soaking in the quiet.

After all, no one was drunk or high or screaming at her while she was there. It was peaceful, and she could lose herself in a story of magic or fantastical worlds or escape into romantic escapades.

Reading had been her life, and the library had been her salvation. While at the library, her head in a book, her mind in a story, she was someone else. She could *be* somewhere else. She could escape.

And that had been nirvana. At least for a couple of hours.

Meeting Jillian had evoked warm memories of those early years because Jillian ran her library the same way Elda had all those years ago. She was fierce and protective and fostered a love of books in every kid she met.

Just walking into the Hope library settled a feeling of calm over her. Josie always thought it was the smell of books that made her feel that way. There was nothing like it anywhere else.

She spotted Jillian in her office at the back of the library, so she headed in that direction.

Jillian was working on her computer. Josie didn't want to interrupt her, but Jillian happened to look up and smiled, then motioned for her to come in.

Josie opened the door, then closed it behind her. "You looked busy. I didn't want to bother you. I just stopped in to say hello."

"It's okay. I was ordering some books."

Josie sighed and took a seat. "Ordering books. How fun."

"Always. How was your day?"

"Good, mostly. Until after school when Zach came into my room and told me I was ruining his football team."

Jillian leaned back in her chair. "Really. And how did you manage to ruin his team?"

"A couple of his players aren't passing my class, so now they're on probation."

"Oh, Josie. How could you? Don't you know football is king here?"

"Uh-huh. Well, in my classroom, literature is king, and I'd like my students to do their assignments. And actually pass the class."

"So did you two have words? Was it a hot and passionate argument?"

Jillian always turned any heated discussion into a hot and passionate argument. In her imagination, anyway.

"No. I gave him their assignments, and he's going to work with them this week so probation doesn't turn into a sus-pension."

"How disappointing. I mean, not for the kids, of course. But I was hoping you two would end up making out on your desk."

Josie laughed. "I don't think the principal would appreci-ate that."

"Who cares what the principal appreciates? I would have appreciated it immensely."

"I think you need a hot guy to come make out with you across *your* desk."

"Don't I ever." Jillian waggled her brows.

"He's out there for you somewhere."

Jillian waved her hand. "Not looking for him. I'm busy."

Josie sighed. "Aren't we both. Which doesn't mean I'd turn down some hot guy throwing me across anything and making out with me."

Jillian pointed a finger at her. "See? You wouldn't have turned down Zach throwing you across your desk."

Josie laughed. "That wasn't the topic of conversation at the time."

"But you like him."

"Yes, I like him. Most days, anyway. Just not this afternoon."

They fortunately got off the topic of Zach and onto other things, mainly Loretta and Deacon's deck party this week-end and what they were going to take, food-wise. Then Josie left so Jillian could get back to work.

But she still stewed about Zach on the way home. He could be so sweet to her when they were all out with their friends. Today, though, he'd been hot.

Angry hot, not sexy hot.

Then again, angry hot could be sexy. Just not when the mad was directed at her.

Of course, at school, they had to be all business. Teenagers had the uncanny ability to zero in on any type of flirting or attraction.

Working with someone you were attracted to had its disadvantages. And she didn't know how she was going to handle it. Because she and Zach had been dancing around each other for months now.

So far, nothing had happened between them other than friendly hanging out in groups with their mutual friends.

Maybe that was all it would ever be. But as she thought back, there'd been glances. And touches that felt like a lot more than just casual friendliness.

So maybe it wouldn't be just friendship between them.

It wasn't like she was looking for a relationship. The last one she'd been in had ended badly—really badly—and she wasn't looking forward to wading in those waters again.

But still . . . Zach was impossibly tall and had great biceps. She really had a thing for biceps. Plus, he was incredibly good-looking, with dark hair and those steely gray eyes that could catch and hold her attention like nothing Josie had ever experienced. That man could make her melt faster than a stick of frozen butter in the hot August sun.

So maybe she'd just dip a toe in and test the waters.

She just wouldn't go for a swim.

Chapter 2

IT HAD BEEN a tough Thursday. Zach had given a test in his American history class, and every kid had groaned about it as if they hadn't known for a week the test was coming. In his other classes his students hadn't been paying attention. Some days it seemed like all he was doing was talking to himself.

Anyone who thought teaching was easy should try it for just a day. It was always a challenge, but then you had that one good day when everything clicked and the kids really got it, and it made all the shit days worthwhile.

After he wrapped up practice for the day, he sat in his classroom with Paul and Chase, who were the only ones who hadn't been grumbling at him this week. Not after he'd laid down the law with them on Monday. He'd pretty much told him they were going to get caught up on their assignments, they were going to do the reading and all the work, and he was going to check their work first. If it wasn't good enough, they'd have to do it again.

He'd had conversations with their parents earlier in the week. Chase's parents were horrified and told Zach he could do whatever needed to be done, and that Chase would spend the entire week and weekend at home getting caught up on all his schoolwork, and that "just passing" wasn't good enough for them. Paul's parents were a little less enthusiastic about academics other than wanting to make sure Paul stayed on the football team.

Since their assignments were due in to Josie by tomorrow, he stayed and read everything. Zach wouldn't have considered anything they had written to be the best prose ever, but he hoped it was enough to get them up to a C grade.

By the time he'd finished with all of that, he needed a drink. He drove over to Bash's bar, hoping for a nice juicy steak and a tall beer.

Since Bash had expanded the bar to include food service, the place had really picked up. The No Hope At All bar had always been a popular place for the drinking crowd. Now it catered to not only the bar crowd but also couples and families.

Lou, Bash and Chelsea's Chihuahua, greeted him with a tail wag when he came through the door.

"Hey, girl." Zach crouched down to give Lou a few rounds of petting before Lou scurried off to chase after a couple of kids who were eating in the separate dining area outside, so Zach made his way up to the bar and pulled up a seat.

Bash was there and had just served a drink to a customer. He spotted Zach and smiled.

"Didn't expect to see you here the night before a big game," Bash said.

"I had a long day. I need a tall glass of beer. And a thick steak."

Bash poured the beer and placed it in front of him. "I'll get that steak ordered for you. Medium rare, with fries, right?"

Zach grinned. "You got it."

While Bash was off putting in the order, Zach swiveled around on the barstool to check out the crowd.

He'd grown up in Tulsa, which was about thirty minutes from Hope. He'd been in Hope about a year, and he was getting to know a lot of people. He frequented Bash's bar on a fairly regular basis, so some of the regulars looked familiar to him. He smiled and waved at a few people he knew.

The door opened, and Bash's wife, Chelsea, walked in. She was pregnant, and she looked amazing, as always, her flaming red hair pulled into a high ponytail, her full-length dress flowing around her ankles as she walked. Normally, Chelsea wore those high heels that women seemed to like, but he noticed lately she'd changed to flat shoes. He couldn't imagine how hard it would be to carry a baby and maintain your balance, though he knew women were capable of anything.

He also zeroed in on Josie as she came in behind Chelsea, along with Jane Griffin. They were all teachers at Hope High, so it didn't surprise him they'd hang out together. Plus, they were all part of the group of friends that Zach hung out with. He was friends with Bash, Chelsea's husband, and Will Griffin, Jane's husband.

Chelsea saw him and headed his way while the other women grabbed a table.

Josie smiled and waved, too. He waved back. He felt a little weird about their altercation at school the other day. Or maybe it had been more of a heated conversation, since it wasn't like they had come to blows or anything.

"What's up, Zach?" Chelsea asked.

"Not much. What are you up to?"

"About fifteen pounds more than I'd like to weigh right now, but, you know. Baby."

He laughed. "You're gorgeous, as always. But don't tell Bash I said that or he might kick my ass."

"Why do I need to kick your ass, Powers?" Bash asked as he reappeared behind the bar.

"Because Zach said I'm gorgeous despite being in my third trimester of pregnancy and feeling as big as a cruise ship."

Bash's lips lifted. "You get a pass, Zach. And yeah, you are gorgeous, babe."

"I'd lean across the bar and kiss you, but . . . ugh."

Bash stepped around the bar and pulled Chelsea into his arms, laying a hot one on her. The entire bar oohed and clapped.

Chelsea blushed. "You did that on purpose."

Bash laughed. "I'll always kiss you on purpose. I'll send Monica over to the table to take your drink orders."

She sighed. "Okay. I'll just float on over to the table. See you, Zach."

"Later, Chelsea."

Lou wandered in through the dog door and followed Chelsea to the table. Chelsea picked her up and set the dog on her lap. His gaze shifted back to Bash, who smiled.

"Yeah, she treats Lou like her kid."

"Ready to add a baby to that?" Zach asked.

"Yes and no. The whole baby thing hit us like a tornado. But I'm so excited to meet our little girl."

"I'll bet you are."

"Chelsea's going to be an incredible mother. She keeps telling me she's out of her element and she has no idea what she's doing, but she's more prepared than she gives herself credit for."

Zach could see that. "She's an incredible teacher. Her students love her. She's relatable, she's got a fun sense of humor, but at the same time, she knows when to draw the line with those kids. She's going to be an amazing mother, Bash. And you'll be a great dad."

"Thanks for that. I'm just ready to hold the baby in my arms, to know she's okay and she's healthy, and to just . . . see her, ya know?"

"Yeah." Having never had kids, Zach really had no idea. But he'd been around his brother and sister-in-law and his nephew, and the whole kid thing was pretty awesome. He could imagine the excitement and anticipation Bash felt. It had to be monumental. He could see himself wanting that, too.

Someday. When he found the right woman.

Right now, all he was interested in was getting through

football season and winning State. His football team was his baby. He might have lost out on the chance to continue his pro career when he'd blown out his knee, but coaching these kids was the second career he'd never thought he'd have. Turned out he was a pretty damn good football coach. And hanging out with teenagers didn't suck, especially teenage boys who loved football as much as he did. He'd spent last season sharpening them up and getting them focused and healthy and prepped.

It was a good team. A unified team. They were tough and formidable, and they could beat anyone.

As long as everyone played.

That part needed some work, apparently.

Despite the noise level in the bar, he zeroed in on the sound of Josie's laughter. Bash had made his way over there. Jane's husband, Will, had come in and was now sitting with them.

Since they were all his friends, normally he'd go over and join them.

So what was stopping him from doing that?

Maybe after he had his steak. After all, they were just drinking, and he didn't want to eat in front of them.

Yeah, that was it.

Or maybe you're avoiding Josie.

He frowned at his inner voice and swiveled around in his chair to check out the TV. There was a baseball game on, so he focused on that.

"Why aren't you sitting with us?"

He looked up to find Josie standing next to him. She looked pretty—hell, she always looked pretty. Tonight she had on a flowery long skirt and a black top, and she wore silver bangles on her wrists that made him want to touch her arm.

Not that she had to be wearing jewelry to make him want to touch her.

Plus, she smelled good, like some kind of seductive wild-flower.

"I was watching the game."

"You can do that with us."

"I ordered a steak, and I didn't want to eat in front of all of you."

She slanted an exasperated look at him. "We've ordered food, too, Zach." She laid her hand on his arm. "Come on. Sit with us."

Obviously, he was being a standoffish jerk for no reason. He grabbed his beer. "Sure."

He followed her to the table.

"Hey, buddy," Will said. "I didn't see you when I came in."

"What's up, Will?"

"Keeping the highways safe, as always."

There was an empty chair next to Josie, so he sat there.

"Tell Zach about the lady you pulled over today," Jane said. "Oh, and hi, Zach."

"Hey, Jane. How are you feeling?"

Jane laid her hand over her belly. "Much better now that I'm through the first trimester. I don't feel like barfing up everything I eat." She winced and looked around. "Sorry I was so graphic."

"Please," Chelsea said. "Quit worrying. You're in tough company. Dudes don't care, and I definitely don't since I've been through it. Unless Josie is squeamish."

"Stomach like iron over here," Josie said. "I don't think you can be a teacher and have a weak stomach."

Chelsea nodded. "Isn't that the truth? I remember my first few weeks as a student teacher. One of the kids had the flu and puked all over his desk."

"He couldn't have raised his hand and asked to leave the room?" Jane asked.

"Come on, Jane," Josie said. "That would have been too easy."

Zach grinned. "At least it came out that end."

Josie gave him a horrified look. "I don't think I want to hear whatever horror story you have."

"No, really, you don't."

"I dunno," Bash said. "I might."

"Let's just say some students take their test taking very seriously," Zach said. "Maybe too seriously."

"Like maybe forgoing an urgent need to use the bathroom?" Will asked.

Zach nodded.

Chelsea wrinkled her nose. "Ew."

Just then, their food arrived.

"On that gross topic, I'm going back to the bar," Bash said with a grin. "Enjoy your dinner."

Bash rubbed Chelsea's shoulder, then disappeared.

"I guess we'll find out just how ironclad that stomach of yours is, won't we?" Zach asked.

Josie looked over at him. "You think stories like that bother me?"

"I don't know. Do they?"

"I'm made of much stronger stuff than that." She picked up her fork and dug into her fish.

"Strong stuff, huh?" Zach asked.

She swallowed and took a sip of her wine. "Yup."

"I'll have to test that theory sometime."

She nodded. "Go for it."

Zach enjoyed a good challenge, so he filed that away in the back of his mind. Will told them his highway story for the day, which had been forgotten earlier, and then they all launched into conversation. One of the reasons he liked his group of friends was the conversation. It always flowed from one person to the next. Everyone joined in, everyone was welcome, and it was always easy, as if they'd been friends forever.

"How's the team, Zach?" Will asked after he swallowed a bite of his burger. "Game ready for tomorrow night?"

"Yeah. Are you all coming to the game?"

"We'll be there," Jane said. "Ryan and Tabby wouldn't miss it, especially with Ryan playing football on the middle school team this year and Tabby cheerleading. Tabby will want to watch the high school cheerleaders. They're like her personal heroes right now."

"Loretta said she and Deacon were coming," Chelsea said. "Hazel loves football."

"Everyone loves football," Bash said as he stopped back by. "Except for Chelsea."

"Hey." Chelsea tilted her head back and leaned against Bash. "I love football. Sort of. I'm learning to love it, aren't I?"

Bash squeezed her shoulder. "You're doing a great job."

"I'll have you know that I am fully aware that Hope High's Eagles are undefeated in the three games they've played this season."

Zach grinned at Chelsea. "See, Bash? She's following the school team."

"I'm impressed," Bash said.

"It's not like I can avoid knowing that. All the kids are buzzing about it. So we're going to do a section on statistics in each of my math classes and start following the team and players. And maybe throw some pro football statistics in there as well."

"Ooh, that's such a great idea," Jane said. "I'm stealing your idea for my math classes."

"Go right ahead."

Zach loved the idea of Chelsea and Jane using football stats. "I like anything that tracks back to football," Zach said. "Unfortunately, I don't think I can make that work for my history classes."

Josie laughed. "Unless you do the history of football."

"I doubt that would fly with the administration."

"Probably not."

"Who wants refills?" Bash asked.

Zach did, and so did everyone else, so Bash waved the server over, and then he left to return to the bar.

"What about you, Josie?" Zach asked.

"What about me?"

"How can you weave football into your language arts classes?"

"I can't. Unless we read some books on some athletes who played football."

"How about a biography on Jim Thorpe?" Jane suggested.

Josie's eyes brightened. "Now, that's an outstanding idea. Native American, Oklahoman, Olympian, pro football player. There's a lot to study."

"So many discussion points," Zach said. "He even played a college football game against future president Dwight D. Eisenhower."

Josie got out her phone and started typing in some notes. "You're so right. I'm going to look up some books and make a curriculum adjustment. I think my students would be fascinated, and you're right, Zach. So many discussion points." She looked up at him. "Maybe I could even get some of your players interested in reading a book about Jim Thorpe."

Zach nodded. "If my players aren't interested in a biography about Thorpe, I'm kicking them off the team."

Will laughed. "Let me know how that goes."

"Oh, he's just mad because a couple of his players are on probation and I put them there."

"Oh yeah?" Will asked.

"That's about to change," Zach said. "I read their papers."

Josie put her phone back in her purse. "So they're caught up?"

"They are. Their writing isn't Hemingway or anything, but hopefully it's good enough. Their assignments will be on your desk in the morning."

"I look forward to reading them. Thanks for caring enough about the boys to work with them this week."

He shrugged. "I need them playing football."

"And that was the only reason?"

The only one he was giving her. "They need to pass. That's all I care about."

"I see. Okay then, I'll grade the papers and let you know."

He caught that look of disappointment on her face and hated seeing it there, but this wasn't the time or place to get into it with her.

Later, he'd talk to her about how important it was to see his kids succeed, whether on the field or in the classroom. His only goal was to graduate these kids and have them live their lives successfully, either as football players or accountants or scientists or baristas or construction workers.

He wanted successful, happy kids. He didn't care how they got there.

After dinner, Chelsea left, and so did Jane and Will since they had to pick up their kids.

Which meant it was just Josie and him.

"Would you like to come over to my place for a drink?" she asked.

He didn't understand her. "I thought you were mad at me."

She frowned. "Why would I be mad at you?"

"About the kids."

"I don't necessarily agree with you about your stance on high school sports and your students, Zach. But that's the teacher in me. It has nothing to do with how I feel about you outside the classroom. In case you didn't notice, we *are* outside the classroom."

"So you can separate the two."

She gave him a direct look. "I can. Can you?"

He wanted to spend time with her, and she was a totally different person outside of school. That was the Josie he wanted to get to know better. "Yup."

"Then is that a yes?"

"It is."

She gave him the kind of smile that made his gut clench. "Then follow me home."

He was looking forward to seeing her house. And seeing where things went with Josie when he got there.

Chapter 3

JOSIE HADN'T HAD a guy over to her house since she'd moved to Hope several months ago.

Actually, she hadn't been with a guy since her breakup with her boyfriend in Atlanta more than two years ago. She hadn't wanted to have anything to do with a man. She'd washed her hands of them, figuring they weren't worth her time. Until she'd met Zach. He'd been kind and funny, and they'd made an instant connection. A friends kind of connection, which had made her feel safe. Though there'd been an attraction between them right away, too. It was just that she hadn't felt pressured to do anything about it, because she'd enjoyed being friends with him, getting to know him a bit.

But that chemistry thing had lingered all through the summer. And now? It was front and center. Like a whoa type of zingy chemistry that had made her take a step back and think about how long it had been since she'd even been kissed, let alone all the other fun things she could do with the opposite sex.

Don't make a big deal out of this, Josie. It's just drinks. With Zach. Who's your friend. That's all.

Who was she kidding? She totally had it bad for Zach and had ever since this past summer when they'd all hung out together. The weekend they'd been together with all their friends at the lake had cemented her attraction to him. Everyone else had been coupled up, and she and Zach had naturally ended up spending time together. It hadn't been awkward at all. In fact, it had been . . . perfect.

Nothing had happened between them. Even the times they'd found themselves alone, Zach had been a total gentleman and had never made a move on her.

Unfortunately. Because if he'd wanted to kiss her, Josie would have been more than receptive to the idea.

She tossed her keys on the table just inside the front door, then turned and watched as Zach pulled his truck into her driveway and got out.

Seriously, he took her breath away. He was tall and lean, and he had muscles, too, but not in that "Hey, where did your neck go?" sort of muscly way. He had the kind of body a woman wanted to get her hands on.

Or at least this woman. Plus, he had a head of dark, thick hair with just a sprinkle of gray at his temples, and that intrigued her in a way that made her want to touch.

Oh, she wanted to touch. All of him. All over.

He smiled as he made his way up the steps and onto the porch. "Great house, Josie."

"Thanks. It's homey. Oh, and be careful of Tumbleweed."

He looked around. "You have tumbleweeds in your living room?"

She laughed. "No. Tumbleweed is the cat. You're not allergic to cats, are you?"

"Not that I'm aware of. But I don't see a cat."

"That's because he doesn't want you to see him. He doesn't particularly like people. Come on into the kitchen. Beer or wine?"

He followed her into the kitchen. She pulled a bottle of wine from the cabinet, then turned to look at Zach.

"Beer is fine with me if you have it."

"I do."

Zach heard a rumbling noise and looked around for the source but couldn't find it. It seemed to be coming from under the dining room table, but since the room was dark, he couldn't tell for sure.

Until he saw glowing eyes looking right at him.

"It's staring at me."

Josie handed him his beer. "What's staring—oh, Tumbleweed. He's not very trusting. His former owner dumped him at the shelter because he's old and his fur was unmanageable. And he had an attitude. Poor baby. He seriously looked like a giant tumbleweed of matted fur when I got him."

"So, what did you do?"

"I took him to the groomer, who very patiently removed about five pounds of matted fur from him. Now he's gorgeous."

"I thought you said he didn't like people."

"He liked Casey, the groomer. She took all day being so sweet with him."

"Uh-huh."

They walked by on their way into the living room. As he walked past the dining room table, a white paw swiped at his feet from under the table. He nearly spilled his beer.

"Shit," he muttered.

The cat growled, low and menacing.

He was going to have to keep a wary eye on that cat.

Josie took up a spot on the sofa, so Zach sat on the other end.

"He really is very sweet and cuddly," she said. "Once he gets to know you."

Zach took a sip of his beer but kept his eye on the dining room table with its glowing eyes.

"You don't like cats?"

He slowly shifted his gaze toward her. "Don't know. Never had one."

"I never had one of my own, but I always loved my friends' cats. And random wild ones I'd meet when I was—"

He waited while she paused and looked at the table, then brought her gaze back to him.

"When I was wandering the neighborhoods as a kid."

"Huh. I never had pets."

She pulled her legs up behind her on the sofa. "Oh, that's too bad. I want to have a lot of animals."

"So, like a cat lady, with your rocking chair and sweater?"

"Funny. No. Just as many as I can handle. Mostly animals that no one else wants."

He cocked his head to the side. "Why?"

She shrugged. "Because everyone wants the cute puppy or the kitten, and they bypass old or frail animals. But those animals need a home and love, too."

There was that clench in his gut again.

"You're something."

She gave him a curious look. "Is that a good something or a bad something?"

He was about to answer, but a flash of something gray and white attacked his tennis shoe. And his ankle. With claws.

He leaped up off the sofa. "Sonofabitch."

"Oh no. Did he hurt you?"

"He dug his claws into my ankle."

"Aww, I'm sorry. Are you all right? Do I need to get you a Band-Aid?"

"It's okay. I'm fine." He glared at the cat.

Josie cast a warm glance at the animal. "That wasn't very nice, Tumbles."

The cat leaped onto the back of the sofa, winding its way toward Josie's shoulder before settling on the arm of the sofa to lick its paws.

The thing that attacked him was a dark white color, had a bushy tail and some bald spots on its skin. And a face that looked like it had been smashed in by a car bumper.

Frankly, it was the ugliest cat Zach had ever seen. If it was even a cat.

Josie swept her hand slowly up and down the thing's back. "Cute, isn't he?"

"That cat is ugly as fuck, Josie."

"He is not."

"Come on. He's a train wreck."

She continued to pet the thing, which made vibrating noises. "Okay, he has some issues. But he's incredibly lovable and affectionate."

"I'm pretty sure my ankle is bleeding."

She looked down at his feet. "Is it really?" She got up, and the cat scampered off to its lair under the dining room table.

She bent down and lifted the leg of his jeans. "Let me see."

"I was kind of kidding about the bleeding part."

"But he scratched you. I'm sorry about that. Cat scratches sting."

Having a beautiful woman on her knees between his legs made him forget all about the sting of a cat scratch and put his mind on other, more pleasurable things.

"My ankle's fine, Josie."

She sat on her heels and looked up at him. "Try being nice."

"I am nice."

The cat growled its disagreement. Zach really wanted to growl back, but instead he held out his hands for Josie.

"Come on," he said, lifting her to stand. "Show me the rest of your house."

"Are you sure you don't want me to put something on your ankle?"

"I think I can handle a couple of scratches, but thanks."

"Okay. Well, you've seen the kitchen and the dining room. There's a screened-in porch that leads out from the kitchen." She opened the door and led him out to what was a small but nice porch.

"I know you can't see it because it's dark, but I have a huge backyard. Great for animals."

"Will you let the Prince of Darkness out there?"

She frowned. "The—oh, Tumbleweed? No. He'll remain an indoor cat. I don't want him disappearing on me."

"Too bad."

She nudged him with her shoulder. "You're mean."

He gave her a gentle nudge in return. "Am not."

"Anyway, there's plenty of room for other animals."

"You have other animals?"

"Not yet. But I will."

"Hopefully they'll be nicer than Beelzebub."

She shook her head. "Come on, whiner."

They went back inside, and she led him through an arched doorway and down the hall. "There's a bathroom here, and two bedrooms, and the master is at the end of the hall."

She paused.

"Afraid to show me the inner sanctum?" he asked.

Her brows popped up. "Is that some kind of euphemism for me showing you my goods?"

He laughed. "No. I meant your bedroom."

"Oh. I don't know. I might want to save that for some other time."

"Why? Do you have some kind of sex dungeon in there?"

Her lips curved. "Do I look like a sex dungeon kind of girl?"

He leaned in closer. "I'm not sure if there's a certain look a woman has to have in order to possess a sex dungeon. I'll bet all kinds of people in all walks of life have one."

"Is that right?"

"Sure. Lawyers and flight attendants and horticulturists and . . . I don't know. Even teachers."

"This teacher does not possess a sex dungeon."

"Okay, so maybe you have some lavender candles and furry handcuffs."

She snorted out a laugh, then turned and walked away. "If you're lucky, you might find out someday."

He'd like to find out now, especially as he watched her walk away. The sway of her hips was mesmerizing.

Instead, he sucked in a breath and followed her back into the living room, trying to ignore the hissing coming from under the dining room table.

He glared at the Evil One. When he took a seat on the sofa, Josie sat right next to him.

"Here," she said, pulling a treat from a bag and handing it to him. "Hold this in your hand, and when he comes out, he'll smell it."

"And then attack me."

She crooked a smile. "No, he'll investigate."

"And then he'll attack my hand."

"Oh my God, Zach." She rolled her eyes. "You're not afraid of a little kitty, are you?"

He refused to answer that. Instead, he took the treat from her and held it in a death grip in his hand.

"No," she said, prying his fingers open so the treat lay in his palm. "Like this."

Josie's eyes were so incredibly blue. He'd never been this close to her before. It was like falling into an azure ocean.

"You have amazing eyes."

She laid her palm across the side of his face. "Yours are pretty spectacular, too. Very stormy and fierce."

His lips curved. "They're gray. Not like yours. Like the most beautiful water I've ever seen."

Her hand lingered, her fingers traveling along his jaw. "Oh, yours are more than gray, Zach. They're expressive. Do you know they change colors?"

"No, they don't."

"Yes, they do. They lighten when you're happy, and they darken when you're pissed. Kind of like clouds in the sky."

"So you're saying I'm moody."

She let out a soft laugh. "No, I'm saying you have a myriad of expressions, and your eye color expresses that."

His gaze shifted to the white demon making its way across the coffee table. He tensed.

"Shhh," she said. "Stay relaxed, and don't make any sudden moves."

Zach looked over at Josie. "That's what people say when they're about to be eaten by a lion."

The cat leaped from the table to Josie's lap. Josie stroked his back.

"This is Zach, Tumbles," she said. "He's a friend. He's very nice, even if he does sound like a mean guy."

"Hey."

Josie looked up at him and gave him a thousand-watt smile that blinded him senseless.

"He doesn't mean to sound that way," she continued. "He just doesn't know you yet. And you don't know him. But he has a treat."

The cat sniffed, and gave Zach an ugly, distrustful glare.

Back at ya, buddy.

But then he inched forward, sniffing a little more.

"Stay still, Zach."

Like he was going to budge when Satan was on the prowl.

The cat gently pawed his hand. Without claws. What a shocker. Then he took the treat, looking up at Zach with his ugly face while he nibbled on the snack.

"You can pet him now," Josie said.

Zach looked over at Josie. "Yeah, I'm good."

"And here I thought you were a tough guy." She swept her hand down the cat's back, making it look easy. Of course it was easy. The cat liked her.

"You would belittle a man who's just trying to make inroads with your cat on his own terms?"

Josie stared at him for a good few seconds. "I'm sorry. You're right. Take your time."

He laughed. "I'm kidding, Josie."

He slid his hand forward, letting the cat sniff it. Tumbleweed leaned his head against Zach's hand and started to purr. Zach rubbed his head and ears.

Success.

And then the cat bit his hand. Not hard, but just enough to let him know not to get too comfortable. But he continued to purr, dropping his head along Zach's hand again.

"I see how it's gonna be, Satan."

Josie laughed. "Oh my God, Zach, that is not his name. And that was a love bite."

"Sure it was."

Obviously bored with the game now, Tumbleweed jumped down and sauntered around the corner. Josie rested her head in her hand, her arm bent and her elbow resting on the top of the sofa.

"So, you never had pets?"

He shook his head. "My dad was allergic to cats, and my mom said dogs would shed and track dirt into the house."

"That's a shame. Did you want them?"

"What kid didn't want pets?"

"True. You don't have any now?"

"No. Just never got around to it. When I was playing pro football, I was too busy, and I traveled half the season. I didn't think it was fair to have a pet in my life then."

"You're not playing pro football now."

She raised a good point. He shrugged. "Still too busy, I guess."

She shifted closer. "Yes, having all summer off was horrifyingly strenuous on your calendar, wasn't it?"

"Okay, fine. I get it. Why are you so pushy about me having a pet?"

"I don't know. I guess I hate seeing anyone be alone."

He gave her a smile. "That's nice of you to be so concerned about me, Josie, but I'm not lonely. And I don't need a dog. Or a cat." He looked over at Tumbleweed, who was sitting in the window, licking his paw and pretending the humans nearby didn't exist.

Definitely not a cat. Ever.

"Wait until I get a dog. You'll change your mind."

"Lots of my friends have dogs. Anytime I want to pet a dog, all I have to do is hang out with them."

"So once I get my dog, does that mean you'll hang out with me?"

He picked up her hand. It was soft, and her short nails were polished a bright shade of yellow. "You don't need to get a dog to make me want to be with you."

He heard the catch in her breath, and when she lifted her

gaze to his, he saw the way the blue in her eyes had darkened to something tempestuous and filled with desire.

"I sure like being with you, too."

One of the things Zach was great at—and he was great at a lot of things—was reading signals. Josie's signal was clanging loud and bright, and it was telling him to kiss her.

He was more than ready to kiss her. He leaned in.

She pulled her hand away and stood. "So, it's getting late."

He read that signal loud and clear, too. It was a big N-O. So maybe his signal reading was a bit off tonight.

Time for him to make an exit. He stood.

"Yeah, sure. Game day tomorrow, so I have some things I need to do to get ready for that."

"I hope your game goes well," she said as she walked him to the door.

He turned to face her. "You should come to a game. See how good the boys are."

"You think that would affect how I grade them?"

He frowned. "No. I meant you should see how good Hope High's football team is this year. I would never ask you to adjust your grade, Josie. And if you don't know me well enough by now to know that—"

She laid her hand on his chest. "I'm sorry. I'm sorry. I guess I'm just a little sensitive about it. It's just that—"

"It's happened before?"

She nodded. "Yes."

"I would never ask you to do that. And when you grade Chase's and Paul's work that they did this week, I want you to know it's their work. They were either on the field with me or in my office all week working on their papers. Papers that I read. And sometimes made them rewrite."

"I look forward to seeing what they've done."

He opened the door, regretting the way they were leaving things. "Good night, Josie."

She leaned her head against the doorway. "Night, Zach."

He walked out and got into his truck. She'd closed the door and turned out the light.

Shutting him out.

Damn.

He started his truck and backed out of the driveway.

Okay, maybe he'd missed that signal by a wide margin.

He might be a little off his game.

He blamed the cat.

Chapter 4

JOSIE FINISHED READING through Chase's and Paul's papers,
then entered their grades into the system.

What they'd written wasn't A-level work by any means.
But their journals weren't half-bad. And their analyses of
the poetry had shown some actual thought.

Zach's influence, no doubt.

At least the boys were caught up now. The work they'd
done was decent, which meant they were now on the passing
side of things in their overall grades. That should make Zach
happy.

Not that she was at all concerned about Zach's happiness.

Since she was finished for the day, she closed her laptop
and grabbed a stack of papers to take home and grade over
the weekend. She slid it all into her bag and turned the lights
off in her classroom, then made her way to the parking lot.

She heard the noise out on the field, just like she heard
it every day. The yelling, the whistles, the sounds of grunts.
Normally she ignored it, but she knew there was a home
game later tonight. She placed her things in the backseat,
closed and locked the door and shoved her keys in the pocket

of her skirt, then walked toward the field, figuring she might as well get a glimpse of practice.

The bleachers were mostly empty except for a few adults sitting in the first row. She didn't recognize them, so she made her way up to the third row behind them and took a seat.

She spotted Zach, who was currently in conversation with one of the players, Paul Fine.

Paul was nodding, and Zach appeared to be lecturing in a very loud voice.

"Isn't he just so hot?" one of the women said.

Josie blinked. Considering the woman had to be about thirty, she certainly hoped she was referring to Zach and not Paul.

"I swear I would let that man do dirty, dirty things to me," the other woman said.

"Not if I got him first." This was said by the first woman, whom Josie decided to call Blond-Haired Woman.

"Not that it matters," Auburn-Haired Woman said. "It's like he doesn't even know we're alive."

Blonde turned to Auburn. "Right? I mean, I was in the front row at open house, talking to him about Scott. He was polite and friendly and then, nothing. He has to know I'm divorced, right?"

Auburn nodded. "You would think a hot single guy like Zach Powers would know who every available woman is in this town. But have you ever seen him out with anyone?"

Petite Brunette, who'd been sitting silently to the right of the other two, finally spoke. "He hangs out in crowds, usually. I saw him one night last week when Tyrone and I were out to dinner at the pasta house."

Blonde grabbed her wrist. "Tell me everything."

Petite Brunette shrugged. "He was with some couples and some women. Drinking beers, laughing."

Josie remembered that night. She'd been there, along with Jillian and several of their friends, both men and women.

"But were any of those women his date?" Auburn asked.

"No clue. Didn't seem that way to me. It wasn't like he was making eyes at any of them or touching them."

"Okay, so just friends," Blonde said. "That's good news. That means he's available, and I still have a shot."

Josie rolled her eyes, determined to ignore the rest of their conversation. She'd mainly just wanted to watch the practice.

She actually liked football a lot, and she noticed Zach organized this practice well. Having experience as a pro football player seemed to have served him well as a coach. Hope High had an excellent quarterback this season, as well as a dynamite defense. From what she'd seen so far, Zach had made serious improvements to this team.

When Zach spotted her, he made his way up to the bleachers, much to the gasping and whispering of the three women below her, who all turned and gaped when Zach sat down next to her.

"Thought I saw you up here."

"I was on my way out but thought I'd stop and see how practice was going."

He made sure to keep his distance, then nodded at the three women who were unashamedly watching them. And when he continued to stare at them, they quickly turned back around to face the field. Only then did he turn his attention back to her.

"Sorry about that," he said, giving a head tilt to the women.

Her lips curved. "Apparently you're very popular."

"Yeah. Whatever. So, are you coming to the game tonight?"

She hadn't intended to. "Do you want me to?"

"Well . . . yeah. I'd really like you to come."

She felt a ridiculous little thrill of excitement zing through her nerve endings at his words. "Then I'll be here."

"Good. I'll see you after the game."

His face lingered close to hers, not too close to be improper for school grounds, but close enough that she wanted to reach up and touch him. Her breathing quickened and his eyes darkened and, oh, this was so, so good.

But like last night, the timing just wasn't right. He backed away. "See you tonight, Josie."

"Sure, Zach."

She watched as he walked away and down the steps. He made sure to wave to the ladies, who waved back.

When she turned her gaze toward the field again, she noticed three sets of eyes on her.

"Are you dating him?" Auburn asked.

Not that it was any of her business, especially since Josie was a teacher and Auburn was a parent. "Of course not. We're both teachers here."

"Oh," Blonde said. "You're my son's English teacher, aren't you? Ms. Barnes?"

"Yes."

"I thought you looked familiar. So you and Mr. Powers aren't . . . together?"

Josie resisted rolling her eyes again. "No. We're teachers and friends."

"I've seen you two together at the No Hope At All bar," Petite Brunette said.

"Yes," Josie said. "We often hang out there with a group of our friends."

"But not alone together," Blonde said.

And she'd had enough. "If you'll excuse me, I have to leave. Enjoy the rest of your day."

She walked down the steps and along the breezeway toward her car. When she got in and started it up, she exhaled.

Geez. Inquisition much, ladies?

Not that she could blame them, really. Zach was a good-looking single guy. Who wouldn't want to go out with him? She did. She'd even had him at her house last night. And had been primed to kiss him.

He'd wanted to. She'd wanted him to. She'd wanted him to kiss her since the summer.

But then those same old fears and the ghost of relationship past had crept in, and she'd stopped him.

She was going to have to put that past to rest so she could have some fun. Because she really needed to have some fun. And who better to have that kind of fun with than Zach?

She started her car and drove off.

Chapter 5

_____

IT WAS FOURTH down and a yard to go on the other team's thirty-yard line. They were deep into the fourth quarter, and Zach knew his guys wanted to go for it. They were up by three points, and they needed this touchdown to seal the deal. But if they lost this opportunity to score, it might be their last chance in the game.

Was he a risk taker?

Hell yes, he was. He always had been. Plus, he needed his guys to know he believed in them. He held up the field goal team and signaled for the offense to stay on the field. He sent in the play, and his guys huddled up.

They got set, and he leaned forward to watch the snap. Robertson, the quarterback, lunged forward, his entire offensive line digging with him, including the backs, who pushed their quarterback over the line.

Zach nodded. Easy first down, and the crowd cheered with approval.

They weren't playing a fluff team. It was a larger school, and a lot of the players were bigger than his guys. The score was close because his team had been going toe to toe on both sides of the ball. He was damn proud of them.

So, when Robertson pitched the ball to Adams, the running back, who ran it in for a touchdown, Zach didn't give the boys a hard time for the end zone celebration. The ref's whistle would pull them back in line.

The defense did their job in the last minute and kept the other team from getting anywhere near Hope High's end zone. When the ref signaled for the end of the game, Zach nodded in satisfaction.

"That was a close one, Coach." Gene, one of his assistant coaches, slapped him on the back.

"Yeah, but we came out on the winning end of it."

"We sure did. The boosters will be happy about that."

Yeah. While he appreciated the boosters, Zach's focus was on his kids. Teaching them football. And winning. And that there was a life beyond football, something he wished he'd learned when he was still in high school.

They still had a lot more games to play, but Zach felt confident about his Eagles. He was determined to take them to the state championships this year.

There were always parents of the kids—and several prominent boosters—lined up on the sidelines after the game. There were the inevitable questions from parents who were pissed off their kid didn't get enough or any playing time, or the ones who wanted his opinion on how their son played. Then the boosters had comments or questions or an invite to an event.

He ignored them, instead heading to the locker room to talk to his kids.

The noise level in the locker room was painfully loud. His boys were hyped, and he couldn't blame them. Beating a great team was always cause for celebration.

"All right, all right, let's bring it down," he said as he walked into the center of the locker room.

The chatter stopped, as it always did when he used the tone of voice that let them know he had something to say.

"Good game. You dug deep and held them when it

counted, and you came up with scores when we needed it most. You worked as a team. That last drive, you stood on one another's shoulders and pushed for that touchdown. And then defense held tough to get us the win. I'm proud of all of you. Now, go out and celebrate, but don't do anything stupid, because there are a lot more games to play. And where do we want to go at the end of it?"

They all yelled, "State" as loud as they could.

"That's right. Have a good weekend."

While they cleaned up and got dressed, he went into his office and made some notes on the game. He wanted to make a few changes in some positions next week. While they had played well, they could do better, and switching some things around would make that happen. He'd discuss it with his assistant coaches on Monday before practice and get a feel for their thoughts on some of the switches he wanted to make.

He finished up his notes, put his paperwork in his bag, and picked up his phone to check messages. There were several. Some he filed away to deal with later, but there was one from Will Griffin.

Good game. We're all headed to Emma and
Luke McCormack's house for pizza and beer.
Come on over.

Since he was hungry, that sounded like a good idea. He checked the locker room first to make sure the kids had all cleared out.

They had, so he locked up and left.

Fortunately, Hope was a small town, and unless you lived on the outskirts, it didn't take long to get anywhere. So within ten minutes he'd parked in front of Luke and Emma McCormack's house.

He knocked on the door and heard Luke bellow, "It's open," so he walked in.

He was immediately greeted by Luke and Emma's three dogs. Luke, a K9 cop, had a beautiful German shepherd named Boomer who greeted him with a fierce tail wag. Emma had a pit bull named Annie and a Labrador named Daisy, and both of them butted in for attention as well.

"Hi, you guys. Aren't you just so cute?"

"Oh, sure, you're all sweet with Emma and Luke's dogs. But you barely tolerated Tumbles."

Josie walked into the entry, holding a bottle of beer. She looked—amazing. He didn't know how someone wearing low-slung jeans and a T-shirt and tennis shoes could look amazing, but she did. Maybe it was the long chain that disappeared into the scoop neck of her T-shirt, or the way the jeans hugged her curves, or maybe the fact that everything about her turned him on.

"That's because none of these dogs tried to attack my ankles."

She shrugged. "Minor details."

The dogs scattered when Luke called them, so Zach walked with Josie into the kitchen.

"Everyone's out back," she said. "There's beer in the cooler outside, and wine in the fridge. Good game tonight, by the way."

"Thanks."

He followed Josie through the door to the backyard. There was a good crowd of their friends out there.

"There's the hero of the night," Luke said. He got up and grabbed a beer from the cooler and handed it to Zach. "Great game."

"It was an outstanding football game," Emma said. "Mikey's sorry he missed the game, but he wants you to know as soon as he's old enough, he's there." She was holding her baby, Michael, who was getting bigger every time Zach saw him.

"It was so awesome, Mr. Powers," Jane and Will Griffin's son, Ryan, said. "And that wide receiver you've got is fast."

Zach pulled up a lawn chair next to where Ryan was sitting on the patio next to his sister. "He is fast. He caught a lot of passes tonight."

"He's Jimmy Fine's son, isn't he?" Luke asked.

"Yeah."

"Huh," Luke said. "Good wide receiver. I hope he does well."

"What does that mean?" Emma asked. "You know Paul's father?"

"Let's just say I know of him."

"Care to elaborate?" Zach asked.

Luke scanned his gaze over the kids, then looked back at Zach. "We'll talk later."

Zach nodded.

If Luke knew of him, that meant Paul's dad had had some run-ins with the local law enforcement. Zach would have to keep a close eye on Paul to make sure he stayed out of trouble, both academically and otherwise.

His gaze shifted to Josie, who also looked concerned after Luke's comment.

Sports notwithstanding, home problems could affect a kid in a lot of ways.

Even though Hope High was a small school, Paul had a really good chance of getting a football scholarship to a decent, if smaller, college. But colleges weren't going to take a chance on kids who had failing grades.

After they talked for a while, Luke got up and went into the garage, so Zach followed him.

"Oh, hey," Luke said, reaching into the garage refrigerator. "Need to restock the coolers."

"Hand something over to me, and I'll help."

Luke straightened. "I'll bet you came in here to ask me about Jimmy Fine."

"I did."

"We arrested him twice for passing bad checks."

Zach grimaced. "Well, shit."

"Yeah. He can't keep a job. Laurel's got hers over at the market, plus, she's working nights at the convenience store, but they're having trouble making ends meet. I think Jimmy's burning all their money on drugs, but we haven't been able to bust him on a drug charge yet."

Not the news Zach wanted to hear. "That's gotta be hard on both the wife and the kid emotionally."

Luke nodded. "We've got a line on a couple of local dealers, so it's only a matter of time until we catch Jimmy."

"Which would probably be the best thing that could happen for both Paul and his mom."

"Yeah, it would be. But only if Laurel will see it as a wake-up call and kick Jimmy to the curb."

"All right, thanks for the info, Luke."

"You bet. Now, help me carry this beer into the backyard."

Zach smiled. "You got it."

ZACH WAS GOING to have to step up and work some extra time with Paul.

He thought about ways he could engage the kid. Chase had been a lot easier to deal with this week when he'd worked with both of them on catching up with their schoolwork. Of course, it helped that Chase's parents had been on board and willing to step in and assist. It had been clear that Jimmy could have cared less other than making sure his kid stayed on the team. And Laurel had just looked nervous. During the game tonight, Zach could tell Paul's head had been somewhere else, which was probably why he was struggling academically.

If he was worrying about money—which the kid shouldn't have to—then it was going to affect his schoolwork—and football.

He needed to find a way to motivate him without making it a negative thing.

He took his seat, and the conversation around him centered on the football game, but Zach's head wasn't in it.

Josie laid her hand on his arm. "You're worried about Paul."

He looked over at her. "Yeah."

"I saw you talking to Luke over by the garage, and I assume that's who it was about. Is it family problems?"

"Yeah."

She sighed. "A screwed-up family life can really drag a kid down."

"He's a good football player and has amazing potential. But if he has to step up and take on more responsibility because a parent isn't doing his job, then it's going to negatively affect everything in his world."

"I know exactly what you mean. It can destroy self-esteem, dig into his concentration, and screw up his future if he lets it. Parents can really do a number on a kid even if they're not directly involved with that child."

"Have you seen that with some of your students?"

"Something like that."

He wondered what she meant by that. Was she thinking of a student? Or maybe she'd experienced something personally.

He needed to get to know Josie beyond just the surface of the "Hey, this woman is hot" kind of getting to know her. Because there was a lot going on.

And he was interested.

Chapter 6

JOSIE WAS GLAD she'd gotten up early this morning to grade papers, because reading narrative story evaluations took a few hours. She knew it was going to be a busy day. She cleaned the house and spent some time chasing Tumbles around because he really enjoyed playing and she wanted to give him a lot of attention. Then she did laundry, though folding towels was something Tumbles enjoyed as well. She'd fold a towel and he'd attack it, and when all the towels were folded, he jumped in the basket and burrowed into it, causing her to have to fold them all again.

But as long as Tumbles had fun, it was worth the extra work. Plus, he was very entertaining and made her laugh.

When she had put away the laundry, she went to the grocery store to get the ingredients to make her watermelon salsa for tonight's party at Loretta and Deacon's house.

She was in the middle of chopping onions when her phone rang. She wiped her hands on the towel and swiped to answer Jillian's call.

"Hey, Jillian. What's up?"

"Making a pumpkin hummus for tonight. How about you?"

"Oh my God, that sounds incredible. I'm making water-melon salsa."

"I am so hungry right now."

Josie laughed. "Me, too. They'll be lucky if any of this dip makes its way to Deacon and Loretta's house tonight."

"Ditto. The drawback of making food we actually like to eat."

"So true. Oh, and speaking of the party tonight, Jillian, what are you wearing?"

"I got these new red-and-yellow-flowered capris and extremely cute new red sandals, and a short-sleeved black top that would look amazing with it."

"Sounds awesome. I'll bet you look fantastic in it."

"Thanks. I know it's fall weather, but I love the sandals. Plus, the weather tonight is supposed to be mild, so I'm wearing them."

"You should definitely go for it."

"I intend to. What about you?"

"I don't know. I have a black-and-white checked dress that I haven't worn yet."

"Is it one of those vintage dress things you like?" Jillian asked.

"Yes."

"Then wear it. You always look adorable in them."

Josie considered it. "Like . . . cute adorable or hot adorable?"

"Well, I think you look cute adorable, but honey, I'm not trying to have sex with you, so I would imagine Zach Powers thinks you look hot no matter what you're wearing."

Josie laughed. "Point taken. Okay, I'll wear it."

"Awesome. I'll see you over there at six thirty."

"Later, Jillian."

She hung up, finished making the salsa, then decided to bake cookies. She knew Megan would make some outstanding confection since she owned the bakery in town, but still, it never hurt to have extra goodies, and her sugar cookies were easy enough to make.

After the cookies came out of the oven, she packaged

them up in a plastic container and went to take a shower. Having short hair didn't mean it took less time to get ready. In fact, she often thought about letting her hair grow out. It had to be easier in some ways to have longer hair. Short hair was a lot of work sometimes. She still had to flat iron or curl it to get just the right look or put a curl just right.

Pain in the butt.

She did her makeup, then put on the dress. She stared at herself in the full-length mirror, trying to decide how she felt about the dress. She loved vintage clothing, and this dress especially. It was black with tiny white squares sprinkled over it. If she was going to be dancing, she'd wear ballet flats or even heels to dress up the outfit. But since it was September and this was going to be a backyard deck party, that meant casual. She put on her red slip-on tennis shoes, and a couple of wide bracelets to finish off the look.

Now she felt good.

Tumbles was currently batting at one of his toys when she walked into the kitchen. She crouched down, and he came over to her, purring. She ran her hand over his head to scratch him behind the ears.

"I'll be back soon. You watch at the window for me, okay?"

He lifted his head against her hand, making her heart squeeze. Funny how it was so easy to fall in love with an animal and so hard to trust a human with your heart. Maybe it was because with animals, there was no hidden agenda, no second-guessing what was on their minds. There was always unconditional love.

She sighed, grabbed the food and put it in a bag, then walked out the front door and got in her car.

When Loretta Simmons had moved back to Hope a couple of years ago, she'd bought some property and a big ranch house. Then her daughter, Hazel, had decided she wanted a dog.

Loretta had ended up with a huge Great Dane named Otis who was just the cutest and sweetest dog Josie had ever met. She wished she had the space for a large dog, but she didn't. While she had a nice-sized yard, a dog that large needed room to run.

Deacon and Loretta, however, had so much acreage, it was perfect for a big loping dog like Otis. And as she pulled onto their property and parked, Otis came running, his deep bark a deterrent to someone who didn't know what a big affectionate baby he was.

She got out of the car and immediately grabbed his face, which reached to her waist. "Hi, Otis. How are you today? Have you been chasing things outside?"

"He saw a rabbit, and I had to run after him."

Josie lifted her gaze to Loretta's nine-year-old daughter, Hazel. "He did, huh?"

"Yeah. He's pretty fast, but the rabbit disappeared into the woods, and Deacon's been training him not to go in there without permission, so he stopped."

Josie patted Otis on the head. "You stopped, huh? What a good boy you are."

Otis's tail thumped back and forth.

"Can I help you with anything, Josie?"

"Thanks, Hazel. That would be great." She handed the cookie container to Hazel, then grabbed the bag containing everything else from the backseat of her car.

"Everyone's out back on the new deck," Hazel said as she led Josie in the front door. "Which, by the way, is so cool. It's big, and you can get there from the kitchen and Mama and Deacon's room. Oh, and you can put the cold stuff in the fridge here in the kitchen or in one of the coolers, and the cookies can go on the table."

Now that they were in the light, Josie noticed Hazel's outfit. "You're wearing a dress."

Hazel never wore dresses. Her father, Loretta's ex-husband, had always insisted she dress up. After the divorce, Loretta swore she'd allow Hazel to dress however she wanted to. Since then, Hazel had shown a preference for jeans or shorts and T-shirts and baseball caps.

Tonight, her silken blond hair was combed out and lay across her shoulders, and she wore a pink-and-white sundress and sandals. She looked so nice.

Hazel shrugged. "Yeah, I thought I'd wear a dress tonight. No reason or anything. So anyway, everyone's out back. Come on."

"Hazel?"

The little girl paused. "Yeah?"

"You look very pretty in your dress."

Hazel grinned. "Thanks, Josie."

Josie followed Hazel outside. She was right. The deck had turned out beautifully. It was huge, wrapped around the side of the house all the way to the bedroom, and stretched out nearly to where the woods started. There were stairs leading down to the yard, and underneath the deck was a covered patio area with a nice seating spot.

Twinkling white lights were strung along the railing and above the deck. When it got dark, it would be beautiful.

Josie found Loretta and Deacon, who were standing over toward the front of the deck, near the new grill Loretta had told her Deacon had bought the other day.

She came over and hugged Loretta. "Congratulations on finishing the deck."

"Thanks," Loretta said. "But save those congrats for Deacon—and for Reid. They did all the work. All I did was nod and smile and tell them everything looked amazing, which of course it does."

"It does look wonderful, Deacon."

Deacon beamed a proud smile. "Thanks. I'm pretty happy with the end result. And that I managed to convince Loretta to wrap the deck around to the master bedroom and add the French doors there."

"I was dubious at first," Loretta said, "but I have to admit it will be nice to walk out from the bedroom at night or in the morning and sit out on the deck."

"I agree," Josie said. "You have a lovely view out here. I can already picture you having coffee out here in the morning."

"Or the last glass of wine at night," Deacon said.

"Plenty of room for a hot tub just outside the master bedroom," Reid McCormack said, coming over to give Josie a hug. "Very romantic."

Reid's wife, Samantha, came over. "Always thinking of romance, aren't you?"

Reid put his arm around Sam. "That's why you married me, isn't it?"

"That and the fact you built me a house."

Josie laughed.

"Did you get something to drink yet, Josie?" Loretta asked.

"Not yet. I wanted to come out here and say hello first."

"Well, come on, I'll go with you."

Josie went into the kitchen with Loretta.

"White or red?" Loretta asked.

"White, please."

"Dry or sweet?"

"Oh, I'm fine with either."

Loretta pulled a bottle from the wine fridge and uncorked it. "This one is already open."

She poured a glass for Josie and handed it to her.

"You're not having a glass?" Josie asked.

"Uh, I already have one . . . somewhere." Loretta laughed. "It's probably outside on the table."

"Which is beautiful, by the way." Josie had forgotten to mention the long pine table in the center of the deck that had obviously been handcrafted.

"Thank you. It's my favorite part of the deck. Deacon made it as a surprise."

"It's lovely, Loretta. And, by the way, you look beautiful tonight. No one told me we were supposed to dress up."

Loretta had on the most amazing sundress that fit her as if it had been made just for her. It was a dusky rose with a lace overlay. And she was wearing a flower in her hair.

"Oh, it's not dress-up. I just bought this new dress, and since we're christening the deck and all, I thought I'd spruce up for the occasion."

"I see."

She'd also noticed Deacon was wearing dark slacks and a white button-down long-sleeved shirt. It was warm out tonight. Most of the guys were wearing shorts or jeans and T-shirts.

Something was up, but since Loretta was already making her way out the door toward the deck, Josie couldn't ask.

Josie found Jillian, who was wearing the cute outfit she'd described earlier.

"You look perfect," she said to Jillian.

"You think so?" She looked down at herself. "I thought the capris might be too loud."

The black capris had huge red and yellow flowers, but they were totally cute. Of course, everything looked adorable on Jillian, who had one of those figures where you could drape curtains on her and people would still say she looked hot. She had hips, boobs, and stunning legs, with everything all in the right places. Plus, she had perfectly styled chin-length brown hair and mesmerizing green eyes. And yet she complained that no guys wanted to go out with her.

Josie didn't get it.

"I totally think that outfit is perfect and makes your ass look great." Josie frowned. "Should I be saying that to you if I'm not dating you?"

Jillian laughed. "I'll take the compliment, no matter who says it."

"Who says what?" Zach asked.

He'd walked over with Dr. Jeff Armstrong.

"I mentioned that Jillian's outfit was stunning and made her ass look outstanding."

Jeff peered around behind Jillian. "I concur."

Jillian's cheeks darkened. "Uh, thanks, Jeff."

"Hey, anytime you want an opinion on what outfit makes your butt look good, feel free to give me a holler."

Josie looked over at Zach, who raised both hands. "I'm abstaining."

She was kind of glad about that, but wow, the looks being exchanged between Jillian and Jeff were incendiary.

Unfortunately, Jeff's phone buzzed. Timing sucked sometimes.

"This is the clinic," Jeff said. "Excuse me."

Since Jeff was a doctor and had opened up an emergency clinic recently, she knew he had to be on call all the time. She also noticed that before he walked away, Jeff gave Jillian what Josie would consider a very promising smile.

Huh. Josie shot Zach a look. Fortunately, he grabbed a clue that she wanted to talk alone with Jillian.

"I'm going to hunt down another beer," Zach said. "Be right back."

Josie grabbed Jillian's arm and dragged her into the house. She led her into the living room since no one was in there and sat her on the sofa.

"What is going on between you and Jeff Armstrong?"

"Between Jeff and me? Nothing. Why?"

"Oh my God, Jillian. The way he looked at you? The way he looked at your butt?"

"How could he not look at my butt considering the comment you made. Anyone would have looked."

Josie shook her head. "Zach didn't look."

Jillian laughed. "Zach didn't look because he's way more interested in *your* butt than mine."

"He is not."

Jillian rolled her eyes. "Girlfriend. Please. When are you going to stop denying what's happening between the two of you?"

"So far nothing is happening between us. We're just friends."

"Yeah, friends who are hot for each other. You know he wants you."

"Maybe."

"So what's holding you back?"

A lengthy list that she really didn't want to discuss with anyone. "I don't know. I'm just . . . hesitant. I've got the new job at the high school. We work together. That's a huge complication."

"And you've already told me there is nothing in your contract that states you can't date a fellow teacher."

"True."

"So, again, what's holding you back?"

"This is my first year at Hope High, Jillian. The last thing I need or want is to give the administration any reason to not want me back next year. I'm trying to build a home here. A future. Having a hot fling with the football coach and a fellow teacher and being the cause of gossip aren't going to endear me to the administrators."

Jillian sighed. "Okay, I can see your point and why you might be wary. But you could be discreet about it."

She leaned against the back of the sofa. "You mean sneak around."

"For a while. Besides, that would make it even more exciting, wouldn't it?"

Would it? Just being with Zach was exciting. Then something occurred to her, and she slanted a look at Jillian.

"You totally got me off the topic of you and Jeff."

"There is no Jeff and me. Nothing's happening."

"But you want something to happen, right?"

"I don't—" Jillian let the sentence trail off.

"Oh, come on, Jillian. There's no way you were going to deny it, right?"

"Fine. He is hot in that Clark Kent kind of way. That thick dark hair, those dark-rimmed glasses he wears. Plus, he's so smart. And funny. And kind of sexy. He stops in the library all the time, and he gives me goose bumps whenever he talks to me."

"Mmm-hmm. So maybe you change the no to yes?"

Jillian frowned. "And maybe you start thinking of a certain teacher-slash-coach as more than just a friend."

"I'll think about starting to think about it."

Jillian rolled her eyes and was about to say something, but then Loretta opened the door. "There you both are. Could you come outside?"

Josie stood. "Sure. You need us to help with anything?"

"Uh . . . maybe?" Loretta gave them both a wide smile. "I'll see you outside."

Loretta shut the door.

Josie looked over at Jillian, who shrugged. "No clue."

Something was definitely up, and Josie couldn't wait to find out what it was.

They went outside. Josie saw Loretta and Deacon, along with Hazel and Otis. They were all standing at the center of the deck.

"I know you all thought we were dedicating the new deck tonight," Deacon said, taking Loretta's hand in hers. "But it's actually more than that."

Deacon looked over at Loretta and gave her a smile, then turned his attention back to the crowd that had gathered. "We're getting married tonight."

Josie gasped. So did Jillian. Pretty much everyone did.

"We wanted to do this at our house, with our daughter present, and all of our friends here as well. We couldn't think of a better way to start our lives together."

"Well, actually, Mama, you and Deacon are already living together here," Hazel said.

"I'm sure we can spare Pastor Fletcher those details, honey," Loretta said, making everyone laugh, including the pastor, who stepped up, Bible in hand.

Josie had never met Pastor Fletcher before. She'd noticed when she'd walked in, there were people here she didn't know, but she was still fairly new to Hope, so there were always people she didn't know.

"Shall we get started?" Pastor Fletcher asked.

"Yes, let's," Loretta said.

Samantha McCormack brought out a box and pulled out a lovely bouquet of white roses and lilies, handing a large one to Sam and a smaller one to Hazel. Sam pulled out boutonnieres and placed one on Deacon's shirt, and then another on Sam's husband, Reid. She also wound a single rose in Otis's collar. Then she pulled out another bouquet of peach flowers that matched her own very cute sundress and stood next to Loretta.

Josie grinned and turned to Jillian. "This is so fun."

"And so unexpected."

Figuring they should let Loretta and Deacon take center stage, they made their way around the couple and toward the back of the deck, where most everyone else had gathered.

Zach came up next to her. "Did you know about this?"

She shook her head. "No. Did you?"

"Nope. Obviously Sam and Reid did, though."

"I guess so."

The pastor started talking, and Loretta and Deacon held hands. What Josie enjoyed most about the ceremony was that Hazel stood between the two of them the entire time. Even though Hazel was Loretta's daughter from her prior marriage, Deacon kept his arm around Hazel's shoulder. Hazel looked up at Deacon like he was her personal hero. It made Josie's eyes tear up, because Hazel needed a hero in her life, and Deacon was definitely that.

Josie sniffled when Deacon and Loretta said their vows, promising to love and care for each other forever. The pastor brought Hazel into their vows, and they both promised to always care for her. That made Hazel grin. It made Josie's heart squeeze.

Then they were pronounced husband and wife, and they kissed—and what a kiss it was. Deacon tilted Loretta back and planted a hot one on her. So hot, Josie was certain the entire outdoors felt like a sudden humid rain forest.

Whew.

Loretta grinned, and Deacon set her upright. Hazel giggled and Otis barked and everyone clapped. Josie leaned against Zach. When he squeezed her arm and looked down at her, she felt a tingle of something she probably shouldn't feel, but she'd think about that later.

Right now there was magic in the air. Magic and love and all kinds of possibilities.

Sometimes happily-ever-after could happen. At least for some people. She believed in those two people who'd just said their vows, and even more, she knew Hazel was in good hands.

Everyone applauded, and then it was just as if they really had come there for a backyard party, because coolers were thrown open, beers were handed out, and Deacon and a few of the guys started up the grill.

Josie and Jillian made their way over to Loretta and gave her a hug.

"I can't believe you didn't tell me," Josie said.

"Tell you what?" Loretta batted her lashes innocently.

"Loretta."

Loretta laughed. "I'm sorry. We didn't tell anyone. We wanted there to be an element of surprise, you know? Except for Sam and Megan and Reid, because Sam did flowers and Megan made a cake. And because we wanted Sam to be my matron of honor."

Josie could only imagine how thrilled Sam must have been about that.

"Okay, you're forgiven. And I'm so happy for both of you." Josie looked over at Hazel, who was currently adjusting Otis's bow tie. "For all of you."

"We wanted to get married in as simple a way as possible, with all of our friends and family who could be here. And now it's done, and we can go have our happily-ever-after."

"Leave it to you to make it simple, yet beautiful and meaningful," Jillian said. "I'm so happy for your new family."

"Thank you. Now we need to go eat before I get all teary-eyed."

"Yes, no tears on your wedding day," Josie said. "After all, Loretta, there's cake. And who can cry when there's cake?"

Jillian nodded. "Especially cake that Megan made."

"You make a good point. Now, let's go get some wine."

They went inside where the bar was set up. Josie poured herself a glass of sauvignon blanc and took a sip.

Yes, just what she needed.

After they filled their glasses, they went outside and found Emma, Jane, and Chelsea, and even Desiree McCormack had made it. They grabbed a couple of available chairs.

"Des," Josie said, "it's good to see you back. How was your trip to LA?"

"Short, fortunately. I met with my agent and the studio only long enough to discuss the shoot coming up in Scotland in a few months."

"Scotland sounds amazing," Emma said. "Will you take Ben with you?"

Des nodded. "Absolutely. It'll be a one-month location shoot, so there's no way I can leave my baby behind that long. And Logan will come out for at least a week while I'm filming."

Josie couldn't imagine being an internationally traveling actress and being able to see the world like Des did. And she got to come home to an amazing husband like Logan and a beautiful baby son. She was also sure it required a lot of juggling, but Des handled it so well.

Josie turned her attention to Loretta, who seemed to be floating on air as she breezed by.

"She looks beautiful," Chelsea said.

"She does," Des said. "Love will do that to you."

"Wasn't that so fun?" Emma asked.

"It was amazing," Josie said. "And a huge surprise. I can't believe they put all this together."

"I'm not surprised at all," Des said. "Deacon would do anything for Loretta."

"It was probably his idea," Chelsea said. "Knowing Loretta, she probably wanted to do it at the courthouse, and Deacon wouldn't hear of it. He'd want it to be romantic for her."

Josie could see that. Every time they were together, it was obvious how much Deacon loved Loretta. He'd want this day to be special. And even though they'd wanted it low key, it had still been sweetly romantic.

"I've never given much thought to the idea of getting married," Josie said. "But I really like how Deacon and Loretta did it. The whole outside-in-the-backyard idea has its merits."

"Agreed," Jillian said. "It was simple and sweet."

Josie nodded. "Plus, I intend to have all my animals involved in my wedding."

"Wait," Des said. "I know I've been out of town the past month filming, but do you have more than just the kitty?"

"No, just Tumbles so far, but I want to eventually have several animals, so I'll want them all to be there, like Otis was here tonight. And most churches frown on having your fur babies at the ceremony."

"This is true," Emma said. "Oh, speaking of fur babies, we got the cutest dog at the clinic this week."

It was as if Emma had read her mind. "Tell me about him."

"One of the rescue organizations has been fostering him. He's an adorable sweetheart, but they've been having trouble placing him because he's only got three legs and has some health issues. But he has the best personality, Josie."

"I'll take him."

Emma laughed. "You haven't even met him yet."

"It doesn't matter. He needs a forever home, and he should come live with Tumbles and me."

"Okay. Come to the clinic and see him, and then decide."

She honestly didn't need to see him. There were already too many animals that had a hard time finding a home. She was that home for those kinds of babies.

"When can I come see him?"

"How about tomorrow morning?"

"But that's Sunday, and don't you want a day off to spend with your family, Emma?"

Emma laughed. "I get plenty of days off. And the foster group often needs to come in on weekend days. They're already planning to be in the clinic tomorrow."

Josie felt a lot less like she was inconveniencing Emma. "I'll be there."

"Where are you gonna be?"

She looked up to find Zach standing over her. "I'm going to Emma's clinic to look at adopting a dog."

"What, the cat from hell isn't enough for you?"

"Aww, Tumbles is sweet, Zach," Chelsea said. "So affectionate and cuddly."

He pulled up a chair next to Josie. "So it's just me he hates."

Josie saw Emma's questioning look, so she figured she should explain. "Zach and Tumbles had a rough introduction."

"Oh." Emma nodded. "Some animals have a hard time with certain sexes. It could be he has trust issues around men. You'll just have to be patient with him."

"So maybe it's not just me," Zach said.

"It's doubtful. I'll bet if next time you go to Josie's you take a bag of treats, he'll warm up to you quickly."

"I'll work on that. Thanks, Emma."

Soon two tables had been pushed together out in the yard, and Josie was surrounded by several of her friends, including Zach, who seemed to be content sitting next to her. Though he spent a lot of time talking with all the guys, he'd occasionally glance her way and smile.

Oh, that smile of his. It was wickedly sexy and filled with promise. Now she only had to summon the courage to actually let go of the last remaining vestiges of hesitation and just go for it with him. After all, what did she have to lose?

Ha. Do you want a list, Josephine? Because you've been down this road with a hot guy before. Remember how that ended up?

She mentally shushed her logical inner voice. And, she reminded logical voice, previous hot guy wasn't at all like Zach. Besides, it was time for some fun, and she already knew Zach was fun with a capital *F*. He didn't seem the serious type, so he was perfect for what she had in mind.

Thoughts of Zach got pushed to the back of her mind as she watched Jillian flirt with Dr. Jeff.

Or maybe Dr. Jeff was flirting with Jillian. It was kind

of hard to tell who was doing the most flirting, because the two of them had their heads together, deep in conversation about . . . something. Given Jillian's initial hesitation to move forward with Jeff, Josie couldn't wait to pull her friend aside and find out what that in-depth conversation was all about.

"Are you really getting a dog?"

She pulled her gaze away from her best friend to answer Zach. "Of course. Why? Do you think I shouldn't?"

"Not my call to make. Other than I would think Mr. Evil is more than a handful."

"Tumbles is no trouble at all. He takes a few meds every day due to his age, and I brush him to keep his coat from getting tangled. Other than that, the only thing he requires is love."

"Yeah, and an occasional blood sacrifice."

She shook her head. "Obviously it's going to take some time for you to warm up to Tumbles. But once you do, you'll love him."

"I can guarantee you I'm never gonna love that cat, Josie."

"Never say never, Zach. You might have to eat those words someday."

"No, I won't."

"We'll see, won't we?"

Obviously, Zach was going to be hard to break down in the pet department. Which gave her an idea.

"Come with me tomorrow morning."

"Where? To the vet?"

"Yes. You can meet the new pup. Well, he's not a pup, according to Emma. But I'd love for you to come with me."

"Sure."

She liked that he didn't even hesitate, and considering how he felt about Tumbles, that made her feel good.

"Thanks. And, who knows? You might find a cute furry baby for yourself while you're there. Emma always takes in unwanted animals."

"That's unlikely."

Josie thought animals brought love and happiness to

everyone who was owned by a cat or a dog or a bunny or turtle or snake or . . . whatever. But she also knew that not everyone was a pet person, so she had to remind herself not to be pushy about it.

Still, it would be interesting to see how he reacted at Emma's clinic tomorrow.

She couldn't wait.

Chapter 7

COFFEE IN HAND, Zach climbed out of his SUV in the parking lot of Emma's veterinary clinic.

Josie's car was already parked in the lot next to Emma's. Since it was Sunday, the clinic was closed. He went to the front door and tried the handle. It was locked, so he knocked and waited.

Emma flipped open the blinds and smiled at him, then unlocked and opened the door.

"Hey, Zach. Josie told me you were going to be here."

"Working all seven days of the week now, Emma?"

She led him down the hall, her two dogs, Daisy and Annie, following along beside both of them. "Actually, I'm working fewer days now that I've hired on another doctor. I'm just here today to check out the foster group's animals and do some paperwork."

"So, who's watching the baby?"

"Luke's off today, so he's at home with Michael. Actually, I'm surprised you're here. Football and Sunday being a solemn religion and all."

Zach cracked a smile. "Amen to that. But it's early, and the games haven't started yet."

"Of course." She gave him a knowing smile. "Come on back. I'm doing some work with a few dogs. Josie's with Marsha from the animal rescue group. She's getting acquainted with the dog I wanted her to see. Though now that they've gotten to know each other, I don't know if there'll be any separating them."

Given Josie's love for animals, Zach could believe that. He already knew how she felt about Beelzebub, not to mention how well she got along with all their friends' animals. So it didn't surprise him to find Josie in the kennel area sitting on the floor with a small white-and-beige fluffy thing, who was currently licking her face. She looked up and smiled at him when he entered the room.

There went that twinge in his gut again, the one he always got when Josie smiled at him.

Emma introduced him to Marsha. She was in her midforties, tall, and very nice-looking, with dark hair pulled back in a ponytail.

"Nice to meet you, Zach," she said.

"Same, Marsha. I admire the work you do."

"Well, you have to be an animal lover. And I am. And so is Josie, who has her hands full with this one."

Josie laughed as the dog licked her chin. God, that laugh of hers made his entire body take notice.

"Isn't he adorable, Zach?" Emma asked. "His name is Wilson."

Zach grinned. "Like the football?"

Josie frowned. "No, like Wilson. He's unique." She ruffled his fur. "Aren't you, baby?"

Zach shook his head. Hell of a name for a dog. Wilson looked up and saw Zach, and he could have sworn the dog smiled. Which was ridiculous, of course. The dog brought a ball over to Zach, his tail whipping back and forth in excited frenzy. He dropped the ball at Zach's feet. Zach looked over at Emma.

"It's fine. You can throw it for him. He's already been

playing with Daisy and Annie, and even though they're bigger dogs with four legs, he's been able to keep up."

Emma told Daisy and Annie to sit, which they did. Zach picked up the ball and tossed it down the hall. Wilson chased it, zipping along just fine. Obviously having only three legs didn't hinder his ability to get around. He ran back to Zach and dropped the tennis ball at his feet, so Zach threw it again.

And again.

And again.

Cute.

"He likes you," Marsha said. "He's open and friendly anyway, but he really likes you."

Zach sat on the floor, and Wilson climbed onto his lap to give him copious licks on the face.

Okay, so the dog was freaking adorable. He was furry and affectionate and apparently craved attention. Zach played with him until Wilson curled up and went to sleep in Zach's lap.

"Huh," Josie said. "I'd say he likes you better than me."

Oh shit. "I don't think that's it at all. My lap is just where he happened to pass out. You probably played plenty with him before I got here, so he's tired."

Josie, Marsha, and Emma exchanged glances. Emma nodded. "We played some with him, but it was like a light switch got turned on when you showed up, Zach. He was a totally different dog. Way more excited and, correct me if I'm wrong, Josie, but he seemed almost . . . happier?"

"I agree," Josie said. "He was much more animated and happy with you. Sometimes a dog just finds its person. You might be Wilson's person."

"I agree," Marsha said. "He seems attached."

Zach looked at all of them. "But I don't want a dog."

The three women looked at him as if to say that was the most ridiculous statement they'd ever heard.

And then Wilson nestled farther into Zach's lap.

Well, hell. He ran his hands down the dog's furry back. So he was cute. That didn't mean anything.

Wilson sighed in contentment.

"If you don't want him, he can come live with me," Josie said. "He has a heart murmur and will have to take meds every day. He'll also need regular checkups to be monitored periodically."

"Which doesn't affect his current level of activity," Emma said. "He should be able to live a very active life. And my clinic will set you up with reminders for when he needs to come in for checkups."

Zach's heart ached for this dog. Wilson already felt like his. "I'll take him."

Emma's smile widened. "Excellent. Sorry about that, Josie."

"Oh, don't be. I'm very excited about Zach taking Wilson. There will be plenty more animals for me in the future."

Josie crouched down on the floor in front of Zach. "You like him."

He shrugged. "I don't know. Never had a dog before."

"Okay, then, let me rephrase. You're going to love him."

Zach honestly didn't know. But he was willing to give this dog a home. "We'll see."

"Yes, you'll see."

He stood and went with Emma to fill out paperwork for the rescue organization while Josie chatted with Marsha about some of the other animals at the rescue. Knowing Josie, Zach figured she'd probably take six of them home with her. He wished he could be as at ease about animals as Josie was, but he didn't have the experience. He looked down at Wilson, who stared up at him with a look of utter trust.

I'll do my best, buddy. But don't expect much.

Since Emma could vouch for Zach, Marsha agreed to release Wilson to him, pending a house visit. Emma gave Zach Wilson's health record, plus a list of things he'd need to buy, like food and stuff.

"Do you have a place for him to sleep?" Josie asked as she stood next to him.

"Uh, the floor?"

She rolled her eyes. "I meant a dog bed or a blanket or something."

"Oh. No." He hadn't thought out every detail.

She looped her arm in his and leaned against him. Not the worst thing that had happened to him today.

"We need to go shopping."

"We do?"

Josie nodded. "At the pet store. You need food and water and food bowls and toys and a dog bed and a crate and collar and a leash and . . ."

He tuned her out as they walked with Emma and Wilson to the front desk.

It looked like Sunday football was going to be delayed.

THEY WERE HAVING an epic trip to the pet store, and Josie was enjoying every moment of it.

She felt kind of bad about it, but she was especially enjoying Zach's discomfort as he wandered every aisle, looking utterly clueless. It was clear he had no idea what to do with a dog. Wilson, on the other hand, seemed perfectly comfortable with Zach, staying by his side the entire time. She had no doubt Wilson would guide Zach on the details of having a dog.

Wilson was a huge hit at the pet store. It was clear he had loads of personality because no one could walk by him without stopping to comment or pet him.

Several single women stopped to pet the dog, and then gave Zach the once-over. Since Josie was wandering the aisles, she observed from a distance, and the women no doubt thought Zach was there by himself.

Josie wondered if Zach knew what a magnet a cute dog could be to a woman. Especially if said cute dog was attached to an extremely hot man like Zach.

He'd seemed oblivious to the women. Friendly, of course, because Zach was always friendly. But not flirtatious. She'd like to think it was because he was with her, since he kept glancing her way when he was talking with the other women.

Maybe it was time to step things up between them and act on those lurking desires that had been building for the past several months. After all, Zach was a hot commodity, and if she didn't grab onto him, it was obvious someone else would. She was certain he'd be down for some fun, sexy action without commitment. Guys always were, right?

"He probably needs this," Zach said as they wandered down the toy aisle.

Of course, it was a fuzzy toy football.

"I'm sure he'll love it."

Josie pulled a knotted rope from the rack, along with a rubber toy to fit treats inside. She also pulled some squeaky toys and chew bones.

"These should be good for a start," she said. "Once you get to know him better, you'll find out his likes and dislikes."

"I thought dogs just liked to chew on things. Mostly shoes."

She rolled her eyes. "You watch too much TV. First, Wilson is roughly four years old, so well past the puppy stage, and Marsha said as long as he has toys, he won't chew on things he's not supposed to."

"Then I'll make sure he has toys to chew on."

Her lips lifted. "Smart man."

"So, you're coming to my place to help me get Wilson settled, right?"

"What? You're inviting me to your secret lair in the woods?"

He frowned. A rather grumpy frown, too, but nevertheless he was still hot.

What would it take to make Zach look less hot? She doubted there was anything.

"Secret lair in the woods?"

"Yes. The women at school are convinced you're some kind of hermit, or a maybe a survivalist who lives in the woods."

"Wait. You and the other teachers talk about me?"

"I didn't say I did. I just listen."

"And they think I'm some kind of survivalist," he said as he handed the most interested college-aged clerk his credit card.

"That's one of the theories."

"Why?"

She shrugged and followed behind him as he walked with Wilson to his SUV.

"I don't know. Something about no one's ever been invited to your place, so you're keeping secrets out there."

"Out there?"

"Yeah. Out there. Or wherever it is that you live."

He looked around, then leaned in toward her. "Well, that's bullshit. I've got nothing to hide. Which is why I invited you to follow me to my house."

"For all I know, you're going to keep me prisoner there."

He rolled his eyes. "I promise to keep the door unlocked so you can flee at any time. So, are you gonna follow me?"

"Definitely. I can't wait to see your survivalist camp or batcave or whatever you've got going on."

He sighed, and she could tell he was exasperated. Good. She liked him off balance.

He put Wilson in the backseat and turned to face her. "Josie, I'm not harboring any secrets."

She laid her hands on his chest. "I'm so disappointed, Zach."

He shook his head, but his lips lifted. "So you're coming?"

She certainly hoped that at some point in Zach's company, she'd definitely be coming.

And hopefully soon.

Chapter 8

WELL, THIS WAS disappointing, and not in a bad way. Admittedly, Josie had whipped up some kind of house on a hill for Zach. A mansion maybe. Instead, he'd led her through long winding roads with beautiful fall scenery and tall trees until they'd gone through a gate and down a road toward some pretty impressive property that she assumed had to be his. Admittedly, she got a little excited when Zach pulled down the long driveway that was obscured by trees on either side. When they got past the thick woodlands, the property opened up onto a beautifully manicured lawn, a winding drive and a good-sized two-story ranch home with an amazing and cozy-looking wraparound porch.

It was perfect. Josie was kind of jealous that Zach had all this land.

It was definitely remote, though. There were other properties nearby, but it wasn't the kind of neighborhood like hers where she could walk out her front door and wave to her neighbors.

He parked in front, and she parked behind him and got out. "This doesn't look at all like a survivalist camp, Zach."

"Not exactly sure what a survivalist camp is supposed to look like, but just in case you're feeling any sense of trepidation, I can assure you I don't have a commune of doomsday preppers hiding in the woods."

She offered up a smile. "I wasn't the one who suggested those ridiculous things, but I'll be sure to put the rumors to rest."

He lifted Wilson from the backseat to set him on the ground, then looked over at her. "By telling people at school that you've been to my house? That'll just start up a new crop of rumors."

"Oh, right. I hadn't thought of that." She twisted her mouth as she thought about the rumor mill on that one, then shifted her gaze to Zach. "No one can know I'm here. You're not going to tell anyone, are you?"

"My surveillance system has already captured you," he said as he led her and the dog to the front door. "There'll be video on my phone, and I'll share it with everyone in the teachers' lounge first thing in the morning."

"That is not funny, Zach."

"I thought it was."

She knew he was joking, but the thought of being stared down by the more conservative teachers at the high school was horrifying.

Yes, she had friends at Hope High. Friends who wouldn't care, who in fact encouraged her relationship with Zach. But there were others who would judge her.

She'd already been judged plenty in her lifetime, so she had zero interest in being the gossip topic of the month. Or, in the case of Zach and her getting together, it might be enough gossip to last the entire school year.

No, thanks.

Plus, she had her students to think about. Her kids meant the world to her. Not all of them loved her, but some relied on her, especially her AP students. Advance Placement classes were intense, and spending the school year with those kids was a lot of work on both sides. She wouldn't let them down. They were her priority.

As she walked through the front door of Zach's house, she was surprised. She'd expected . . .

She had no idea what she'd expected. Some . . . man house, she supposed. Dark and chrome and dripping testosterone.

This place was nice. It had medium-stain wood floors throughout, a ton of full-length windows to let in light, and the furniture wasn't overly manly at all. Instead, the living room featured a pretty dark blue sectional and a decent-sized TV mounted over a beautiful porcelain tile fireplace. There were comfortable chairs, and the entire room felt welcoming.

It all looked expensive as hell.

"Can you take Wilson while I grab the other stuff out of the car?" he asked.

She pulled her attention from the designer living room and onto him and nodded. "Sure."

After Zach left the room, Josie looked down at Wilson. "I don't know what's going on here, Wilson, but this place is huge, it looks expensive, and I'd say you landed yourself in some comfy digs."

Wilson wagged his tail.

"Let's go check out the kitchen."

Since she had the dog on a lead, he had no choice but to follow. Which he did without balking. A good sign for Zach.

The kitchen was just as impressive, with a chef's stove, an oversized island, a large-sized stainless fridge and freezer, gorgeous white quartz counters, and dark blue cabinets. It was the kind of kitchen anyone who loved cooking would own.

"Okay, I've got everything," Zach said as he came back in. "I guess his food and water bowls should go in here?"

"Yes, they should. You should probably take him for a walk around the house first, and acclimate him to his surroundings."

Zach's lips lifted. "Is the house tour for Wilson or for you?"

She moved close and slipped her arm in his. "Both, of course."

"Fine." He leaned down and slipped the leash off the dog. "Come on, Wilson. Let's check out your new digs."

Josie watched as Wilson parked his butt on the kitchen floor.

"Wilson, let's go," Zach said, starting out of the room.

The dog just sat there and cocked his head to the side. Josie fought back a smile, and when Zach looked to her for help, she shrugged.

"What am I supposed to do now?" Zach asked.

"If it were me, I'd get down to his level and make friends with him."

Zach frowned. "Didn't I do that at Emma's clinic?"

"It takes more than one attempt, Zach. He has to trust you to want to follow you."

Zach heaved a sigh. "Fine."

This whole day didn't go like Zach had planned. He thought he'd go with Josie and help her pick out a dog. Kind of like his good deed for the day.

Instead, now he had a dog, and he was missing today's games on TV.

Not that he was complaining. Wilson was cute as hell, but they needed to get things off on the right foot if he and the dog were going get along.

So he crouched down on the floor and eyeballed the dog.

"Look, Wilson. I'm new at this whole dog thing. I know this is probably strange and a little scary for you, too. So we're in this together, you and me, right? We're going to be best buds, but you gotta trust that I'm never gonna hurt you. And that means you have to go where I go, okay?" He finished off by rubbing Wilson's back.

Zach was sure Wilson had no idea what he was saying, but when he stood and took a few steps back, the dog followed. And when he started out of the room, Wilson came along, staying right by Zach's side.

Josie came up beside him. "You did that perfectly."

"I don't even know what I did."

"You talked to him. Honestly. Affectionately."

He laughed. "I did, huh?"

She grasped his arm, and he had to admit he really liked her touching him. "Zach, dogs know when people are being genuine. And Wilson could tell by the tone of your voice. That's how you'll earn his trust."

"I'll keep that in mind."

He gave Josie—and Wilson—a tour of the house. He took them upstairs, mainly to get a feel for how Wilson would take to the stairs.

The dog was tentative at first, taking the first couple of stairs slowly. But once he got the hang of it, he bounded up the rest of the stairs and barked at Zach and Josie from the landing.

Josie laughed. "I don't believe there's much that dog can't do."

"I don't think so, either."

There were three bedrooms upstairs, and two bathrooms, one for guests and the master. He noticed Josie made herself at home peering into all of the rooms.

He liked that she wasn't hesitant. He wanted her to feel comfortable at his place. And when she stepped into his bedroom, he could already imagine her in his bed. Hell, it wasn't the first time he'd thought about her in his bedroom. In his bed.

His jeans tightened, and when she turned around and gave him a heated smile, it didn't help the current situation with his rapidly expanding dick.

"Nice room," she said, then made her way into the master bathroom.

"Thanks."

"Oh, you have a huge shower," he heard her say.

And there went his imagination again. Josie, naked, in his shower, pressed against the wall, the water pouring over her while he . . .

He didn't follow her into the bathroom because he needed a minute to get his overcooked visions under control.

When she came out, she grinned. "I'd love to take a steam shower in there sometime."

"You're welcome to get naked in any part of my house anytime you want to."

Her gaze stayed on his and her lips lifted. "I'll keep that in mind."

She was making him sweat. He wondered if she was doing it on purpose.

He led her downstairs, keeping watch on Wilson, who took going down the stairs like a champ. Zach made sure to praise him at the bottom of the stairs, and the dog's tail whipped back and forth.

Zach tended to spend most of his time downstairs, in the living room and the kitchen, along with his office where he worked out plays for the football team and graded papers. There was a bathroom on the first floor, and outside the French doors leading from the kitchen there was a great backyard with about five acres of land. Wilson ran outside and sniffed everything.

After his sniffathon, Wilson peed on every shrub and tree until he had nothing left to sprinkle.

"I guess the backyard is his now," Zach said.

Josie nodded. "Yes, it is. This is a great yard, Zach. I love the patio, and the outside kitchen is amazing. You must host some killer parties out here in the summer."

"Thanks. And no parties. You're actually the first person who has been here."

She turned to him. "Really? Why?"

He shrugged. "I don't know. I guess I like my privacy."

He caught the look of concern on her face.

"Oh no. If you didn't want me here, you should have said something."

"No, it's not that, it's just—"

"I was pushy, wasn't I? I invited myself over. I'm really sorry. I had no idea you wanted to keep your home life private."

"Josie, I—"

"I'll just go." She turned and started inside.

"Josie. Dammit. I invited you here, remember?"

She stopped. "Oh, that's right, you did."

"So relax, okay? How about something to drink? We'll get all of Wilson's stuff set up, and we can chill."

"Okay."

She helped him with Wilson's water and food bowls—there was a great nook between the kitchen counter and the back door that was the perfect placement for the bowls. Zach led Wilson over there. The dog sniffed both bowls, took one bite of food, a couple of laps of water, then sat and stared at them.

Josie broke out a ball from the bag and rolled it across the floor. Wilson chased it, grabbed it, and hopped up onto the sofa.

"If you don't want him on your furniture, now's the time to let him know that," she said.

Zach looked over at her. "Why wouldn't I want him on my furniture? That's where I hang out. He can sit there, too."

Her lips quirked. "See, I knew there was a reason I liked you."

"Only one reason?"

"What, you want a list?"

"A list would be good. You can start anytime."

She rolled her eyes. "I don't think your ego needs the stroke."

There were parts of him that definitely needed stroking by Josie, but he'd leave it alone for now. He moved to the island and leaned his hip against hers. "Oh, come on. I'm sure the list is endless. My good looks, my charm, my sense of humor, not to mention my expert kissing skills."

"Now, those I don't have any experience with, so I wouldn't put those on the list just yet."

He turned to face her and pulled her against him. Her body was hot, and he wanted to touch her skin without the impediment of clothes between them. His fingers roamed her back, and that heat licked along his fingertips, making him itch to explore her further.

"I'm happy to help enhance your kissing experience."

She tilted her head back. "I have experience with kissing, Zach."

"I imagine you do. We should put our experiences together and see how that goes. If you're interested."

"I'm interested, and you should most definitely kiss me."

He moved in, but then Wilson butted in between them and barked.

That heated moment dissipated in an instant.

Josie laughed and took a step back. Zach frowned and stared down at Wilson, who was dancing between them.

"I think he might need to pee," she said.

"Dude, we were just outside. You peed on everything."

Wilson continued to wag his tail, so Zach went to the back door and opened it, then went outside with the dog, who dashed over to a nearby tree and, sure enough, peed on it.

"Okay, Wilson. I'm noting you have the smallest bladder in town."

"Hey, at least he let you know he had to go out," Josie said, coming up beside him and sliding her hands into the pockets of her jeans. "That's more than most dogs would do on day one at a new place. You should praise him and give him a treat."

"For using a bush as a urinal?"

"Yes. That's how you encourage him to do the same thing the next time."

He brushed his thumb over her bottom lip. "The next time I want to kiss you?"

She laughed. "These lips aren't going anywhere. Except inside. It's getting a little chilly out here."

"Okay. Go pick out a bottle of wine. I'll hang out here with the dog for a while and see if there's anything else he wants to do."

"See? Now you're getting the hang of being a dog daddy."

He grimaced. "Dog daddy? Please don't ever call me that again."

She grinned, then disappeared. Zach wandered the yard with Wilson, who, despite sniffing every blade of grass, every bush and tree trunk, did nothing else remarkable, so they finally went back inside. Josie had some stuff piled up on the kitchen island.

"Hey, I rummaged while you and Wilson were outside. Hope you don't mind."

"I don't."

"Good. I figured you'd want to watch the game—" She lifted her head up. "Some game or whatever. If you're not particular about what game, I have suggestions."

He walked into the kitchen. "You do, huh?"

"I do. Anyway, I found cheese and fruit and awesome crackers in your pantry. You are well stocked. I'm impressed."

"I like to eat, and it pisses me off when there's no food in the house."

"Good food, apparently."

Wilson trotted over to the water bowl and took several long drinks. Zach pulled his attention back to Josie, who had apparently found the bottle opener, because she was pulling the cork out of a bottle.

"Something wrong with good food?" he asked.

"Not in my book. You want wine?"

"Sure."

She'd made herself at home in his kitchen. He didn't know how to feel about that. His kitchen—hell, his entire house—was his domain.

He liked people just fine, enjoyed entertaining them and hanging out with them, but usually never on his own turf. There were a lot of reasons for his choosing to keep his home base to himself, and Josie's making herself comfortable here was a . . . thing.

But he'd invited her over, so any way he felt about it, he was going to have to keep it to himself.

And as she laid the tray on the coffee table, kicked off her shoes, and pulled her feet up on his sofa, Wilson having jumped up and curled alongside her, he had to admit to feeling a kick of something he'd never felt before. He couldn't pinpoint exactly what that feeling was, only that watching Josie petting Wilson made him ache for something he was sure he'd never had before.

"You going to stand there and stare at us, or are you going to come over here and sit down?"

He blinked at Josie's words, but he didn't move. For some reason he felt frozen, unable to take that step forward.

Come on, idiot, you can do this. It's not like she asked you to get married or move in or anything. It's just sitting on the damn couch together.

Whatever this *thing* was, he needed to get over it. Forcing his feet to move, he made his way to the couch and sat between Josie and the dog. Wilson got up, turned around in a circle three times, inched over a bit toward him, and went to sleep, his body nudged against Zach's right thigh.

Zach picked up the remote and flipped through channels until he found a football game.

"Oh, my favorite team," Josie said.

Zach arched a brow. "Yeah? Which team?"

"San Francisco, of course. Mick Riley was the quarterback until two seasons ago. Now his son, Nathan, has taken over as quarterback. He put up amazing stats last year, and the team finished thirteen and three, and they made the play-offs, only to fall in the second round. This year they're unbeaten through four games. I think they're going all the way. They've shored up some holes they had in their secondary and added some key players on the offensive line. They're tough."

Zach leaned back and stared at her. "I'm impressed."

Josie popped a grape into her mouth, then took a sip of wine and smiled at Zach. "You thought I was just pretty, but a woman. And like most guys, you think we're out shopping when football's on or watching something else on TV. Women enjoy sports, too, Zach."

And like a lot of women, he was often misjudged, too. "Yes, you are pretty. And you are definitely a woman. And I don't judge the sexes and their knowledge and enjoyment of sports, or lack thereof. I never assume anything about anyone, especially women. I don't judge you, and I'd appreciate you not judging me."

Now it was her turn to give him the once-over. "Sorry, you're right. I assumed. Oh, please forgive me, Zach."

She batted her lashes at him in a way he found charming and utterly insincere.

"I think you're giving me shit."

"Good to know you're so smart."

"And you're a smart-ass."

"See, now we're getting to know each other." She laughed and handed him a cracker with some cheese. He popped it into his mouth and washed it down with some wine.

"You make good snacks, Josie."

"Thanks. And your taste in wine is excellent, Zach."

"Thanks."

She swirled the liquid around in her glass. "This one is an Oklahoma brand I'd never heard of."

"Yeah, there are some great wineries in Oklahoma. We should hit a couple of them some weekend. There's an amazing winery in the central part of the state that grows some incredible grapes. They even do weddings."

"Really?"

"Yup. I took a tour there over the summer. Great family-run business. I met all three of the sisters who were involved in the operation."

Josie arched a brow. "Three sisters, huh?"

"Yeah. Real pretty sisters, too."

"You trying to make me jealous, Zach Powers?"

"I wasn't, but are you?"

"Maybe." She leaned forward. "But you know what really, really interests me right now?"

She was close enough now for him to breathe her in. She smelled clean and a little bit citrusy. He wanted to take a swipe of her neck with his tongue.

"What interests you?"

She lifted her long lashes and gazed at him with those amazing eyes of hers.

"This football game."

He laughed. "Are you sure you're not a guy?"

She leaned back. "Positive."

At halftime, he grilled chicken tenderloins outside while Josie fixed them a salad and made some incredible vinaigrette to go over it. He chopped up the chicken, and Josie added it to the salad.

"This is really good," he said as they ate. "I like the fennel in here."

"Thanks. I like it, too. As well as your fully stocked fridge."

"Hey, you're welcome to come over here and cook anytime."

"I might hold you to that, because I like to eat."

She ate with enthusiasm, something he enjoyed watching.

"What's your favorite food?" he asked.

She paused, thinking, then said, "Spaghetti and meatballs."

He nodded. "Good call."

"Yours?"

"Easy. A nice, juicy steak."

She nodded. "I like a good steak as well."

"Come over sometime and I'll grill one for you."

She shook her head and smiled, then mumbled, "Like a dream come true" as she went back to eating.

"What does that mean?"

"Oh. This place. This food." She looked around, pointing to his kitchen with her fork. "If you'd seen where I grew up . . ."

He cocked his head to the side. "Tell me about it."

She shook her head. "Some other time, maybe."

"That bad?"

"Let's just say it wasn't like this."

He looked around at the fancy appliances and spacious kitchen and shrugged. "Josie, this is just stuff. It's meaningless without . . ."

He trailed off. No point in going down that road.

"Without what?" she asked.

"Nothing."

"You started the conversation, Zach. Finish it."

"Warmth, A sense of belonging. Of family."

She sighed. "Okay, I understand that. But you had everything, didn't you?"

"You'd like to think that. But let's just say I didn't have the warmest family. You don't have to come from a poor family to have a shit upbringing. My father's disapproval over my life choices still echoes in my head all these years later."

She laid her hand on his arm, sympathy written all over her face. "I'm sorry. I know what that's like. I mean, not the same situation, but . . . same, you know? Pain is pain, Zach, no matter the circumstances."

"Yeah."

They looked at each other, and Zach could tell Josie was as uncomfortable about the topic as he was. So they both turned and focused on the TV. He knew he was glad to get off the subject of family. Josie probably was, too.

They watched the rest of the game and argued over several calls. Not only did Josie know football, but she knew penalties as well. They'd gone about fifty-fifty on those as far as who was right, but she stood her ground and refused to back down, even when he told her she was full of it.

She'd even gloated when San Francisco won the game, and she made no apologies for it.

Josie was quite possibly the perfect woman. She was beautiful, smart, she loved sports and animals, and she didn't mind arguing with him over anything, both at work and outside of school. Plus, she'd asked about his family. Not that he'd wanted to talk about them. But he wanted to get to know her better, so the family discussion was going to come up again at some point. And if he wanted to get her to talk about hers, he'd have to talk about his.

Yeah, he liked her. Of course, he'd already known that before. But now he liked her even more.

"We should put the leash on Wilson and take him for a walk," Josie said. "Get him used to his surroundings and to walking with you."

"Sure."

At the pet store earlier, Josie had told him since Wilson was a small dog and had only three legs, a harness would work best for walking him. She'd helped Zach pick one out that would fit him, and now she showed him how to put it on him.

Zach had to give it to the dog. For his first day with new people and in a strange place, he was awfully patient. He sat while Zach fumbled with the harness a few times until he got it right.

"You sure are easygoing, buddy," Zach said as he kneeled in front of Wilson and affixed the leash to the top of the harness. "Thanks for being so patient with me."

After he stood, Josie wrapped her arm in his. "I think the two of you are going to get along great."

Zach looked down at Wilson, who he could swear was smiling up at him.

"I hope so."

They opened the door and headed outside.

Chapter 9

THE NIGHT TEMPERATURES were on the cool side, so Josie grabbed her sweater from her car before they set out on their walk.

For a three-legged dog, Wilson had some speed. He tugged on the harness like he had someplace to go. Josie showed Zach how to rein him in and make him walk at their speed.

It took some doing and about a mile for Wilson to realize he wasn't in charge, but he finally expended enough energy that he began to walk at Josie and Zach's pace.

She had to give Zach credit. For his first day as an animal owner, he was pretty zen about the whole thing.

"So, you've really never had a pet before?"

"No."

"You're doing great, Zach. Wilson's really taken to you. And animals know when people are jerks."

"They do, huh?"

"Yes."

"That must be why Beelzebub likes me so much."

She laughed. "He's a unique case. And Tumbles doesn't hate you."

"Sure he doesn't."

"Bring Wilson over, and he'll get used to both of you."

"Does he like dogs?"

She shrugged as they turned the corner to walk around the block. "I have no idea. I guess if you bring Wilson over, we'll find out."

"You'd torment your cat like that?"

Josie looked down at Wilson, who seemed as chill as any dog she'd ever known. "I think Tumbles can handle himself just fine."

"You're right. I should be worried for my dog."

"Wilson will be fine. I promise Tumbles will be on his best behavior."

"I'll withhold comment until I actually see that happen."

The conversation lulled, giving her time to survey the neighborhood. What neighborhood there was, anyway. There was a lot of real estate in between lots, and Zach's house was separated from . . . well, from everyone. Not that there was a lot of everyone to speak of. Josie could count the number of houses they'd passed on one hand. She supposed it was great to have so much land, to have the ability to plant a garden, build a shed, do whatever he wanted to do.

"You must like your privacy," she said as they turned the corner and made their way back to his house.

"Yeah. That's the reason I chose this neighborhood. It's quiet, there aren't a lot of people on the block, and the house sits back at the end of the road all by itself."

Zach opened the front door, then bent and released Wilson from his leash. The dog dashed inside and headed straight for the kitchen, where Josie heard him lapping up drinks of water. She was happy he was already learning where his stuff was.

She followed Zach inside. "You're reclusive, then."

He frowned. "No, I'm not. I just like my privacy and don't want to have neighbors being able to see into my kitchen from their kitchen."

"No chance of that happening with you being the last house at the end of the road."

They stopped in the kitchen, and Zach refilled their wine-glasses. "You're being snarky."

"You caught that, huh?" She took a sip of wine and set the glass down on the island.

Zach moved into her. "So you think I'm some pampered recluse?"

"I didn't say that. But I will tell you this place is huge and remote, and you could do with a little warmth and some companionship."

He put his arm around her and pulled her to him. "I'm not cold."

He was right about that. The blast of heat she felt from being close to him took away all the chill she'd felt on their walk. She put her hands on his chest, drawing in some of that warmth. "No, you aren't."

"Plus, I got a dog today. He'll warm things up around here, and he's a companion."

"Is that the only reason you decided to adopt Wilson?"

Wilson had made himself comfortable on the sofa and was now passed out on his back, his legs up in the air, which meant he was comfortable, and that made Josie happy.

"I'm pretty sure Wilson adopted me," Zach said.

Josie smiled. "This is true."

"Oh, and also? You're here."

She lifted her gaze to his, losing herself in the warmth of his eyes. "Which means what, exactly?"

"You warm up my house."

His words made her feel . . . unsettled, but also welcome. Something she hadn't often felt in her lifetime. "But I don't live here. I'm not going to be the one to give your house the warmth or companionship it needs."

He moved into her, his body aligning with hers in a way that made her aware of every inch of him.

Every delicious, hard inch.

"I don't know about that, Josie. You're here now. And things seem to be heating up just fine between us. Isn't that enough for the moment?"

The moment. She liked living in the moment. She wasn't much for looking into the future.

But tonight? It was definitely enough.

"Yes. It's enough."

He lowered his mouth to hers, and her breath caught.

Oh yes, in the moment was exactly where she wanted to be.

With Zach's lips on hers.

Chapter 10

ZACH TOOK IN the way Josie hesitated, the way she held her breath when he kissed her. He paused, waiting to see if she'd back away.

But then she melted against him, and he knew she was all in.

He was thankful for that because he'd wanted to kiss her for months now, and if she'd backed off again, he was going to be really disappointed.

Her lips were soft, and she tasted intoxicating, like wine and cinnamon. She was damn delicious, and he wanted more.

Kissing Josie was perfect, as if her mouth had been made for him. Her body fit perfectly against his, like they didn't have to adjust to each other. Instead, her curves slid right into his angles, and as he leaned against the island, she naturally slid into his body in a way that made him feel like this was meant to be.

He wasn't much of a meant-to-be kind of guy, except right now Josie's breasts were mashed up against him and her hipbones were kind of doing an undulating thing as they were kissing, and frankly, he was having a really hard time not grabbing a handful of her delicious ass cheeks to draw her closer, but he was trying his best to keep his hands to himself and make this all about the kiss.

She had a great mouth and she tasted really good, but if she kept moving against him like that, his dick was going to get hard.

Okay, he was already hard. Difficult not to be when a hot woman made moaning noises and writhed all over you. And when she tangled her fingers in his hair and gave his hair a hard tug, his erection went from "oh yeah" to "oh fuck yeah," and he needed to take a step back.

He gave her a gentle push to break the electrifying contact, and she licked her lips. He tracked the movement of her tongue, his mind traveling in some very dirty directions about where he'd like to see her tongue go next.

"You stopped," she said.

"Yeah. I thought maybe you'd like to clear your head and think about things. About where you wanted this to go."

Her lips curved. "I was thinking maybe this could go to your bedroom next. Provided that's what you want."

He sucked in a breath and leaned his elbows on the island, trying not to hyperventilate. "You know damn well I want you, Josie. I want you to be sure about it."

"I appreciate you giving me time to think about it, Zach, but I'm a grown-ass woman, and I would very much like to get naked with you."

That was all he needed to hear. He pushed off the island and took her hand. "Okay. Let's go."

Except the next thing he heard was this horrible yakking sound coming from the living room.

He turned to see Wilson barfing up a hunk of . . . something on the floor.

"Oh. Yuck," Josie said, moving away from him and rushing to Wilson. "Come on, baby, let's go outside."

She disappeared through the doors, shooting Zach a regretful look.

He grabbed paper towels and cleaned up the mess on the

living room floor, never more grateful to have wood floors and not carpet. Once that was done, he stepped outside. Josie was walking the property with Wilson, who was sniffing the area.

"He okay?"

She nodded. "No more vomiting. It might have been the food, or a combination of that and the anxiety and newness of moving in with you."

"So you're saying I cause anxiety?"

She laughed. "No. But it often happens with animals when they have a lot of new life changes to deal with. And anyway, Wilson seems fine. Do you need me to clean up the area where he barfed?"

Zach frowned. "I already cleaned it up, and why would you need to do that?"

"You'd be surprised how squeamish some people are about things like that."

"Yeah? I'm not one of those people."

"I'm glad to hear you have a strong stomach."

"Stronger than you think." Zach watched Wilson go over to his water bowl and take a couple of laps. Then he went back into the living room, hopped onto the sofa, curled up into a ball, and went back to sleep. Zach was glad his dog wasn't sick.

His dog. Huh. He had a dog, someone to care for. That was going to take some getting used to.

Josie came over to him and pressed her palm into his stomach. "Listen, I'm going to go."

"Why? Because my dog threw up?"

She gave him a look.

"Okay, I'll give you that. It's a buzz killer, and I should probably give him some time with me."

She smiled at him. "Exactly. Go cuddle Wilson. We'll try this again some other time."

He wasn't going to press the issue because obviously the mood had been broken. And he needed to make sure Wilson was okay.

This must be what it was like to have kids. If a dog was

this much of a distraction, he sure as hell wouldn't be ready for kids any time soon.

He walked Josie out to her car. She turned to face him. The wind had picked up, and Zach could tell the direction had switched to the north. The edges of Josie's sweater tried to make an escape, flapping behind her.

She shivered. He grasped the edges of her sweater and tugged her against him, then briefly brushed his lips across hers.

"Get in your car and get warm."

"I don't know," she said, tilting her head back as she moved in closer. "I'm pretty warm right here."

"Yeah, and the closer you get? The harder I get. And that's a problem."

She looked down to where his erection bulged against the zipper of his jeans. Then she lifted her gaze to his, and her lips curved.

"That is a problem. You should do something about that."

He laughed. "Thanks. I'll do my best."

She gave him a hot look and he groaned, opening her car door so she could get inside. And away from him, because she was too damn tempting.

"Good night, Josie."

"Night, Zach."

He waited while she drove away, hoping the stiff north wind would deflate his erection.

No such luck.

With a disgusted sigh, he turned and walked into the house. Wilson lay on the couch, looking morose. He sat next to him and rubbed his back.

"Rough first day, huh, buddy?"

The dog's tail thumped up and down.

"You're gonna be fine. We're both gonna be fine."

Zach picked up the remote and put on tonight's football game.

Chapter 11

JOSIE PACED BACK and forth in front of her classroom. When she turned to face them, she was happy to see that all of them were paying attention.

They should. *The Things They Carried* was a great book, and she hoped each of her students took something important away from it.

"As you're reading, I want you all to think about why the narrator describes the weight of the objects each soldier carries. A weapon, a radio, a grenade. Why is their weight so important to each of them? Two-page essay on the reasoning behind the descriptions of weight. That's your assignment for this week, due Friday.

"Really delve into the story, the reasoning behind it. What is the narrator trying to convey?"

The bell rang, so she took a step back so her students could hustle out.

Since this was the last class before lunch, she knew how important it was to maximize their free time.

For her, too. She gathered up her things and made her way into the teachers' lounge.

Jane waved her over to the table she was sharing with Chelsea, so after she grabbed her lunch container from the refrigerator, Josie made her way over to them and slid into an empty chair.

"How's your day going?" she asked them.

"Good," Jane said. "I'm hungry and no longer sick, so things are looking up."

Josie smiled. "That's definitely pregnancy progress."

"I thought so," Jane said.

"I'm hungry, too," Chelsea said. "All the time. Also, the kids in third period are on my last nerve. But I don't think that's pregnancy related."

"It isn't," Jane said. "That's your calculus class, and those kids are always a pain in the butt."

Chelsea sighed and picked up her sandwich. "True."

"Why are calculus kids a pain?"

After she swallowed, Chelsea said, "They're so smart. It's hard to challenge them. They get bored easily, finish the work fast, and then they start annoying me."

Josie dipped her fork into her chicken salad, then paused. "So keep challenging them. Hit them with something even harder to give their brains a workout."

"The curriculum only offers them so much," Chelsea said.

Josie gave her a look.

"Okay, fine. I could start printing out some worksheets I saw online. College-level coursework like advanced calculus and linear algebra. Not for credit, of course, but just to keep them busy."

"And challenged," Josie said.

"Like a math Olympics," Jane said with a grin.

Chelsea popped a grape into her mouth and smiled. After she swallowed, she said, "Yes. Anything to keep them from getting bored. And to keep me sane."

"That would work," Josie said. "I have the same issue with some of my AP English students. They've read all the material, they work ahead on their projects, and sometimes it's hard to challenge them with our core curriculum. So you have to think outside the box. I'll give mine outside projects, or I'll let them assist in grading papers from my freshman classes, and we'll talk about what works and what doesn't in terms of what another student has done. They often have a fresh perspective on a student's work that I haven't thought of. I love that my kids make me think."

"That's because they're all smarter than we are," Chelsea said. "Which I'm equal parts grateful for and terrified of."

"We want upcoming generations to be smarter," Jane said. "We want all our kids to be smarter. They're our future leaders. We don't want dumb future leaders, do we?"

Josie laughed. "No, we definitely don't. So let's keep challenging these kids."

"I hope my kid is smart," Chelsea said. "Then again, what if she figures out my laptop password by the time she's five?"

Jane laughed. "She'll do that anyway. They all do."

Josie nodded. "This is true."

Chelsea laid her head in her hands. "I'm doomed. Doomed, I tell you. And she'll probably have better shoes than I do."

"No doubt," Jane said.

Chelsea lifted her head. "I hate you both."

Josie laughed. Eating lunch with these two was always so much fun.

After they ate, Jane and Chelsea went back to their classrooms. Josie stayed in the lounge to check her phone. She had a text from Jillian who said she had something to tell her.

Now Josie was intrigued. She sent Jillian a reply.

What's the news?

Jillian texted back. You'll have to wait till Wednesday.

Josie scrunched her nose, tapped her nails on her phone, then sent another text.

You're tormenting me.

Jillian replied with a laughing emoji and: I know.

She made a few notes in her teacher planner, determined not to go back to her classroom until it was time.

When she saw Zach come in, she tried her best to ignore him. He smiled at her and she smiled back, but then he made his way to a table where the other history teachers were eating.

She knew it was best they not be seen fraternizing, but it was difficult to keep her distance from him. Especially today, when he looked so fine in his jeans and black button-down shirt. The sleeves were rolled up to expose his forearms. He had very nice forearms, but she couldn't help but stare at his mouth, remembering how soft his lips were when they had been pressed against hers.

She felt a sudden rush of heat and looked around to see if anyone had noticed her looking at him. Of course they hadn't. Everyone was absorbed in their own conversations.

Except Zach took that moment to glance her way and give her a knowing smile.

No one else had seen her ogling him. But Zach had.

Bastard.

How dare he be so good-looking and so hot? And how dare he distract her so much? She knew better than to let a guy get into her head like this.

With a disgusted sigh, she cleaned up the remains of her lunch and left the lounge, determined to focus on schoolwork and not Zach for the remainder of the day.

She set up her plan for the next class with five minutes to spare. Her phone buzzed, so she took a quick glance at the message. It was from Zach.

I saw you watching me. What was on your mind?

There was that swell of heat again. From a text.

She had it so bad. And she needed to get it under control. She typed a return text back to him.

I was deep in thought about a test I'm giving this period. Sorry if you thought it was about you.

She sent the text and smirked.
He replied right away.

Lying will give you warts.

She blurted out a laugh.
"What's so funny, Ms. Barnes?"

She looked up to find Keith, one of her students, had come in. She shoved her phone into her purse and shut her desk drawer.

"Oh. Just a text from one of my friends. Go ahead and take your seat, Keith."

She gave tests in two of her classes, giving her time to catch up on planning and paperwork, which meant the afternoon breezed by. Instead of going home after school, she headed to the library. She had books in her car that needed to be returned within the next couple of days anyway, so she figured she'd kill two birds with one stone. She could return the books and at the same time see whether she could wrangle some info out of Jillian. Because there was no way she was waiting until Wednesday.

After returning the books, she wandered toward the back of the library. Jillian was in her office with someone having a discussion, her glasses perched on top of her head. The employee was gesticulating wildly with his hands and looked upset, while Jillian, as always, kept her demeanor calm, nodding and talking softly.

It was one of the things that Josie liked best about her friend. Jillian had a zen-like quality about her. Nothing rattled her.

The door opened, and the employee stood there. "I will win this, Jillian."

"I'm sure you will, Greg."

Uh-oh. That didn't sound good.

After the employee left the office, Josie walked in.

"Is everything okay, Jillian?"

"Oh, hey," Jillian said, smiling. "Everything's fine. Just doing a new-employee six-month evaluation."

"Is this a bad time?"

"Actually, no."

"It looked like your employee was upset."

Jillian waved her hand. "Greg is never upset. Except with the Keurig in the break room. It keeps going on the fritz and he has to continually reset it, and he's made it his personal mission to make the damn thing work."

Josie blinked. "He was complaining about the coffee-maker?"

"Yup."

Josie shook her head. "So it had nothing to do with his evaluation? Not that it's any of my business."

"Nothing at all to do with that. He's a great employee. He's just at war with the Keurig, and I have to constantly hear about it."

"The things you have to deal with."

"Tell me about it. And I thought being head librarian would be all about the books."

Josie laughed.

"So, are you here for more books?" Jillian asked.

"Aren't I always here for more books?"

"Yes. It's one of the reasons we're best friends."

This was true. "I'm also here so you can spill your deep, dark secret."

Jillian gave her an innocent stare. "What deep, dark secret?"

Josie shot Jillian a look. "Don't make me hurt you."

"You think I won't make you wait until Wednesday?"

"You think I won't camp out here in your office until you tell me?" Josie crossed her arms and planted an "I'm dead serious and I'm not budging" look on her face.

Jillian sighed. "And you would, too."

"You know it."

"Fine. You drive a very hard bargain, though this would be a way more fun story to tell with wine."

Now Josie was even more intrigued. "Ohhh, it's a wine kind of story."

"It is."

She considered for a minute that Jillian was stalling. Then again, it was wine. Jillian would never joke about that. "I can wait for wine."

"You sure?"

"Absolutely. I'll go home and change, feed Tumbles, and meet you for drinks after you get off work, if you're free tonight."

"I am free tonight. It's a date."

"Awesome."

They made plans to meet at six o'clock at the No Hope At All bar, which gave Josie plenty of time to feed Tumbles and play with him for a while, plus do some of her prep work for tomorrow's classes before she had to change and leave to meet Jillian.

The bar was already full when she got there. She remembered Bash offered half-priced beers and a burger special on Monday nights.

She caught sight of Bash as she waited for her table. He looked slammed, but he waved and she waved back. She didn't see Bash and Chelsea's dog, Lou, at the bar, so Lou must be home cuddling with Chelsea tonight.

Josie managed to wrangle a small table in the corner and ordered two glasses of pinot grigio since Jillian had texted that she was on her way just as Josie had left her house. By the time the server delivered the wine to the table, Jillian was walking in.

"My timing is perfect," Jillian said, sliding her purse onto the vacant chair.

"It is. How did the rest of your day go?"

"Busy, but good. Children's story hour is all set for Saturday, inventory is going well, and I've started working on the budget for next year. So I'm actually a little ahead of schedule instead of scrambling to catch up."

Josie took a sip of the wine. It was excellent. "That's a good thing. Nothing worse than feeling like you're lost and falling ever behind."

"Isn't that the truth?" Jillian took a drink of the wine. "Oh, this is good, and a perfect way to start off the week."

"I think so, too. Now, spill."

Jillian laughed. "We're getting right into it, are we?"

"You seriously don't expect me to wait it out while we chitchat about nothing, do you?"

"Fine, then. Jeff Armstrong asked me out."

Josie's brows shot up. "Shut the front door. He did not."

"He did. I ran into him at the grocery store over the weekend, and we got to talking over the mangoes. Then we had an in-depth discussion about fruit salad."

"Fruit salad? Really?"

"Yes," Jillian said with a laugh. "He's going to some country club fundraiser party thing this coming weekend with a bunch of doctors. But it's kind of casual, like partly catered, and partly bring a side dish. He's not really much of a cook, so I gave him some ideas, figuring fruit salad would be easy enough for a non-cooking doc. Then one thing led to another, and he asked me to come help him fix something and go with him to the party. I said yes, of course, and I will not be making a fruit salad."

"Of course you won't." She was beyond stoked that her friend had a date with a guy she was interested in. "That sounds so fun."

"Doesn't it? I'm equal parts nervous and excited to spend some time with him."

"He is very hot, Jillian."

Jillian sighed. "He is, isn't he?"

"I'll want a full report of your date. I'm only sorry I can't go with you."

Jillian seemed to consider the idea. "Hmm, you know what, I could probably wrangle you an invitation. There are lots of single doctors. And I could use the moral support."

Josie grabbed her arm. "No. I was joking. You can handle this."

"But I want you to go with me."

Josie had zero interest in meeting single doctors. There was only one guy she was interested in, and he wasn't a doc. But she'd do anything for Jillian. "Sure. If you want me to come with you I will, but I don't think you need me there."

"Oh, come on. We'll see how the other half lives."

Josie laughed. "I don't think all doctors are as rich as you might think."

"You never know. Not that money makes any difference to me at all. I just like Jeff. He's funny and warm, and he really cares about the people of Hope. He worked hard the past few years to get that urgent care center up and running. He's very devoted to it."

"And it's always busy, so obviously it filled a need in our town."

They ended up eating dinner at the restaurant. Bash's chef always made the best poached salmon, and it had become one of her favorites.

As she ate, she noticed the football game was on.

"I'm surprised Zach hasn't shown up," she said.

"Should he have?" Jillian asked.

"It is Monday night, and football's on. I would think he'd be up here watching the game and hanging out to watch it."

"Oh, is that why we're here?"

Josie laughed. "No. I happened to make the connection when the game came on. Just surprised not to see him."

"And maybe a little disappointed?"

She slanted a look at Jillian. "I didn't say that. I see him every day at school."

"How's that working out?"

She looked up from her plate. "How's what working out?"

"You know, seeing him at school."

"I don't know what you mean."

"Oh, come on, Josie. You know what I mean. The two of you are dating, right? So you have to keep that a secret at school."

She didn't know what they were doing. "We're not dating. We just hang out sometimes. And we kissed. But dating? I wouldn't exactly call it that."

Jillian laid her fork down and took a sip of her water. After she set her glass on the table, she asked, "Then what would you call it?"

Josie thought about it for a few seconds, then shrugged. "I . . . don't know. Like I said, we're hanging out."

"Hanging out is what teens do, Josie. You're hardly in that category."

Jillian was right. Her relationship with Zach was beyond labeling, because nothing was progressing with them. Some of that was due to circumstance, but a lot of it was due to her own hesitation.

She should change that, because kissing him had felt so good. She'd like to do it again.

After she and Jillian finished dinner and said their good-byes, Josie went home. When she got there, she was going to settle in to read a book, but she picked up her phone.

It wasn't that late. She should check on Zach's dog, Wilson, and see how Zach was faring with him. Maybe Zach hadn't been at the bar tonight because something was wrong with Wilson.

She hoped not, and now she was worried.

She sent Zach a text message asking how Wilson was doing, figuring that was innocuous enough. If he was busy, he wouldn't text back. If he wasn't . . .

Her phone buzzed. It was Zach, so she pressed the button.

"Hi, Zach. I didn't expect you to call."

"You texted, so I figured you weren't busy. What are you doing?"

"I just got home. Jillian and I had dinner at Bash's bar tonight."

"Yeah? What did you have?"

He would ask that. "The poached salmon."

"Good stuff. Anyway, Wilson's doing great. I thought maybe he'd be lonely being home all day, so I went home after school and brought him to practice with me."

She loved that he'd thought of Wilson. "You did?"

"Yeah. I figure all day is long enough."

"How did he do on the football field?"

"He did great. He barked at all the guys while they ran the field."

"So he's taken on assistant coaching duties."

"Something like that. He liked watching them throw the ball around. I think he wants to get his teeth into his namesake."

Josie laughed. "I guess you'll have to get him his own football."

"That might be a disaster, because I intend to take him to the games. The last thing I need is him chasing a thrown pass."

"Oh, I hadn't thought about that. You're right. Footballs should probably be off limits."

"Yup. Besides, he seems to be enjoying his other chew toys. Right now, he's sitting on the couch next to me and gnawing on his bone."

She could picture Zach's feet up and Wilson lying right next to him, totally content. She was happy about that visual. "Sounds perfect."

"So, hey, as long as you called, I was wondering if you were busy Saturday night."

She paused. "Actually, yes I am."

"Got a hot date?"

"Not really. Just . . . something. I'm not sure it's something yet, but I need to keep it open."

"That's vague as hell."

"Sorry. Jillian has a date with Jeff Armstrong. It's some party with a bunch of doctors, and she's trying to wrangle me an invitation to go with her."

"Oh, yeah? Sounds fun."

"It could be. I'm just going to be her moral support."

"Or maybe you'll pick up a doctor."

"I'm not going to pick up a doctor, Zach." And he was being an ass about it.

"Sure. Anyway, I gotta go. Wilson just went to the door, so I think he wants to go out."

"Okay. I'll talk to you later."

"Yeah, thanks for calling to check on Wilson."

He hung up, and she stared at her phone. Was he upset she'd told him she was busy? And why had he acted like she'd offended him? Or maybe she'd just read something into their conversation that wasn't there.

This was why she hadn't dated anyone since her breakup. Relationships were confusing and always made her feel bad. And she had zero time to feel bad. She'd done plenty of that throughout her entire life, and she was over it.

So maybe she *would* pick up a hot doctor at the party Saturday night. And she might fall in love with him and have a happily-ever-after with him.

Or maybe she wouldn't. Maybe she could be happily ever after all by herself, because she was awesome like that.

Either way, Zach could suck it.

Chapter 12

ZACH STARTED SATURDAY in a good mood. It had been a long, tough week, and last night's game at Northeast High had been a hard-won battle against a very good team.

He'd taken Wilson with him to the game. It had been a risk, but it had worked out perfectly. Zach felt bad about leaving him home alone while he worked during the day, so he'd started going home after school to pick him up and bring him to the field for practices this past week. Wilson had gotten to know all the players and had gotten used to the football field before game night.

Of course, they'd had an away game, but it hadn't seemed to matter. Last night's game had turned out even better than he could have hoped for. The cheerleaders had adopted Wilson as sort of a mascot and watched over him so Zach could concentrate on coaching. After the game, his social media had blown up, not just about the win, but also with pics of Wilson with the cheerleaders, his dog sitting next to the players on the bench, and with kids who'd come to watch the game, along with a lot of comments about "Coach Powers's new dog, Wilson" and what a welcome addition he was to the Hope High Eagles team.

Not a single negative comment about having a dog on the field. He'd asked permission from the other team's coach before he brought Wilson, and Coach Simmons had told him he had no problem with it.

He was grateful for that. Wilson had a great time. His dog needed some love, and he'd gotten plenty last night.

This morning, they'd gone for an early run outside. There was definitely a chill in the air, and Wilson wasn't a fast runner, but he did pretty damn well considering he had only three legs. Zach decided he'd treat Wilson just like any other dog, and he'd let Wilson tell him what he could and couldn't do. So far, it was working out.

After they finished their run, Wilson ate his breakfast, went outside for a short sniff-and-pee around the yard, then curled up to sleep in what was fast becoming his favorite spot in the corner of the couch.

Which meant Zach could sit at his desk and work up some new plays for the team. They'd been working hard, but there were still some areas that needed tweaking, especially at wide receiver. Paul had dropped three passes he should have caught last night, and Zach felt his concentration was off. Paul was normally the one kid he could count on, but lately it hadn't been that way. It was getting worse, too, and Zach knew it had to be issues at home affecting his field play.

The question was, what to do about it. The kid obviously needed some help, but what could Zach do without directly interfering? Maybe he just needed someone to talk to. The only thing Zach ever did was ride the kid's ass about his play and his homework. Maybe it was time to dial it down some and see if he could get Paul to open up.

He thought about calling Josie to talk to her about it, but they hadn't talked since their conversation the other night.

He smiled about that. Yeah, he'd put that conversation about Paul on hold. For now.

He had some things to do to get ready for tonight.

NOT WANTING TO feel like the third wheel she obviously was, Josie declined when Jillian offered to come by with Jeff and pick her up. Instead, she got the address and drove over to the golf course, then wound her way around the streets until she found the clubhouse.

Though "clubhouse" didn't really do it justice since it was a long, sprawling building that kind of reminded Josie of a castle. She hadn't even known this place existed. The golf course was situated amidst a new community that had been built just a few years ago, according to Jillian. The houses were new, huge and looked like they cost a small fortune. It was an interesting contrast to her neighborhood, which was one of the older ones in town.

She loved her street, with its charming brick and frame homes that were nestled close to one another in such a neighborly fashion. She'd met the neighbors on either side of her, and they were great people. One was a retired couple who took walks every morning, and she'd often see Dave outside working on the house or the yard, while Amanda sat on the porch reading. The couple on the other side were around her age, had been married four years, and had a two-year-old daughter who was simply adorable.

Here, everyone was spread out, and the houses weren't close enough to walk outside and talk to your neighbor, but maybe that was the way the people who lived here wanted it. Though she supposed if you liked golf, it didn't suck to have a golf course out your back door. It all depended on what you were looking for in a home. For her, it was that feeling of belonging, something she hadn't felt when she was growing up, and why she'd chosen her neighborhood and her particular house when she'd moved to Hope.

The wind whipped her sweater back as she got out of the

car. She looked up and saw no stars. Instead, thick clouds cluttered the sky.

She could smell the impending storm, that scent of a coming shower that always felt so renewing. She loved rain, and a cleansing rainfall was the best. But before it decided to dump a deluge of water on her, she reached into the backseat, pulled out the food she'd made, and hurried toward the front door.

There was a sign leading her to the room where the party was taking place. Music was playing, and the room was already filled with people. She hoped Jillian and Jeff were there, because she didn't want to feel like an intruder.

She didn't have to, because Jillian spotted her right way and came over to greet her.

"I'm so glad you came. Here, let me help you with those," she said, taking one of the dishes from Josie and setting it on the table near the wall. "I made a carrot-and-beet salad because I didn't want to make anything unhealthy and be judged for it."

Josie laughed. "You think doctors don't eat junk food?"

"No clue, but I wanted to make a good impression. I'm so nervous. How do I look?"

Josie could tell from Jillian's nonstop barrage of topics that she was, indeed, nervous. She gave her friend the once-over. Jillian looked beautiful in a pale lavender shift dress that hit her just above the knees. Her white sandals were the perfect complement to the dress, and her green eyes sparkled with excitement.

"You look beautiful. You always look beautiful."

Jillian grinned. "Thanks. That's what Jeff said."

"He did? That's great. Where is he?"

She pivoted and pointed over to a circle where some people stood talking. "Over there with several doctors who work at the emergency clinic. Doesn't he look amazing?"

He did, dressed in dark pants and a navy button-down shirt. "He does."

"I could barely breathe on the drive over, Josie. Just sitting in the car with him made my pulse race. And there were no awkward silences, either. He asked about my work at the library, told me about the book he was currently reading, asked about my life here in Hope. We talked, you know? I mean we really got to know each other better on the short drive over."

She was so happy to hear that. Oftentimes you could build up in your head what you thought could be a great date, only to have it fizzle out when you spent time together and realized you had nothing in common. She had high hopes for Jillian and Jeff.

"Come on, let's go get a drink and join the fray," Jillian said.

"Sure."

Josie opted for a wine spritzer since she was driving. That way she could at least feel like she had a drink, but the alcohol content would be low.

Once they had their drinks, they wandered over to where the group was still talking.

"Hey, everyone," Jillian said. "This is Josie Barnes. She's my best friend and a teacher at Hope High."

"Hey, Josie," Jeff said.

"Hi, Jeff."

"Let me introduce you to everyone here."

She met a couple of doctors and their spouses, and a few more doctors who were there alone—two women and three men.

"Like you, Stephen moved here not long ago," Jillian said, nodding toward one of the doctors—a tall, good-looking guy with sandy blond hair and compelling green eyes.

"You did? Where from?"

"Bismarck."

"Oh. That's quite the change."

"Yes. I got a divorce and decided to move back home."

"You grew up here?"

He nodded. "Just outside of Hope, actually. But I got a job here so I'm glad to be back."

"Hope's a great town. You didn't have family in Bismarck?"

Stephen shook his head. "My ex and I are both doctors, so we ended up there because of a practice opening. I'm an obstetrician. So, after the divorce, I knew I didn't want to stay—for more reasons than just the weather."

"It's really nice here in Hope. And not just the weather."

Stephen laughed. "Yes, I like it here. And not just the weather. It's nice to be around family again."

"Then I'm glad you're back home."

"Thanks. Me, too. You want to head over to the buffet table and grab something to eat?"

"Sure."

She searched the room for Jillian, who had disappeared into the crowd. There were a lot more people here than she'd anticipated. She'd expected some stuffy gathering with a lot of dry conversation about gallbladders. She didn't know why. Preconceived notions of what doctors did, she supposed. Instead, there were music and dancing and lots of animated talking and laughing. As she and Stephen headed toward the buffet, she heard one guy tell another guy about his two-year-old daughter's antics, one woman tell another about how hard it was to get grape juice stains out of the carpet, and the beginning of a dirty joke she really wanted to stop and hear the ending to.

This was a fun crowd. She was having a great time. Even more important, Jillian was having fun. Josie finally found Jillian and wandered over, mostly listening to the conversation. She noticed Jeff kept his attention almost entirely on Jillian. He never left her side to go off and hang out with his doctor friends, and always included her in conversation. He even talked up the fact that Jillian was the head librarian and all the fun things she did for kids there, since so many of the doctors had children.

"We have to bring the twins for story time next Saturday," a man named Harrison said. "Don't you think they'd love it, Tess?"

The gorgeous redhead next to him nodded. "Definitely.

Libraries meant everything to me as a child. I know Marcus and Mandy will love the library."

Jillian smiled. "You're both welcome to come with the twins. We have coffee and tea and baked goods for the adults, and I have a couple of my assistants who help out with the kids. You can sit with the kids or browse books while we do story time."

"It sounds perfect," Tess said. "The kids will enjoy that. And so will we."

"We should make plans to go together," another guy said. "You know if Tess goes, Wendy will want to go, too."

"I'll call her and tell her about it," Tess said. "We'll make plans."

Jillian beamed a smile over at Josie, and she couldn't have been happier for her friend. Building up the library's programs was one of her main goals for the year. There were library regulars, of course. Josie had been one of them as soon as she'd moved to Hope. But infusing the library with new patrons would be fantastic, especially if Jillian could foster a love of books in children. It was one of her favorite things, and something they both talked about often at book club.

Josie followed Stephen to the buffet, where she piled her plate high with shrimp and crab and all the wonderful sides.

"Which one did you make?" she asked him.

"Oh, this one," he said, pointing to the stuffed crab. "But I have to confess I didn't make it. I'm not much of a cook."

"So you bought it?" They made their way over to a table.

"No, my mom made it. She's a great cook."

"Lucky for you, huh?"

He laughed. "Yeah."

He hadn't asked what she'd brought so he could taste it. She also noticed he filled his plate with nothing but meat and seafood dishes.

"You don't like vegetables?" she asked, nodding toward his plate.

"Oh no. I mean, yes, vegetables are fine. I'm trying out this diet. I'm training for this ironman triathlon and working on adding some proteins into my diet, so a lot of lean meats and fish dishes."

"But wouldn't vegetables fill your body with some necessary vitamins for fuel? And don't you need carbs?"

He gave her an indulgent smile, the kind a parent would give a child. She instantly lost interest in him. "People who don't know anything about how an athlete trains would think that."

As they ate, he proceeded to educate her about his diet and his training routine. In detail. He seemed nice enough, but it was clear that working out, training, and eating were his entire life. He never once asked her about her life or her interests.

Right now, one of her interests was not being the least bit interested in Stephen. She hoped her boredom wasn't evident on her face. She tried to look interested, but after being lectured at for thirty minutes, she was ready to flee. Unfortunately, Jillian was locked into a deep conversation with Jeff, so she wasn't able to make eye contact and send a visual signal for help. Not that she could blame her friend. Jillian was in the initial stages of attraction with a very hot guy, which meant she had eyes only for Jeff.

Which also meant Josie was on her own. She looked over at Stephen. "Excuse me. I'll be back."

She stood and Stephen looked anxious. "Where are you going?"

She resisted the urge to roll her eyes. "The restroom."

"Oh. Okay. I'll hold your seat."

"You do that."

If she was lucky, maybe one of his friends would sit down and engage him in conversation about beef protein shakes or something and he'd forget she existed.

She hightailed it out of the main room and down the hall, taking as long as she could in the ladies' room. She washed her hands, retouched her lipstick, fluffed her hair, and checked her earrings. She looked at her phone, and, dammit, not a single text message.

Giving up, she finally exited the bathroom and wandered

the clubhouse, deciding to check out the window display at the shop.

Golf clubs were *so* interesting.

"Thinking about taking up golf?"

She quickly turned around at the familiar voice. Zach stood there with a plate in his hand.

"Hi, Zach. I didn't know you were going to be here."

"I am. And I'm late, too. I'd better take this plate inside. Want to go inside with me?"

"Uh . . ." She looked at the main doors and hesitated, figuring Stephen would pounce on her as soon as she went back in there.

He frowned. "Something wrong?"

"I met this guy. He kind of attached himself to me, and he and I have nothing in common. Like, really nothing in common."

"Oh. Easy enough to rectify." He took her hand and led her inside.

She was right about Stephen. As soon as she walked through the doors, Stephen leaped from his seat and came over to her. He noticed Zach holding her hand, too.

"I thought maybe you got lost."

"No, I ran into Zach. Zach Powers, this is Stephen. Sorry, Dr. Stephen . . ."

"Belson," Stephen said.

Zach handed over his plate to Josie in order to shake Stephen's hand. She noticed he hadn't let go of Josie's hand.

Interesting.

"Nice to meet you, Stephen. Josie tells me you kept her company while she was waiting for me."

"Oh. You're her date?"

"Yup. I'm her guy."

Josie resisted the urge to let out an audible sigh of relief. Instead, she leaned into Zach. "Yes, he's my guy."

"Oh. I see. Well, you two have a fun night."

"Thanks, Stephen. I enjoyed—"

Stephen had already made his exit.

"Talking to you," she finished.

Zach looked over her. "No you didn't."

Her lips curved. "No, I didn't."

"That bad?"

"He runs triathlons. Eats a lot of meat. Big into his . . . physical conditioning. He knows nothing about me because he never asked."

"Oh. One of those."

"Yes. Anyway, what did you bring? And are you secretly a doctor and never told me?"

He laughed. "I made a prosciutto and fennel salad with pomegranates."

He laid his plate on the buffet table and popped the top off the container. The salad looked amazing. Though she'd already eaten, Josie intended to take a taste.

"This looks delicious, Zach." She grabbed a plate and scooped some onto it.

"What did you bring?" he asked.

And he'd asked her what she'd brought. Of course he had, because Zach was that kind of guy. Which was why she liked him. She smiled up at him. "The lemon pie."

He nodded. "Nice. I'll have a slice. Or maybe two. And no, obviously I'm not a doctor. But I contribute to the charity, so they invite me. This is the thing I was going to invite you to tonight."

Since she was at the buffet, she went for seconds on the crab salad as well. She glanced over at him. "Ohhh."

"And we ended up in the same place anyway. Kind of like it's meant to be, huh?"

"Funny how that turned out." Happily, too. He was her rescuer, and, she had to admit, she was happy to see him. For more reasons than just the rescue.

They took a seat at an available table. Josie looked around for Stephen but didn't see him anywhere. Maybe he'd left. She hoped not. He wasn't for her, but she didn't want him to feel left out, since this was his event, not hers.

She finally spotted him at a table talking to a pretty redhead. The two of them were engrossed in conversation with each other, and the woman didn't appear to be looking for an escape route, so Josie was happy about that.

"Where's Jillian?" Zach asked.

"On the dance floor with Jeff," she said. She'd been keeping an eye on her friend, figuring it was her duty to make sure Jillian was having a good time, but not act as third wheel and hang around too closely. She scooped up a forkful of the salad Zach had made. It was delicious and flavorful. "Your salad is really good. You made this?"

"You sound surprised. I have skills, you know."

"I'm sure you have many skills. I just didn't know that cooking was one of them."

He dipped his chin and leveled the kind of smile at her that made everything inside her quiver in response.

"I know many things. Can do many things. I'm extremely talented with my hands."

"Now, there's an innuendo I can get behind."

"Can you?"

"Definitely. I mean, we keep ending up in the same places. It's like fate is throwing us together. Like we're meant to be."

He gave her an odd look, so she knew she had to clarify. "I mean 'meant to be' in the sense that we should have sex."

He coughed and grabbed for his water, taking a couple of large swallows. "Okay. Didn't expect that."

"I didn't expect to say it. Not like . . . all out there like that. I'm usually more subtle." She looked around to make sure no one had heard her boldly proposition Zach like that.

But instead of pushing the issue, he let it drop, which surprised her. Most guys would have pressed it, suggesting they leave after she'd thrown out that not-even-veiled suggestion. Instead, he stood and held his hand out toward her.

"Would you like to dance?"

He was a constant surprise. She stood and slid her hand in his. "Sure."

The music was slow and easy, a song she recognized and happened to love. Zach pulled her close and they swayed together, giving her a chance to breathe him in. He smelled clean and crisp and very male. She wanted to get closer, to put her nose in his neck and inhale deeply of whatever that scent was. Soap, probably. Whatever it was, it was the sexiest damn soap she'd ever smelled. She resisted the urge, because she was still a little embarrassed about blurting out the "let's have sex" thing. Instead, she focused on the feel of his body pressed against hers, how tall he was in comparison to her, and how firm his thighs were, all which did nothing to change her focus from all things sex to something a little more innocuous.

She had to face it. She had sex on the brain whenever she was around Zach. Hence the blurting. It was probably time to do something about how she felt. It wasn't like it was a big deal. They could keep emotion out of it, have some fun, and maybe it would clear her head. After all, sex had been off the table for a long time for her. Some no-holds-barred, all-night sex was probably just what she needed. And with someone like Zach, who smelled great and felt good and was fun? She knew she could have a good time with him. Plus, he never seemed to take anything too seriously. It wasn't like he was out there scouting out a potential wife or anything. So her heart would be safe.

He leaned back so he could look at her. "Lost in the music?"

She smiled. "Something like that. I do like this song."

"Me, too."

The music ended, so they headed off the dance floor, running into Jillian and Jeff along the way.

"Where are you sitting?" Jillian asked.

Josie pointed out their table, so Jillian told her they'd meet them there.

"Would you like a drink?" Zach asked.

She nodded. "A glass of sauvignon blanc would be great, thanks."

"Okay, I'll meet you back at the table."

She went over to the table and sat. She noticed a missed call on her phone, so she took a look, surprised to see it was a call from her mom. It wasn't too late, so she went out into the hall and hit the CALL button.

Her mother answered right away.

"Jo Jo, my baby girl. You didn't answer when I called you."

"Hi, Mom. I was out."

"Oh. What are you doing? You out with some guy?"

She was not about to give her mother any details. "Just hanging with friends. What's up?"

"Oh, you know. Everything's the same down here. But I've run into some problems. They're cutting my hours at the market because Bill is a dick. He never liked me, you know, and, honey, it's really hard to make ends meet as it is with that shitty wage they're paying me. I shouldn't even be working there. I can do hair, ya know? But I've been to all the salons here in town, and no one's taking on new stylists. Anyway, I was wondering if you could help me out, you know? I mean, it wouldn't be for long because I've already got a line on another job. It should come through in no time at all, and I'll be up on my feet again."

Josie rubbed her stomach where an ache had formed. When her mother talked nonstop like that, she knew without a doubt she was using again. And if she was on drugs, she was missing work and using any money she had on coke or meth or whatever she could get her hands on.

"Mom, are you high right now?"

"Me? Of course not, honey. I'm doing just fine. I mean, I partied a little with Ronnie and Lil and the crew the other night, but I'm clean. I'm totally clean."

Josie sank into the nearest chair and rubbed her brow with her finger. "You promised, Mom."

For a few seconds, there was silence on the other end of the phone. Then, "I know, Jo Jo, but it's hard, ya know? And I try to be good, but it's really hard. And I get lonely, and Ronnie and Lil are my buds."

"Your buds are drug addicts, Mom. You need to stay away from them. Find new friends."

"Straight people are assholes."

Josie took in a deep, slow breath, resisting the urge to tell her mother what she really wanted to tell her, what she'd wanted to tell her her entire life. How often she'd let Josie down, how weak she was.

But that would be pointless because the one thing her mother lacked was the ability to take responsibility. Her mother tried and she failed. She tried again and she failed. And it was always someone else's fault. It was a cycle Josie was used to. She should walk away, but she couldn't. Because somewhere over the years, she'd become the parent.

"You're going to have to go get clean again, Mom."

"Yeah, yeah, I will. But you'll send me some money, right?"

And this was where it got really hard. "No, Mom. You know I can't send you any money."

"But I need it, Jo Jo. I don't have anyone else. You know that."

She heard the crack in her mother's voice, knew she was crying. It wasn't the first time. It wasn't even the twentieth time. In fact, her mom would always fall into tears when she didn't get her way. Over the years, Josie had grown immune to the tears.

Mostly.

"I'm gonna die here without your help, Jo Jo."

Then the pleas.

And the ache of guilt in Josie's heart that would never go away.

"I have to go now, Mom. Go to the free clinic down there. They'll help you get clean."

"I don't wanna go there. I just need some money."

It always hurt her to walk away. But she had to. "I love you, Mom. I have to go."

"But I need—"

She hung up, knowing her mother would continue to beg without stopping. She let her phone fall into her lap and stared down at it.

Things had been going well. When she first moved to Hope, she'd driven down to the southern part of the state where her mother lived. The job in Hope had been a blessing. Her mom had been clean for a while and Josie was hopeful things would work out. Hope was close to her mom but still far enough to give her the space she needed.

Over the years, her mother had been in and out of rehab multiple times. Josie gave her credit for trying, but until she got clean and stayed clean, Josie intended to keep her distance. She'd been hurt too many times to bear witness to her mother destroying herself over and over again. Still, she wanted to be close—just in case.

In case of what, she didn't know. She'd learned over many years that she couldn't help her mother. Only her mom could help herself. The only thing Josie could do was offer her love and emotional support.

And even that wasn't enough to keep her mother away from the lure of drugs.

Tears pricked her eyes and she shook her head, refusing to shed another tear because of her mother. She was stronger than that. She'd vowed long ago that no one would ever hurt her again.

She needed to remember that vow.

ZACH HAD BEEN deep in conversation with Jeff and Jillian, and he realized it had been a while since he'd seen Josie.

"Do you have any idea where she went?" Jillian asked.

He stared over at her untouched wineglass, then shrugged. "I thought she said she was going to meet us here at the table, but when I got back here with her drink, she wasn't here. I figured she was in the ladies' room, but she never showed up."

"Hmm," Jillian said. "I'll go check."

Zach nodded and watched Jillian disappear to the far corner of the room. When she returned a minute later—without Josie—he started to worry.

"She's not in there."

He stood. "I'm going to go look for her."

"She probably just ran into someone she knew," Jeff said.

"Yeah, probably," Zach said. "I'll be right back."

"Bring Josie back with you, okay?" Jillian asked.

He offered her an encouraging smile. "You bet."

He wandered the room. Since it was fairly dark in there, it was possible he could have missed her. But once he did a walk around twice, it was obvious she wasn't in there. He stepped out through the doors and into the hall and spotted her sitting in one of the oversized wingback chairs.

She was staring down at her phone in her lap, but she wasn't talking to anyone. And he could tell from the look on her face that something was wrong. She looked . . . upset. Devastated. Downright sad. Whatever had happened, it was bad. Seeing her like this was like a punch to his stomach. He walked over and squatted down in front of her.

"Josie."

She lifted her gaze to his. "Oh, I'm sorry, Zach. I lost all track of time."

"What's wrong?"

"Nothing."

"Bullshit. What's wrong?"

"I'm okay, really." She started to get up, but he laid his hands over hers.

"Just stay there and talk to me. Something's obviously upset you."

She sighed. "I. . . can't. Not here."

He nodded. "Jillian's worried about you. Let me go tell her you're okay, and that we're leaving."

She gave a short nod. He went back into the ballroom and told Jillian that he found her, that she wasn't feeling well and that they were leaving. Jillian wanted to go to her, but he explained Josie was all right, that she just had a headache. He told her that she should stay and have fun with Jeff and that he had it handled, and he'd have Josie text or call her tomorrow.

Okay, so he lied. But he knew Josie would be okay with that explanation and that she'd feel bad if Jillian cut short her date with Jeff to be with her. Plus, he did have it handled.

Whatever *it* was.

When he went back, he grasped Josie's hands and pulled her up. "You okay to drive?"

"Of course."

"I'll follow you home."

She shook her head and frowned. "You don't have to do that."

"I'm following you home."

"Okay."

It took only about ten minutes to get from where they were to Josie's house, which was good, because his imagination went into overdrive on the short trip to her place. He couldn't fathom what had made her so upset. And instead of conjuring up all kinds of tragic circumstances in his head, he needed to hear it from her.

He was right behind her as she pulled into her driveway. He walked up next to her when she made her way to the front door. When she pulled her keys from her bag, he took them from her. "Let me do that."

She easily gave them up to him, so he unlocked the door and she stepped inside, flipping on the lights.

First thing she did was kick off her heels and drop her purse on the table by the door.

"I need a drink," she said. "How about you?"

"A beer would be good."

Tumbles came out from wherever he'd been hiding and rubbed up against Josie's leg as she pulled a glass from the cabinet. Surprisingly, the devil didn't attack him when he took the wine bottle she'd grabbed. He opened it and poured a glass for her while she went to the refrigerator to grab him a beer.

"Let's go sit on the sofa," she said, her voice more subdued than he'd ever heard her.

"Sure." He followed, waiting for her to make herself comfortable on the sofa. She pulled a blanket from the back of the sofa and draped it over her bare legs. He sat next to her and took a long pull of his beer and stayed quiet, figuring she might need a few minutes to gather her thoughts before she started talking.

Tumbles walked over him—without an attack—and curled up, purring, next to Josie. Huh, that was a surprise.

Maybe the cat was tuned in to Josie's mood and figured now wasn't the time to cause trouble. Josie absently stroked the cat's back.

Josie finally shifted to face him. "My mother called while we were on the dance floor, so I went out to the lobby to call her back. It didn't take long for me to figure out she was high."

Ouch. "I'm sorry."

"Me, too. She's been an addict since—most of my life, actually. She's gotten clean off and on, but the sober part typically doesn't last long."

"So she's the family that lives in the southern part of the state?"

She nodded. "I was happy to have an opportunity to move back here. She'd been sober for two years, the longest it's ever lasted. I've been down to visit her, and we've been getting along really well. I had high hopes that eventually— maybe—she could move up here, and maybe we could be close again. Or maybe close for the first time ever.

"It was a dream, of course. She's fallen off the wagon again, and the only reason she called was to ask me for money."

He rubbed her back, knowing full well what it was like to have family disappoint you. Different reasons, of course, but the same result. "I'm sorry, Josie. That has to hurt."

"My entire childhood and a lot of my adult years have been spent taking care of her, worrying about her, wondering if she's even alive. When I was a kid, she'd go off and get high and leave me alone."

"Where was your dad?"

She shrugged. "I don't have any idea who my father is. By the time I was old enough to know that most kids had two parents and when I asked my mother about that, she just said he was gone. His name isn't on my birth certificate, so my guess is that she never even knew him."

Christ. "So, what, she just left you alone?"

"Not at the beginning when I was a baby. And before. When she found out she was pregnant, she swore off the drugs. And when I was an infant, she was more responsible. She went years without using, got a job, and I remember some really good years in there. We were happy. It was only when I started school that she started using again. I'd come home from school, and she'd either be high or passed out or just . . . gone. Sometimes she'd leave food . . . sometimes not."

That punch to his stomach felt like a burning hole now as he tried to imagine what kind of childhood Josie had had. "Did you have anyone else to lean on? Any other family?"

"No. No other family. We had some nice neighbors at the apartment who would feed me and let me sleep over during the times she disappeared so that the Department of Human Services wouldn't take me away from her. Because it was never more than a night or two. Then she'd show up again, and she'd somehow manage to scrape together enough money to keep a roof over our heads and put food on the table. I never asked how she managed that. I figured she was probably dealing or . . . something else. I never asked. I didn't want to know."

Christ, he couldn't imagine living like that. "Hard life, babe. No wonder you're so tough."

"Not as tough as you might think. I studied hard, applied to every university I could that was out of state. When I got a scholarship to the University of Georgia, I fled and got as far away from her as soon as I could." She offered up a tremulous smile. "I abandoned her. What kind of person does that make me?"

"A survivor. You had to look out for yourself because your mother wasn't looking out for you."

She let out a soft laugh. "I ran, and I didn't look back for four years. I buried myself in college life, and for the first time, I felt like I could breathe. I worked two part-time jobs while I was in college, and I squirreled away money while I lived in the dorms. I had never felt so free as I did then. And not once did I check on her."

He could see where this was going. "And the whole time you felt guilty about it."

She stared down at her hands. "Yes."

"You were young. Traumatized. I'd have done the same thing."

She shrugged.

"You still feel guilty. Why?"

She lifted her gaze to his. "Because we took care of each other all those years. She wasn't perfect, but she never abandoned me."

"Oh, come on, Josie. She abandoned you every time she used drugs. She's your mother. You were supposed to come first. You didn't. Never feel guilty for thinking of yourself during that time."

"I don't know. I'm exhausted, and I'm tired of thinking about it."

"Come here." He took the glass from her hand and laid it on the coffee table, then pulled her against him so her head rested on his shoulder.

"I wish I had the answers. All I know is we keep taking the same ride on the merry-go-round over and over again, and I just can't do it anymore, Zach."

"Then get off the merry-go-round. It's time to let go of that feeling of responsibility for your mother."

He felt her inhale deeply, then let it out. "Maybe."

She didn't say anything else, so he smoothed his hand up and down her arm until her breathing grew more even. When he took a peek about ten minutes later, she was asleep.

Zach rubbed his hand over the softness of her skin and listened to the sound of Tumbles's purrs.

And did a lot of thinking.

Chapter 13

JOSIE WOKE UP in her bed, though she didn't remember going to bed. Her dress from last night lay over the arm of the chair in her bedroom.

She would have hung that up. And she still wore her bra.

Okay, she never slept in her bra. When she smelled coffee—and food—she knew she wasn't alone in the house.

She got up and went into the bathroom, brushed her teeth and washed her face, then ran a comb through her hair. Then she grabbed a pair of sweats and a tank top and pulled those on before heading into the kitchen to find Zach there making breakfast, Tumbles meowing and winding himself around Zach's ankles.

"Good morning," she said.

He turned and smiled at her. "Hey."

"Did you stay here last night?"

"I did."

"What about Wilson?"

"I went home early this morning to let him out and feed him breakfast. He's out in my backyard right now, chasing birds."

"You didn't have to stay. Or come back."

"I know I didn't have to. I wanted to. You were upset last night."

She went to the coffeemaker and poured herself a cup of coffee, added sugar, and took a sip. Just what she needed. She leaned against the counter. "Did you put me to bed last night?"

He flipped the bacon. "You passed out on the sofa. I thought you'd be more comfortable in bed."

"That was nice of you. And thanks for not letting me sleep in my dress."

His lips curved. "Yeah, it was a real hardship taking your clothes off."

She smiled back at him over the rim of her coffee cup. "Sorry about last night."

"Never apologize for being honest about who you are and where you've been."

It made her feel raw. Exposed. She'd never told anyone about her past, yet for some reason last night she'd told Zach everything, and she had no idea why. Maybe it had been the phone call from her mother, leaving her feeling so vulnerable. And maybe it was something about Zach that made her trust him.

"Come on," he said, "let's eat something."

He'd made fruit salad and eggs, bacon and English muffins.

She took a seat at the table. "Just helped yourself to my kitchen, huh?"

He grabbed a spot next to her and poured her a glass of juice. "Yup. You have a problem with that?"

She picked up the glass and looked over at him. "Not at all."

Tumbles meowed at Zach's feet. Josie looked down at her cat. "I also see you've made a friend."

"I fed him this morning. He likes me now."

"It takes more than food to make a friend of Tumbles. Did you cuddle him?"

"Me? Cuddle Beelzebub? No way."

She tilted her head to the side. "Confess, Zach."

"We might have cuddled a little. But if you tell anyone, I'll deny it."

She cast a grin at him. "Your secret is safe with me."

"Good."

She dug into the food. It was good. "So, you can cook."

He scooped eggs onto his muffin, then looked over at her. "Doesn't take much skill to make bacon and eggs."

"Oh, trust me. I've known people who can screw that up." She waved her fork at him. "The eggs are creamy. What do you do with them?"

"Now, that's my secret."

"Hmm, you are full of secrets."

He popped a piece of bacon into his mouth and chewed, then swallowed and gave her a sexy smile. "You have no idea of my hidden talents, Ms. Barnes."

"Really. Do tell."

"I'm actually more of a show than tell guy."

"I'll just bet you are." She liked this easy banter between them. She also appreciated that he didn't pressure her first thing this morning with more questions about her mother. She had already overshared.

After breakfast, she did the dishes while he finished coffee.

"I need a shower," she said.

"Yeah, me, too."

Oh, that sexy look he gave her, the one that offered up so much promise. The thought of him taking a shower with her conjured up heated images she wasn't ready for. She already felt at a disadvantage, that she'd already given him too much of herself.

She walked over to him and placed a hand on his chest, feeling the fusion of warmth from his body to her hand. "Thank you for breakfast."

He picked up her hand and folded it between his much larger hands. "You're welcome. Are you okay now?"

As okay as she was going to be. "I'm fine. Thank you also for being here with me last night."

"I'll always be here for you, Josie."

She'd heard those kinds of promises before. "Thanks."

He went to the door, and she wished she could trust in her feelings. In Zach.

She opened the door and leaned against it. "See you later?"

"Sure." He pulled her into his arms and laid one toe-curling kiss on her, the kind that made her rethink asking him to leave. When he pulled back, she was breathing hard, her body on fire from being close to Zach. But still, he didn't let go of her. Instead, he tipped her chin up so she had to meet his gaze.

"I'm not going anywhere, Josie. If you need me, just call."

Dammit. Her eyes filled with tears. She gave him a quick nod. "Okay."

He brushed his lips across hers and let her go. She watched him walk to his truck and drive off, and with every breath she took watching him go, she wished she had been strong enough to ask him to stay.

Chapter 14

THE ENTIRE SCHOOL had been focused on homecoming this week. Mainly the parade and the dance, while Zach was focused on the football game. In the meantime, there were classes to get through before they could get to the rest.

He'd been working on some extra-credit stuff to keep Paul Fine's grades up. This week they were doing assignments on the Preamble to the Constitution, so he gave Paul some added assignments. He'd expected Paul to complain, but so far he seemed to be doing okay with the extra work. Maybe it was the one-on-one attention Zach was giving him. They'd spent some time before football practice discussing the Constitution, personal freedoms, and Zach tried to relate the subject matter to Paul as an individual. The kid seemed to get it. Or at least Zach hoped he did. It seemed to be working, and that was all Zach cared about.

In the meantime, today was game day, and he had to get through classes and keep all his kids focused on actual schoolwork when he knew damn well their heads were filled with homecoming. Hell, that was where Zach's head was, too, so they all had to employ some extra effort today.

So he made a bargain with every class. If they dedicated the first forty-five minutes of class to schoolwork, he'd cut it short, and they could chat up homecoming the last fifteen minutes. But no focus, no free time.

So far, it was working. He'd had full attention spans and class participation from every class—plus a lot of clock watching. But if he could get forty-five minutes of actual involvement from his students, he'd call it good.

When he finally got to his free period, he breathed a sigh of relief. He left the classroom, intending to head to the athletic office to go over the plays for tonight's game. Since they had all the pomp and circumstance of the parade before the game and introducing the homecoming court, and since several of his seniors were in the court, there wouldn't be a lot of time with them prior to the game. He had to make sure he knew what he wanted to say.

On his way out the door, he ran into Josie.

He smiled. "Well, hello—" He looked around and noticed students milling about, so he finished with "Ms. Barnes."

She gave him a curt nod. "Mr. Powers."

And then she walked right past him. No smile, no stopping to talk. Nothing.

He shook his head and continued on to the athletic office. But that short meeting with Josie bugged him. Was her response to keep their personal relationship away from the prying eyes of students and administration, or was she pissed at him for some reason?

He pulled out his phone to send Josie a quick text, then thought better of it.

This might be a high school, but his relationship with Josie wasn't high school. He tucked his phone away and pulled up the plays on his notebook. He had a lot to do before the game tonight, and his feelings about Josie were just going to have to go on the back burner for now.

* * *

"YOU'RE GOING TO the game tonight, aren't you, Ms. Barnes?"

Josie looked up from her notebook. "I'm not sure, Dominique."

"Oh, come *on*, Ms. Barnes," Melody said. "It's homecoming. Everyone goes to homecoming. Plus, the parade. The marching band. The cheerleaders."

Melody was dressed in her cheerleader uniform today since it was school spirit day. Josie had never gotten into homecoming when she'd been in high school, but she understood the allure. "I'll definitely think about it."

"I think you're, like, required to be there since you're a teacher," Edmond said.

She fought back the need to roll her eyes. "It's not a requirement for teachers to be there. But I will do my best to come."

"Got a hot date?" Melody asked.

"That is not your business."

"Oh, it is a hot date," Dominique said. "What else would keep you from homecoming, Ms. Barnes? Who's it with? Anyone we know?"

She sighed. What was it with these kids? Everything always had to revolve around something dramatic.

"I do not have a date. If I come to the parade, I'll be alone."

"Bummer," Edmond said. "My older brother is twenty-one. Has a job and everything. Want me to fix you up with him?"

Oh, dear God. "No, I can get my own dates. But thank you, Edmond. Now, let's get back to the book, shall we?"

She had to get a handle on this class before they dug deeper into her personal life. How had she lost control so quickly? Teens were wily and could spin a topic off course faster than a rocket launch.

By the time school let out, she was breathing a sigh of relief. Every class had been wound tight today, and their excitement level had given her a massive headache. All she wanted to do was go home, take something for her headache, and lie down in a dark room. The last thing she wanted to do was go stand on a street and watch a parade go by—or even worse, listen to a screaming crowd at a football game.

She went home, dropped her purse, and picked up Tumbles to give him a cuddle, carrying him into the bathroom with her. She put him down to open the cabinet and grab some acetaminophen, downed two pills with a glass of water, then went into the bedroom.

Tumbles had already hopped on her bed, so she kicked her shoes off and joined him.

She was out cold within minutes.

When she woke, she felt disoriented and had no idea how long she'd slept. It wasn't dark yet, which was good. Her headache was gone, too, which was even better. She got up and went in search of her phone, which was still tucked inside of her purse.

She'd missed a couple of calls and a few texts. The calls had been from Jillian, who had also texted, asking why she wasn't answering her phone. The texts were from Jane and Chelsea. Both were asking her about coming to the parade and the game tonight.

She sighed and punched the button to return Jillian's call.

"I was worried about you," she said.

"I had a headache after school today, so I took a nap."

"Oh, I'm sorry. Are you okay?"

"Fine now. What's up?"

"I was checking to see if you were going to the parade and the game."

What was it with homecoming? "I don't know."

"Come on. Get out of the house, breathe some fresh air. There will be stuff to eat and drink, and we'll have some fun. Jeff is meeting me there."

"Then you certainly don't want me there."

"Don't be ridiculous. Of course I do. Meet me."

If she didn't meet Jillian, it was likely both Jane and Chelsea would bully her into going anyway. "Fine."

They made plans on a time and place to meet for the

parade. After she hung up with Jillian, she texted both Jane
and Chelsea and told them where she'd be. They replied that
they'd meet up with her there.

Then she texted Zach.

I know you're busy with game prep. Just wanted
to say good luck tonight.

She didn't expect a reply, so she was surprised when he
sent one a few minutes later.

Thanks! You coming to the game?

She smiled and sent a reply: I'll be there.
He answered her text again: I'll look for you.
For some reason, that sent warm tingles across her skin.
She shook her head. Ridiculous. He would have zero time
to search the stands for her. He was just being nice.
But still, those warm tingles lingered while she got ready
for the parade and the game.

Chapter 15

JOSIE DIDN'T KNOW what to expect out of this whole homecoming thing. She'd never participated when she'd been in high school, and she'd totally passed on all the college homecoming stuff. She'd always gone somewhere off campus during the festivities because all the nonstop partying just hadn't been her thing. She'd had enough of the overindulgence and excessive partying in her own house growing up.

But this was a total family atmosphere. It was raucous in the best way. Kids from toddlers to teens were running about yelling and laughing, vendors sold drinks and food and balloons, and the parade started with the Hope Fire Department's truck blaring its sirens to lead the floats and bands down Main Street. The parade was about to start, and she felt that shock of excitement drilling through her veins. There was a giant banner across the front of the street that read *Hope High Homecoming*, and a grandstand had been set up with bleachers. The park was filled with people who occupied the benches, and every available curb was taken.

It was a cool fall night, perfect for a parade and football.

How utterly fun.

She walked over to the park and saw Chelsea and Bash. Jane and Will were there along with their kids, Ryan and Tabitha.

"Hi," she said as she came up to them. "This is all very exciting."

"It is," Jane said. "Is Jillian coming?"

She nodded. "She had to close the library and run home to change clothes, so she said she might be a few minutes late."

"We should go find a spot in front so the kids can see," Will said.

Bash nodded. "Lead the way."

They all followed Bash and Will as the two tall men made a path in the quickly gathering crowd near the street. They'd managed to eke out a tight spot near the main corner, but then Josie noticed four teen girls abandoning a nearby bench with a perfect view of the street, so the three women pounced on it.

Chelsea crossed her tennis-shoed feet. "I miss my high heels."

Jane patted her hand. "After the baby comes, you'll be rocking your heels again. While carrying the baby and a diaper bag."

Josie grinned. "And you can do it, too."

"Of course I can. I'm a woman, and as we all know, there's nothing we can't do. Except, of course, wear heels when our ankles are swollen."

"It's a temporary thing, honey," Josie said. "In a couple of months, you'll have a beautiful baby girl in your arms and amazing shoes on your non-swollen feet."

Chelsea sighed and lifted her feet up to inspect them. "I can't wait—for both of those things."

Josie got a text from Jillian, so she gave her directions to their location. Jillian found them a few minutes later and sat on the bench with them.

"How did you all score this awesome spot?"

"Some teens kept it warm for us," Jane said.

The parade had started, so once the noise from the fire engine had passed, they sat back and enjoyed the floats and bands and cars and civic organizations.

It was a colorful array, and Josie loved every second of it. She enjoyed the small-town atmosphere, how watching the members of the city council go by in cars and wave to the crowd could prompt so many cheers and excitement.

She didn't know anyone on the city council. Were they really that popular, or did they somehow elicit some sense of celebrity to people in Hope?

She leaned over to Jillian. "Is the city council popular?"

"Why?"

"They got a lot of cheers."

"Oh. This group has done a lot of good for Hope. Revitalization of downtown, enhancement of the parks, construction of a new dog park, increased personnel in the police and fire department, and a general push for safety and recreation. People seem to be taken with them."

"I can see that. And those are all good things."

"Yes, they are."

"It's often hard," Chelsea said, "especially in small towns, to get progress of any kind going. I grew up here, and for the longest time nothing was done. Then, for the past ten years or so, there's been amazing growth and revitalization."

She looked around at the beautiful tree-lined streets, the brick storefronts with colorful awnings, the movie theater, bookstore, bakery and flower shop, all owned by people who lived in this town. And for the first time since she'd moved here, Hope had started to feel like home to her.

It was a dizzying sensation. She shifted her attention back to the street and smiled as the middle school choir's float went by, the children loudly singing. Someday she might get married and have children, and years from now, one of her kids might be on that float.

It was a dizzying sensation, the idea of Hope being her forever home.

But she was getting way ahead of herself, and dreams often didn't materialize into the sweet fantasy of reality.

Her mother might have had those same dreams. A husband. A daughter. That small-town happily-ever-after. And somewhere along the way, those dreams had been crushed into dust.

Josie knew better than to trust in fairy tales, because she knew better than most that there was no such thing as a happily-ever-after.

But as she watched Bash hand Chelsea a cup of ice cream and looked at the way Chelsea smiled lovingly up at her husband, she realized that some people had figured out how to grab onto that happiness with both hands.

Chelsea and Bash were happy. Married. About to have a baby.

Her gaze shifted to Will and Jane. Will had hoisted Tabitha up on his shoulders so she could watch the parade, and Ryan stood in front of Will, while Jane and Chelsea chatted on the bench.

She wasn't jealous of their happiness; she just wondered if she'd ever find something like that.

"I love the school band," Jillian said, pulling her out of her thoughts. "They're so well taught. And several of the students come to the library on a regular basis."

Josie nodded. "Quite a few of them are in my AP English class, too. I don't know how they manage to juggle it all."

"Me, either. When I was in high school, it was all I could do to just do homework."

"Oh, come on. You're brilliant."

"You're my friend. You have to say that."

Josie laughed. "No, I don't."

"Well, you're pretty smart yourself. And the kids love you."

"Thanks for saying that. I do love what I do. And I like this school."

Jillian grabbed her hand. "I'm so happy to hear you say that, because we're all happy you're here."

"Ditto," Chelsea said.

"And ditto," Jane said.

There was that swell of warmth again, that feeling of belonging.

"Don't make me feel all warm and welcomed."

"Or what?" Chelsea asked. "You might start to like us?"

"I already do. But you don't want to have to deal with a blubbering woman on the street corner."

Chelsea waved her hand back and forth. "Please. You have two hormonal, pregnant women with you. We're used to tears."

Jane nodded. "True. We wouldn't even notice you sobbing."

Josie laughed.

"I don't know if I want to wade into crying waters," Jeff said.

Jillian practically leaped off the bench at Jeff's arrival, but Josie noticed she resisted. Barely.

"Hey, Jeff," Chelsea said. "No one's crying here. We're just giving Josie a hard time because she's being senti-mental."

Jeff smiled down at Josie. "About?"

"Friendship," Josie said. "Home."

"Aww, that's sweet."

"It is, kind of. How are you, Jeff?"

"Good."

He was talking to her, and even focusing his attention on her, but she could tell he wanted to get to Jillian, who was practically vibrating.

"I think I'll go get something to drink," Josie said, getting up so Jeff could sit by Jillian. "Anyone want anything?"

No one did, and Jeff slid into her spot on the bench, so she headed across the street to one of the vendors to get herself a cappuccino. The sun had gone down and it was getting cooler outside, so she wanted something to help warm her up.

Instead of heading back to the group, she wandered down the street, realizing she hadn't taken a lot of time to get to know the town since she'd moved here. Other than Loretta's bookstore, Megan Lee's bakery, and Sam McCormack's flower shop, which she visited regularly, she didn't stop in and frequent any of the other stores.

She was going to have to change that. As she wandered down the street, she noticed an antiques shop. She loved antiques. She made a mental note to stop by soon. There was also a place that sold pet supplies. She should definitely drop inside to see what they had. Frequenting independent business owners in her own town was more important than throwing money at the chain stores.

She ended up going around the block, making mental notes to visit many of the places she saw.

"We thought you'd gotten lost," Jillian said when she made her way back to the bench.

Josie smiled. "I went for a walk."

Bash and Will came back with the kids. "You all ready to head to the game?" Will asked. "It's that time."

They followed the crowd toward the school and the stadium, which, based on the crowd they were following, was going to be packed with people.

Zach would like that.

After they settled in their seats, Josie searched the field for Zach. He was out on the field with his players, walking back and forth. Despite the crowd noise, she could hear him barking out orders.

Her lips curved as she could imagine him fired up about tonight's game, about the overfilled stadium. He had to be incredibly energized.

"This is so exciting," Josie said. "My first homecoming game."

"Seriously?" Jillian gave her a wide-eyed look. "You're joking."

"Not joking. In fact, I went to one of Hope High's games recently, which was actually my first high school football game."

"Wow," Chelsea said. "So that means you never went to homecoming games when you were in high school."

She shook her head.

"In college, either?" Jane asked.

"Nope."

Jillian gave her a smile. "Well, then, you're going to love this. The energy just crackles. Everyone from the smallest kid to the oldest adult gets into the spirit of watching these kids fight for a win. And with it being homecoming and the stadium being so full, it'll make the experience that much richer."

"I'm looking forward to it."

Jillian went back to watching the action on the field. Josie appreciated that her friends didn't press her about the reasons why she'd never been to a game in high school or college.

Maybe they all thought Josie didn't enjoy football, which wasn't true, of course. At the time, she'd had more on her mind than having fun.

Now, though, fun was for sure on her list.

The first quarter of the game was definitely fun. Bremerton High was a good team with a tough defense. Hope High's offense was better, and by the end of the first quarter, Hope had scored fourteen points.

Having a core group of friends to watch the game with made all the difference. Loretta and Deacon Fox had also joined them along with their daughter, Hazel, and they all cheered and screamed every time Hope's quarterback connected with a pass, or when one of the receivers caught the ball.

At halftime, Hope High was up twenty-four to seven. Josie was on her way down the steps to get a coffee as the team started heading off the field.

It was then she locked eyes with Zach. He smiled at her, and for that quick second she felt a jolt of electricity, as if she'd been struck by lightning. She grabbed onto the railing and watched him follow his team into the locker room.

Wow. That zing lingered all the way through waiting in line at the concession stand until she made it back to her seat. Okay, she still felt the heat from his gaze.

Had that been her imagination? Had that quick smile been nothing more than a "Hey, I see you. How's it going?" on his part? Or had it been more?

For her, it had definitely been something more. And that something more was both interesting and thought provoking.

Either way, she was a lot warmer now, and it had nothing to do with the cup of coffee in her hand.

She couldn't wait to see him after the game.

ZACH HAD COACHED a lot of games. He'd played in a lot, too. But this one had probably been the best on record.

And not just because they were deep into the fourth quarter and were up by three touchdowns. Though that sure helped. The tight knot of tension that had lodged in his throat at the start of the first quarter had finally dissolved. Now he could concentrate on finishing off this game.

His boys had been hot since the start of the game. Warrick Robertson, Hope's quarterback, had fired bullets with every throw, and his receivers had caught each one. Their running game had been perfect, and defense had been monsters.

Paul Fine had caught six passes, one for thirty yards and a touchdown. He'd been focused and disciplined and had played the best game Zach had ever seen him play. Plus, he'd turned in all his work this week. So far, things were working for the kid.

And now there were four minutes left, and his team had the ball on Bremerton's thirty-yard line.

Zach took a quick glance over on the sidelines. Wilson was currently sitting with the second team, seemingly as engrossed in the game as everyone else. Which Zach knew had to be crazy, but then again, maybe his dog had become a football dog. He turned his attention back to the field.

Robertson tossed a shovel pass to Adams, their star running back, and Satterfield opened up a wide hole for him at center, allowing Adams to sprint into the open field and run for another touchdown.

Yes! Zach tried to keep his emotions in check, but he couldn't resist the slight pump of his fist. That touchdown was the nail in the coffin for Bremerton. Not that they hadn't already buried them anyway, but now it was official.

He pulled his starters and gave his second string some playing time for the remainder of the game. After all, it was homecoming, and he wanted all his guys to be able to say they got to play in the game.

When the clock ticked down to zero, the crowd erupted. Man, he loved the sound of a full stadium and the effusive cheers. He crossed the field to shake hands with Bremerton's coach and told him his team had played tough. He shook hands with several of Bremerton's players as well. They were a good group of kids, and everyone had played clean, something he always appreciated. After he congratulated his guys and coaches and let them go off and celebrate on the field, he searched the stands, remembering where he'd spotted Josie earlier.

She was celebrating hard, clapping and hugging everyone around her. When she turned to search the field, she found him, grinned, and waved.

Yeah, that felt good. He wanted to see her. Locking gazes with her before halftime had left him with a jolt of need to get close to her.

He smiled and nodded to her, and reluctantly filed that need away for later, because he had business to attend to first. He walked off the field toward the locker room, Wilson right by his side.

The celebration going on in there was akin to winning state. Except they hadn't won state. Not yet, anyway. They still had half the season to go. But he understood their enthusiasm. Homecoming was always a huge celebratory week, infusing everyone in the school with excitement and spirit. It always fired up his players, and now that they'd won, they felt like kings of the world. He'd let them have this, at least until practice on Monday.

Then he'd bring them back down to earth.

He walked into the locker room. "Okay, okay, okay," he said, raising his hands to quiet down the rowdy boys. "It was a good win tonight. Everyone was firing on all cylinders."

He looked around the room. "I'm proud of all of you. You played hard, and it showed. I've got a couple of game balls to give out. First ball goes to Macintosh for that interception."

A round of applause and yells went out as he came up to get the ball.

"Second game ball goes to Robertson for a perfect throwing percentage and four TDs tonight."

Lots of woo-hoo's on that one.

After Robertson took his seat, Zach picked up another ball. "Last ball tonight goes to Fine."

Paul shot his head up, looking shocked.

"Not only have you improved in your position as wide receiver, but tonight you caught six passes, went over a hundred yards and one touchdown. Well done."

Paul got up and made his way to Zach. Zach handed him the ball.

"Good job tonight," Zach said, smiling at the kid.

Paul grinned. "Thanks."

On his way back to the bench, he got claps on the back and good-natured shoves. Zach could tell Paul was enjoying the attention.

Great for the kid. He needed to feel good about himself. He'd worked hard this week.

"Okay, that's it. Have fun the rest of the weekend. Don't burn anything down."

Everyone laughed. Wilson barked at all of them.

Wilson ended up getting a lot of attention from the players. One of the team parents had made him a scarf to wear that was emblazoned with the Eagles logo. His dog wore it proudly. Plus, he looked damn cute in it.

Zach briefly talked over next week's practice scheme with his assistant coaches, but he knew everyone wanted out, so he kept it short. The locker room emptied in a hurry.

He went to his office and cleaned up the paperwork he'd left askew in his hurry to get out to the field. His phone buzzed, so he grabbed it to take a look.

There were several congratulatory messages from his friends, and an invite to a "private celebratory party" from the mother of one of his students who somehow had gotten hold of his number. He shook his head and deleted that one.

There was also a text from Josie that said, Congrats on a great game! Going to Bash's bar to celebrate. Come join us.

Then there was a follow-up text from Josie. Oh, and Bash said to bring Wilson with you.

His lips curved. He stood, shoved his phone in his pocket, and grabbed his keys.

By the time he got to the No Hope At All bar, the parking lot was full. Which didn't surprise him since it was ten o'clock on a Friday night. Plus, a lot of people from the game were likely here.

"Okay, buddy," he said to Wilson, attaching the leash to his harness. "Everyone in here is friendly, and you'll get to meet Lou, Bash and Chelsea's dog. She loves every dog who comes in here, so the two of you are going to get along great. You ready for this?"

Since Wilson hadn't yet met a stranger he didn't like, Zach didn't think a full bar was going to be a problem. Still, he intended to stick close to his dog.

He opened the door and was greeted with several rounds of cheers and applause.

He grinned. Wilson barked, and Lou came running over to greet his dog. They did a mutual sniffing, and Zach released Wilson from his leash. Lou ran off toward the back room, and Wilson followed.

So much for sticking close to his dog. It was as if as soon as Wilson had met Lou, Zach had ceased to exist.

"I see our dogs have met," Bash said, coming up to shake Zach's hand.

"Yeah. Wilson seems taken."

"Don't worry. Lou will keep him amused. Congrats on the great game."

"Thanks."

"First beer's on me. There's a table in the back corner." Bash motioned with his head to the southeast corner of the bar where all his friends were seated at an oversized round table.

"Got it. Thanks."

"I'll be right back."

He started in that direction, smiling when he saw Josie tilt her head back and laugh at something Chelsea said.

Her laugh got to him, the way she let go so fully with her friends. She gave all of herself in everything she did, from her work to her playtime. He'd really like to engage her in another form of playtime and see how much she let go.

And before those thoughts went any further, he dismissed them and made his way to the table.

"Hey," Deacon said, standing up to shake Zach's hand. "What a great game."

"Thanks. Where's Hazel?"

"Will and Jane took her home with them since she and Tabitha are best friends," Loretta said. "She's having a sleepover there tonight. So we're taking advantage and having a kid-free night."

"Which means we can actually have adult conversation," Deacon said.

Zach had taken a seat—luckily the empty one next to Josie. He grinned at Deacon. "Got some cussin' to do?"

Deacon laughed. "No, but conversation at our house tends to revolve around things a nine-year-old finds interesting."

Loretta leaned into Deacon. "Hey now. Said nine-year-old likes a lot of the same things you do."

"That's true. She does like football and soccer and baseball and all things construction."

Loretta looked over the group. "She also likes the Vamps."

"Who?" Chelsea asked.

"It's a music group," Deacon said. "And she talks about them all the time."

"Oh." Josie looked over at Zach, who shrugged.

"Well, aren't we all officially old," Chelsea said.

Bash laughed. "Hey, I knew who they were."

Chelsea arched a brow. "Really."

"Yeah, really. We do play music here at the bar, ya know. And a lot of it is contemporary."

"Huh," Chelsea said. "I guess I never pay attention to the music playing."

Josie looked over at Zach. "How about you?"

"Don't look at me. I'm a classic rock guy."

"Really."

"Yeah. Why? Does that surprise you?"

She twirled the wine around in her glass. "Kind of. I guess I saw you as a country music kind of guy."

He laughed. "Nope."

"You'll have to share your favorites with me."

"I'll do that. And what about you?"

She shrugged. "I like music. All forms."

"So you're saying you're easy."

She had been taking a drink and swiped her mouth as she laughed. "I did not say that at all, and you know it."

"That's too bad."

She leaned over and laid her hand on his forearm, the contact burning through the material of his shirt. "Nice try, though."

He'd noticed Jillian and Jeff weren't there, and asked Josie about it.

"They begged off," she said. "Jillian said they wanted some alone time."

The heated look she gave him made him want some alone time, too. With Josie.

They ended up ordering some appetizers to munch on because everyone was hungry. Everyone rehashed tonight's game, which didn't hurt Zach's feelings at all.

"So, undefeated so far, Zach," Bash said, sliding back in his chair after checking on things behind the bar. "Does that feel more like smooth sailing to the end of the season or more pressure?"

Easy question to answer because it ate at him after every game. "More pressure. They know they're good, and they've got a shot at making it to state this year. If they fail, it'll crush them."

"But they're good," Deacon said. "So you just have to keep telling them that, and work with them the same way you have been doing. They've got this."

Zach nodded. "That's my intention."

Josie gave him a concerned look. Her fingers crept closer to him, but she didn't make that move. He understood why. They weren't a couple, and she wasn't ready to take that step to make whatever it was between them public.

"Are you going to the homecoming dance tomorrow night?" she asked.

He nodded. "Chaperoning. Figured I could keep my eyes on my players that way."

"Me, too. Though I don't have players, of course. But it'll give me a chance to go to a homecoming dance."

He shot her a curious glance. "What do you mean?"

"I never went to my own. Or prom."

"No kidding."

"You didn't go to prom?" Chelsea asked.

"No. I wasn't into that kind of thing in high school."

He saw Josie's lips close up tight, realized there was more she wanted to say, but didn't.

"Well, honey, you definitely have to go to this one," Chelsea said. "Bash and I will go, too, won't we, babe?"

"Sure. Wait, what?"

Zach grinned at Bash's deer-in-the-headlights look.

"Come on, you always wanted to take your pregnant wife to the homecoming dance, didn't you?"

Bash gave Chelsea a smile. "Anything for you. I'll arrange for Dave to cover here tomorrow night."

"Perfect. I'll squeeze my pregnant belly into a killer dress and sparkly sandals since I can't wear heels. And we'll tell Jane she's going, too. We'll all chaperone."

Josie nearly quivered in her chair. "Oh, now it's going to be fun, won't it, Zach?"

Not exactly the one-on-one date he was looking for, considering there'd be more than a hundred teens there, plus faculty eyeballing the two of them. But he might be able to sneak a dance with Josie. And that would be a start.

"Yeah, it'll be fun."

Chapter 16

JOSIE SPENT THE better part of Saturday hanging out with Chelsea and Jane because Chelsea insisted if they were going to the homecoming dance, they had to get manicures and pedicures and decide on clothing options.

Plus, Chelsea said she needed the moral support more than anyone because she couldn't decide what to wear that would make her look pretty in her very pregnant state. So Josie and Jane went over to her house while Bash disappeared to do some things at the bar.

"I don't know why you're worried," Josie said. "Even as far along as you are, you're still gorgeous."

Which was true. With her red hair, intense blue-green eyes, and a body that, despite the pregnancy, still smoked hot, Chelsea had nothing to be concerned about.

Chelsea stood in her bedroom, hands on her hips. "My ankles are swollen."

Jane looked down at her feet. "Only a little, honey. And you had tiny ankles to start with, which is why you could wear those tall heels all the time."

Chelsea waved her hand at Jane. "Pfft. Anyone can wear heels. It just takes practice."

Jane was lounging in the oh-so-comfortable-looking oversized chair in Chelsea's bedroom. "Uh-huh. Wait till you have a toddler to chase after. Those heels will quickly lose their appeal."

Chelsea raised her chin. "Heels will never lose their appeal to me, and I can chase after my kid no matter what I'm wearing. I will not be defeated by a tiny replica of me."

Josie laughed. "I can already picture an adorable red-headed toddler."

Chelsea sighed. "Me, too. And she'll likely have Bash wrapped around her little finger."

Josie could picture that. "Doesn't she already?"

"Yes. He reads to her in bed every night. Well, he reads to my belly. And sings to her. It's kind of adorable. I have it on video to show her someday."

"Aww, that's so sweet," Josie said.

"Will does the same thing," Jane said. "He'll talk to our baby and sing songs, and no matter what he's reading, even if it's a sports article, he'll read it to my stomach."

Josie couldn't imagine what that must be like. She never knew her father, so having that kind of bonding with a father figure had to be . . . incredible.

Josie looked over at Jane. "Does he want a boy or a girl?"

"He's stepped up and been such a great father to both Ryan and Tabby, and I've seen him with both of them. He's just as happy taking Tabby to her dance recitals as he is taking Ryan to football games. He's so excited about this baby that he doesn't care about the sex."

"And your kids are okay about Will having a child of his own?" Josie asked.

"Since my ex is out of the picture forever, they already think of themselves as Will's kids. He is their father in every way. So this is just another sibling to them."

She was so happy life had worked out so well for Jane and Will. "Perfect. I'm so excited for all of you."

"Thanks. Me, too."

"Me, three," Chelsea said. "But in the meantime, you both have to help me choose a dress."

Fortunately, Chelsea had an extensive closet. There was a mauve short-sleeved dress that was modest enough for a high school dance, but fit Chelsea perfectly and was drop-dead gorgeous on her. And she had a pair of sparkly gold sandals that were just the right touch.

After that, they had some tea and butter cake that Chelsea had picked up from Megan's bakery that morning.

Josie bit into the cake, and she swore it simply melted on her tongue. Delicious.

"What are you wearing tonight?" Chelsea asked them.

"Probably a tarp from the garage," Jane said.

"Please," Josie said. "You're petite and adorable, and you barely even have a belly."

"I have enough of a belly that none of my clothes fit anymore."

"You'll wear something from my closet, then," Chelsea said.

Jane's eyes lit up. "Ooh. I accept."

"What? No arguing? Usually you argue."

Jane shrugged. "I'm pregnant and nothing fits and I'm frustrated and I need a pretty dress. No arguing today."

Josie grinned. After seeing Chelsea's closet, she didn't blame her at all.

They ended up agreeing on a beautiful copper dress for Jane with scalloped sleeves and a scoop neck that fit her perfectly. She looked at herself in the mirror and smiled.

"Will's eyes are going to bug out of his head when he sees me in this."

"I'll bet his eyes do that all the time."

She turned to Josie and grinned. "Well, yeah. They do. What can I say? He loves me."

"You're just mushy in love, Jane," Chelsea said. "It's disgusting."

"Oh, and you're not? Last time the four of us went out to

dinner, you and Bash were nuzzling up to each other so much I blushed throughout the entire meal."

"Hey, we're newlyweds."

"Uh-huh. But not new to each other." Jane looked over at Josie. "Seriously. He had his hand on her neck, she had her hand on his lap doing—God knows what?"

"Well, it wasn't *that*. I was rubbing his thigh."

Jane held up her hand. "Don't even want to know."

Josie laughed. She could tell these two had been friends for a long time. Their banter was like a comedy show.

"What about you, Josie?" Jane asked. "What are you wearing tonight?"

"Oh, I haven't thought about it yet. I have a nice black dress. I'll probably wear that."

Chelsea arched a brow. "Is this one of those standard black dresses you wear to weddings and funerals?"

Josie cracked a smile. "Maybe."

"That's what I thought." Chelsea gave her the once-over. "We're about the same height."

"Yes, but you're way curvier than I am." In other words, Chelsea had boobs. Josie definitely did not.

"This is true, but I have a couple of dresses I think would look amazing on you."

"Oh, it's okay, you don't—"

Before she could finish her sentence, Chelsea had disappeared into that huge magical closet.

"No point in arguing with her," Jane said. "When she wants to outfit you, you kind of don't have a choice."

Josie relaxed. "So I've noticed."

Chelsea came out with three dresses, all stunning and not one of them the kind of dress Josie would wear. Josie's tastes ran more along the lines of vintage and hippie wear. But when Chelsea threw a cream-colored sparkly dress at her, something about it captured her attention. She couldn't resist trying it on.

"It has a vintage feel," Chelsea yelled at her from the other side of the bathroom door. "It's always been a little tight on me at the bust, so it should fit you perfectly."

It fit her like it had been made for her. And the sequins over the lace had a faded pearlish look that made them look vintage, which was right up her alley. Plus, the long sleeves came to a bell at the wrist, which lent a seventies vibe to the entire outfit. And she had the perfect shoes to go with the dress.

She opened the door and stood in the doorway.

Jane gasped. "Wow."

Chelsea grinned. "I knew that dress was perfect for you. With your short black hair and your lithe body, it's like the dress has been sitting in my closet all this time just waiting for you to wear it."

Josie lifted the tag from inside the cuff. "I noticed it still had the tag on it."

"Many of Chelsea's dresses do," Jane said.

"I found bargains, and I buy things I love." Chelsea shrugged. "Which doesn't mean I'm ever going to wear them."

"Wherever did you find this?" Josie asked.

"There's an amazing secondhand store that sells the most incredible dresses. We'll have to go shopping there because I think you'd love their clothes."

A shop like that would be perfect for her. "In town?"

Chelsea nodded. "It's a block off the main street, so you wouldn't notice it unless you were specifically looking for it. I'll give you the address so you can go. It'll be a few months before I'm ready to dress-shop again."

"I'll mark you in my calendar for two months after the baby comes," Josie said.

Chelsea laughed. "You're on. By then, I'll be ready to leave her with Bash and take a shopping excursion."

Jane snickered.

"What?" Chelsea asked.

"Or you'll be taking her with you because you won't be able to stand leaving her for even an hour."

Chelsea's lips curved, and she rubbed her belly. "You might be right. For someone like me who's been so independent her whole life, I've gotten used to carrying her around with me. I can't wait until she gets here."

"The last trimester always goes by the slowest," Jane said.

Josie was excited about both Chelsea and Jane having their babies. She might not be popping out babies herself any time soon, but she couldn't wait to hold her friends' little ones.

After she left Chelsea's house with the exquisite dress in tow, she walked home—courtesy of living right down the street from Chelsea. The crispness of fall had hit Hope, and the leaves were finally turning. She slowed her walk and admired the gold, scarlet, and magenta colors that lined her beautiful street.

She loved autumn. There was something about the change of season from sticky, hot summer to breezy, cool fall that felt renewing to her. Maybe it harkened back to spending summers at home, where she had frequently been stuck with her mother, who was often out of work. She had tried to hang out with friends or at the library, but inevitably she'd had to stay home to take care of her mom. So while a lot of kids had fond memories of youthful summers, most of Josie's memories were of her mother's drugged-out escapades and her worrying that her mom was going to overdose and die and leave her alone.

By the time she got home, her stomach had knotted up from the unpleasant stroll down memory lane, and her happy fall feeling had dissipated. And now she felt like she should call her mom and check on her, even though she knew she should let it go. She wasn't her mother's keeper.

Not anymore.

She hung up the dress and did a load of laundry. After she got the first load into the dryer, she sat at the kitchen table to make a grocery list on her phone. While she was thinking of the ingredients for the quinoa salad she wanted to make, a text message popped up from her mom.

She immediately clicked over, her heart sinking as she read it.

Hi, my little Jo Jo. So, I was wondering if you had
a little cash to spare. They cut my hours at the
store, and I'm having trouble making rent. Just to
hold me until next month, you know? I love you,
baby.

Josie sighed. It was as if they hadn't had that phone conversation last week. Then again, her mother had almost
assuredly been high at the time and likely didn't even
remember that phone call.

She fiddled with her fingers, debating whether to call her
mom, but figured if she sent a text reply, maybe her mother
would see it and remember this time.

She started typing.

Hi, Mom. I'm sorry, I can't send you any money.
You know why.

She started to send the message, but hesitated, then added
I love you, too at the end.

She went back to her grocery list, then finished her laundry. Every now and then she'd stop and go back to stare at
that text message, not sure if she wanted a reply from her
mother.

When it was time to get ready for the dance, she knew
the nonresponse from her mom was the best answer.

Chapter 17

ZACH FIDGETED WITH his tie and searched the room, wishing Josie had agreed to let him pick her up. Instead, she told him she was going to drive herself to the dance so it wouldn't look so conspicuously like they were dating.

Logically, he knew she was right, but he'd wanted to pick her up. He'd wanted to kiss her and maybe make out a little before driving over to the Hope Community Center for the dance.

Instead, he stood near the entrance, watching the kids come in to have their photos taken. That was fun, too, especially seeing some of his burly linemen in suits, straining the seams of their jackets as they posed like uncomfortable sticks with their dates, who looked much more chill than the guys. But his guys' body language during these photos spoke volumes.

The ones who were on first dates? Hands in pockets, or they didn't know where to put their hands. And the girls were kind of shy as well. It was cute.

The ones who were couples, on the other hand, were all over each other, hands-wise, and he'd had to step in a couple of times to put a stop to hands on the ass or other suggestive poses.

He was definitely going to have to be on his game tonight. The last thing he needed was to have one of his players called out by the administration for inappropriate behavior.

He shifted his gaze to the front door as a couple came in. It was Bash and Chelsea, along with Will and Jane. He nodded and smiled at them, then masked his disappointment by shaking his head when Delbert Nottingham dropped his hand over his date's shoulder and let his fingers trail a little too close to her cleavage.

He could not believe he'd gotten so old, he was relegated to ass-and-boob patrol. It wasn't that long ago he'd been chasing tail. Now he was protecting it.

"Lookin' for a date, honey?"

Someone slung an arm around his shoulder. He looked over to find Bash standing next to him.

On the other side of him, Will, shaking his head. "I've never seen a sadder spectacle of manhood. All alone, hugging the wall, unloved. It's kind of pathetic."

He frowned. "Speaking of dates, don't you two have some?"

Bash grinned. "We do. They're off checking themselves in as chaperones."

"We, on the other hand, are not chaperones," Will said. "And you looked kind of lonely, so we thought we'd see if we could help you out."

"I'm not lonely. I'm keeping an eye on the students."

"Looked to me like you were keeping an eye on the door," Will said, sliding his gaze to the double doors. "Got a hot date?"

"No." These guys saw way too much. Was he wearing his thoughts on his face? If so, he was going to have to work on being more guarded.

"Want us to fix you up with someone?" Bash asked. "Chelsea said Bekka Sims is available. She's a fellow history teacher, right?"

"I don't date other teachers."

His gaze snapped to the doorway, where he saw Josie walk in and slide off her coat, revealing a knock-him-dead lacy dress that clung to her body.

"Damn."

Will snorted out a laugh, then leaned in toward him. "Yeah, you don't date other teachers."

Shit. He turned to face the guys. "So, you want to go check out the food table?"

Bash shook his head. "Nuh-uh. We want to watch you drool over Josie and pretend you're not interested."

He pushed between the two of them. "I'm going to the food table. And to get some iced tea."

What he really wanted was a beer, and maybe a shot or two of tequila. Unfortunately, there was no alcohol at a high school dance. So he made his way to the table and grabbed some chips and a tiny sandwich, then followed some of the students to the drink table, keeping a side eye on the kids lurking in the corner.

There was a situation brewing back in one of the corners with a couple of guys who appeared to be having words. So while he chewed his sandwich and drank his tea, he wandered that way.

They must have seen him coming, because one kid went north and the other headed south before he could get there. That suited him just fine, as long as no fight broke out. But he'd linger in the open anyway just to make sure they didn't reconnect as soon as he turned his back.

"You're taking your job very seriously."

He hadn't even noticed Josie coming up to stand beside him. "I thought I saw an argument brewing between a couple of students."

"Well, you look plenty menacing, even in that very nice suit."

"Menacing, huh?"

"Yes. And extremely well dressed. I like that tie."

"Thanks. You look devastatingly gorgeous, and I'd very much like to put my hands on you in this very inappropriate venue."

Even though the lights had been turned down, he caught the telltale blush on her cheeks. "Oh. Then, thank you for thinking inappropriate thoughts about me."

He wanted to give her a look. The kind of look that would tell her just the kind of inappropriate thoughts he was having. But not here, not when so many kids could zero in on the two of them chatting. So instead, he nodded. "Any time."

Fortunately, the music started up, and most of the kids hit the dance floor, so they were less on display.

"Would you like something to eat?"

She laid a hand on her stomach, then grimaced. "No, not right now."

"Drink?"

"Not unless it's vodka."

He laughed. "Yeah, I know that feeling. Want to take a lap and see what's going on in the dark corners?"

She tilted her head. "Is that your way of dragging me into a dark corner?"

"I wish. Come on."

Something was obviously on her mind, or else she wasn't feeling well. He skirted a glance at her while they walked. She looked too damn good to be sick. Her full, pouty lips were painted a dark, burnished, kissable shade that made him want to capture her lips to see if she tasted like cinnamon.

Just thinking about it made his pants tight, so instead, he kept his focus on watching those dark corners and frowning when he saw students doing things they shouldn't be doing. It was amazing how just a frown could get kissing or handsy kids to pull apart.

"I think I've inherited my father's stern frown," he said as they wound their way near the dance floor.

"Is that right?"

"Yeah. I've discovered I've got the trademark Powers glare. Very effective on teens."

She stopped and turned, tilting her head back to search his face. "Show me."

He gave her the look.

She laughed.

"Hey."

"Sorry. Not effective on me."

"You're not one of my students, and your passing grade doesn't depend on me."

"True. But I have to tell you that glare makes you look a little . . . How can I say this without offending you?"

He crossed his arms. "Go on. Say it."

She chewed on the lower corner of her lip, once again pulling his attention to her mouth.

"Constipated."

"What?"

She shrugged. "Sorry."

"And to think I wanted to kiss you."

"Oh, but now you don't?"

"Nope."

She offered up a sexy smile. "Liar."

She turned and walked away, forcing him to follow her. They ended up at the table where their friends were.

Bash came back with a tray of lemonades and iced teas. Josie took a seat so Zach made sure to sit next to Bash because he knew she was jittery about people possibly thinking they were together.

"So, when are you going to ask Josie out on a real date?" Bash asked.

Zach shrugged. "I have asked her."

"Oh. So she doesn't like you?"

He furrowed his brows. "It's not like that. There've been scheduling things and timing issues."

"Uh-huh."

He leaned back to glare at Bash. "Why do you even care?"

Bash shrugged. "Maybe I think you need someone."

"Really. Why?"

"I don't know. I'm happy. Will's happy. All of our friends have found someone."

"I don't need anyone."

"Yeah, that's what I used to think. Until this insanely beautiful woman forced me to fall in love with her."

Chelsea turned her head. "Wait. What? Forced you? There was no forcing, mister."

Bash laughed. "I knew you were listening."

She lifted her chin. "I never eavesdrop. It's rude. And Bash is right. Ask Josie out on a proper date."

Zach rolled his eyes. "Thank you. I'll give it some thought."

Josie leaned near Chelsea. "What are you all talking about?"

"Football," Bash said.

"Oh."

Zach got up and went over to Josie. "Let's dance."

Her eyes widened. "Here?"

"Sure. Great way to keep an eye on the kids on the dance floor."

"Oh. Okay, sure."

She laid her napkin on the table and stood, following him onto the dance floor. There was a fast song playing, so they moved in time to the music. He had no complaints about watching Josie's hips sway.

She got in closer to him. "You are not watching students. You're looking at me."

"Okay, fine." He turned around and scanned the dance floor. Everyone seemed to be behaving, for the most part, so he pivoted again to face her. "Nothing scandalous going on."

"Did you expect there to be?"

"You never know. But not really."

The song switched to something slow. Josie started to walk off, but he grabbed her hand and tugged her close, moving her into the center of the dance floor.

"One more."

"We shouldn't," she said, tilting her head back.

"Probably not. Just glance around and look mean, like you're scanning for inappropriate dance behavior."

She stifled a laugh. "Okay."

He enjoyed the feel of her against him, though he couldn't really pull her as close as he wanted to because he didn't want the students—or faculty—getting any idea that there was something going on between them.

But there was definitely something going on between them. He was having a hard time focusing on anything but the way her dangling earrings teased the column of her neck, or that one hair curled possessively against her earlobe, making him want to tease his tongue there. Or the sweep of her dark lashes whenever she made eye contact, and the utter sea blue of her eyes that never failed to draw him in. Not to mention the softness of her hand or her sweet scent.

"So, what exactly should we be looking for?"

He snapped himself out of his mental inventory of Josie. "What?"

"You know, on the dance floor. The students?"

"Oh. I don't know. Inappropriate touching, kissing, those kinds of things."

"I see. Okay, I'll be on the lookout for those things, but so far everyone seems to be behaving."

She was right. The only one who wasn't behaving—at least mentally—was him. So he pulled his focus from the beautiful woman in his arms and back to scanning the dance floor. He realized a few of the other teachers and parental chaperones had taken to the floor to dance, including Chelsea with Bash and Jane with Will, which made Zach and Josie stand out a little bit less, thankfully.

Not that it mattered. The kids were looking only at one another. Adults were practically invisible to them.

"Would you like to go out with me?"

Josie snapped her gaze back to Zach.

"What?"

"You know, on a date."

"We are out."

He slanted a look at her. "This is not a date. This is chaperoning the homecoming dance."

Her lips curved. "I don't know. I've never been to homecoming. It's kind of romantic."

"Come on, Josie. I mean a real date. Just the two of us. Out to dinner or to a movie or something you'll enjoy doing."

"Well, first, I am enjoying myself. Second, I'd love to."

He hadn't realized he'd been holding his breath until she said yes. "Great."

"How about Tuesday?"

That was random. "Why Tuesday?"

"The movie theater has movie noir night."

He grimaced. "You mean old movies in black and white."

She laughed. "It'll be fun. And there's popcorn."

"Sounds awesome."

The song ended, so they made their way back to the table. Josie excused herself to go to the restroom, and Chelsea and Jane went with her.

Zach went to refill drinks for the two of them, and grabbed another sandwich while passing by the food table.

When he sat down, he smirked at Bash.

"What?" Bash asked.

"I have a date with Josie."

Bash leaned back in his chair. "Asked her out, huh?"

"Yeah."

Will leaned forward. "When?"

"Tuesday night."

Bash laughed.

"What's so funny?"

"You're taking her out on a work night?"

"Yes. So what?"

"Dude. Nothing hot can happen on a work night."

"I don't know about that," Josie said, giving Zach a wink as she walked past the three of them on her way back to her chair.

Chelsea took her seat. "If I recall correctly, Bash, we had no problem with Monday dates. Or Tuesdays. Or Wednesdays. Or—"

Bash raised his hand. "Yeah, yeah. I get it."

Zach laughed, then skirted his glance across the table at Josie, who gave him a heated smile.

Tuesday was going to be a good day.

Chapter 18

JOSIE WAS ENJOYING the quiet time of her prep period Tuesday afternoon, grading papers in her classroom, when the door opened and Zach walked in. She could tell from the look on his face he was not happy.

"Three players on probation, Josie. You put three of my players on probation."

She leaned back in her chair and studied him, noticing how sharp he looked in his dark jeans and black-and-white-striped button-down shirt with the paisley tie.

So. Hot.

"First, I did not put your players on academic probation, Zach. They did that to themselves by either failing tests or not turning in assignments. And second, you already know that, so I don't know why you've barged in here being all accusatory with me."

His face scrunched up with bottled rage. She sat back calmly while he worked through his anger, because she knew he wasn't pissed at her, but rather at his players. So she let him walk it off by pacing back and forth in her classroom for a few minutes.

"What was it this time? They had to write some freakin' play? Or was it that damn poetry shit again? I mean, that's torture, Josie, you know that."

"Let me see the student names."

He walked by and dropped the partially crumpled report on her desk. She picked it up and scanned the list.

"Abe's in my eleventh-grade language arts class. He didn't turn in two papers last week on theme and archetypes."

"What? He didn't do the work at all?"

"No. He didn't do the work. And Paul was supposed to write an analysis on the second half of the book we were reading in class, describing the narrator's point of view. It was worth three hundred points. He failed to turn it in."

"Like, he didn't turn it in on time?"

"No, Zach. He didn't turn it in at all."

"Shit."

"And Warren didn't turn in a single one of his homework assignments last week."

She heard his heavy sigh, knew how much this must weigh on him. The football team relied on him, but all the players had to be on the same page. And when two or three fell, they crumpled the entire team.

She pushed back from her chair and looked up at him. "I'm sorry. What can I do to help?"

He shook his head. "Nothing. They either do the work or they fail and they're off the team. I'm getting tired of kicking their asses every damn day."

She grasped his arm. "They're worth it, you know. Every one of them is worth the effort you put into them. They know you care, Zach. You have no idea what that means to them. If the two of us talk to these boys, maybe we can convince them to put in some extra effort."

"I'm not sure I even care anymore."

"Of course you do. If you didn't care, you wouldn't be standing in my classroom yelling at me about them."

He looked down at her. "I'm sorry. I just—I'm running out of ideas on how to help them."

"Then let me help you help them. I'll give you some assignments that'll equal the credit they've lost. But you have to make them responsible for doing the assignments. And don't help them. Then they sink or swim on their own."

He seemed to consider it. "All right."

"I'll get something together and have it for you before the end of school today."

"Thanks." He started toward the door, then stopped and turned to her. "We're still on for tonight?"

She smiled at him, happy that he could separate school from their personal lives. "I can't wait for tonight."

For the first time since he'd stormed into her classroom, his lips curved into a smile. "Me, too."

There was something about that man's smile that made her heart flutter. Which was utterly ridiculous, but there it was. She felt it, so she wouldn't discount it.

After he left, it was time to get back to work. Since she had a little extra time before her next class started, she put together those assignments for Zach's players. She was bound and determined they were going to get back to passing her class.

She made the assignments doable, but not simple. When her next class started, she had one of her students run the envelope to Zach's classroom so he'd be sure to have it to distribute it to the boys after school today.

Then it would be up to them to do the work. There was nothing else either she or Zach could do.

After school ended, she went home and did her grading for the day, then fed and played with Tumbles and Arthur, the blind bunny she'd adopted the other day.

Arthur was settling in surprisingly well. She was happy about that. Tumbles seemed to have taken to him, too. He followed Arthur all over the house as the bunny learned his way around. Tumbles seemed to be aware that Arthur had special needs, so he took extra care to make sure the bunny didn't run into walls or anything that could hurt him.

Animals were such special creatures. Her heart swelled with love for her two babies. As she sat cross-legged on the floor and watched Tumbles redirect Arthur away from the wall so he could hop toward his food bowl, she could envision a house filled with children and animals someday. The kids would crawl all over the floor, laughing as dogs and cats and bunnies played with them.

And, of course, there'd be a man who loved them all.

It was a nice dream. Maybe someday it would come true.

In the meantime, she needed to get ready for tonight's date. She decided on a long, flowered skirt with a white top, then added a pair of ballet flats and her favorite silver chain necklace and hoop earrings. She did her makeup and fixed her hair, then got dressed. She put Arthur in his crated area and poured herself a glass of wine while she waited for Zach.

When he rang the doorbell, she checked her phone.

He was right on time. She opened the door, surprised to see him holding a bouquet of stunning wildflowers.

"You don't seem the roses type," he said.

"I'm not. Those are gorgeous. Come in."

He walked in and handed the flowers to her.

"Let me put these in some water."

Zach looked around—mostly for the cat—and didn't see him.

"You need a dog."

She was at the sink and turned to gape at him as he made his way into the kitchen. "I can't believe you said that."

"Wilson barks—loud—when someone rings the doorbell. I don't suppose the devil cat even meows to alert you."

She snickered. "Hardly. But it's good you have a guard dog."

Zach leaned against the counter. "Not sure he'd do anything other than run and hide if someone broke in, but he's loud, and that might give someone a second thought."

"Hey, the burglars don't know that. And he obviously thinks he's fierce. Would you like a beer or a glass of wine?"

"Beer would be good, thanks."

She pulled one from the fridge and handed it to him.

"How's he been getting along?" she asked as she followed Zach into the living room.

"Like he's been living in my house his whole life. He loves all his toys, which are littering my entire house now. Along with his favorite blanket. And his chew bone."

Josie curled a smile across her beautiful lips. "I'm really happy that he's doing so well." She looked over at him. "Are you happy?"

"Surprisingly, yeah. I never knew how quiet my house was until Wilson came to live with me."

"Dogs are good at letting you know you were once lonely."

"Didn't say I was lonely, just that it was quiet."

"I stand corrected, then. Big tough guy isn't lonely." She repositioned herself so she leaned her body against his. He didn't mind that at all.

"Yeah, that's me. Never lonely. Kind of like you, right? Minus the big-tough-guy part."

"Hey, I freely admit I like the company. Tumbles is great company. So is the bunny."

He arched a brow. "You got a bunny?"

She nodded. "His name is Arthur. He's black and white with floppy ears, and he's so soft and totally adorable. The rescue organization called me two days ago and said they were having trouble placing him because he's blind and his radar isn't all that great, so he needs some assistance maneuvering around his designated areas."

He gaped at her. "You adopted a *blind* bunny?"

"Of course I did. He's so sweet, Zach. He's over here. Come meet him."

They got up, and Zach followed Josie into the corner of the living room. He hadn't noticed the fenced-off area earlier. Sure enough, a long-eared black-and-white rabbit was sound asleep in there.

"He's really cute. Will he take a bite out of my ankle like the Prince of Darkness?"

She straightened and rolled her eyes. "You're such a baby."

No one had ever called him a baby. "I am not. I've been tackled by a two-hundred-seventy-pound lineman. I think I can handle a little pain."

"Uh-huh. Except from a ten-pound cat."

"Cat scratches sting."

"Don't I know it. He scratched me while we were playing today. But you don't hear me whining about it, do you?"

"He scratched you?" He visually searched the exposed parts of her body. "Where?"

She shook her head and led him back to the sofa. "That's how cats play, Zach. Sometimes play gets rough. You're going to have to toughen up."

The last thing he wanted to do with Josie tonight was discuss her cat. He decided it was time to shift the conversation. "Oh, so you're tough, huh?"

He reached for her and pulled her onto his lap. Her head nestled in the crook of his arm, the soft curves of her body pressed against the hard planes of his.

This was better than talking about cats. Looking down at her made him forget about everything other than wanting to kiss her. Her lips were partially open, painted pink, and she was breathing fast. So was he, the blood rushing through his veins in anticipation of what was to come.

"Got me right where you want me now?" she asked.

"Mostly." He lifted her slightly so her face was closer, and then he brushed his lips across hers, taking a tentative taste. He didn't want to push her into anything she wasn't ready for. Her nails dug into his chest, and she moaned, flicking her tongue out. He opened her mouth with his, and her tongue slid into his mouth. He resisted the urge to groan as his dick hardened instantly. Something about her taste, the sweet scent of her, did a number on him. She was the sweetest candy, a temptation he couldn't resist. He'd wanted her for months now, and to be kissing her now, to feel her body moving so willingly against his, was everything he'd been dreaming about.

He lifted his head. "It's movie night."

She splayed her palms against his chest, her eyes laden with desire. "What movie?"

He sucked in a breath and dove in for another kiss, lost in the wicked taste of her, the promise of more, the need to delve into the secrets he could uncover in the soft curve of her neck as he made his way down there to breathe in her scent, then lick his way to her collarbone. He was impeded by clothes, and that was a damn shame, because he wanted to taste every inch of her skin.

She pulled back and stared up at him. "Zach. I don't know about you, but I'm okay with forgoing movie night."

He was about to bust the seam of his jeans, and all he could think about was getting Josie's clothes off. "Like you said . . . what movie?"

"Okay, good. Are you sure about this?"

She'd asked him for consent. That was different. "Damn sure. How about you?"

"I'm so sure that I might die if you don't get me naked."

That was about as definite a yes as she could give him. He stood and pulled her up, then swooped Josie up into his arms and headed down the hall.

"Are you crazy? You don't have to carry me to the bedroom," she said.

He glanced down at her but didn't stop. "Don't ruin my romantic moment here, woman."

"Sorry. In that case, I'm swooning with desire. Take me, caveman."

He rolled his eyes at her. When he got to the bedroom, he nudged the door with his shoulder and set her on her feet in front of the bed. He swept his hand along the side of her neck and kissed her again. She moaned against his lips, and he soaked in the taste of her, the sound of her, the way her body molded against his.

And then he heard a meow. He pulled away from Josie and looked down to see that Tumbles had made himself at home in the center of Josie's bed.

She smiled at Zach. "Give me just a minute."

She turned and scooped up the cat, petting and murmuring to him as she left the bedroom. She came back a few seconds later and shut the bedroom door, then came over to him and splayed her hands on his chest.

"I gave him a treat. He's happy now."

"Does that mean I get a treat?"

She lifted her shirt over her head and let it drop to the floor. She was wearing a satiny, bronze-colored bra that barely covered her breasts. "What did you have in mind?"

"What you're doing right now is perfect."

"Then let's continue." She kicked off her shoes, pushed her skirt to the floor, and stepped out of it.

Panties matched the bra, and he liked the ensemble very much. She had a hell of a body. Slender but curved in all the right places, and he couldn't wait to get his hands—and his mouth—on all those places.

She toyed with the long silver chain that dipped between her breasts. "Your turn."

He gave her a half smile, then pulled off his shirt and threw it on the pile on the floor, enjoying the way her gaze roamed over his chest. He toed off his tennis shoes, then undid the button on his jeans and drew the zipper down. He shoved the jeans to the floor and kicked those onto the pile. Left only in his boxer briefs, he waited while she walked over to him.

She sighed as she raked a nail across his naked chest. "This is much better than I imagined."

He liked that she'd imagined the two of them like this. "I'm happy to hear that, but we haven't even started yet."

"So it gets better than just you, mostly naked, standing in my bedroom."

He reached around and unhooked her bra. "Oh, yeah."

And then she pulled the straps of the bra down her arms and flung the bra onto the growing pile on the floor, leaving her beautifully, perfectly naked.

"Damn." The word came out in a whisper. And when she shimmied out of her panties, he was afraid he might not be able to form coherent words.

The last thing to go was that sexy silver chain, which she laid on the nearby dresser. Then she moved closer until their bodies touched, her hand cupping his erection.

"You're still wearing clothes."

He managed to swallow past the golf-ball-sized lump in his throat to answer her. "Not for long."

In an instant, he'd shucked his boxer briefs, his erection a testament to his desire for Josie.

"Well now," she said, rubbing up against him. "It's about damn time we did this, isn't it?"

Typically, he was the one in control, the one doing the seducing. But with Josie, he felt off kilter, and totally seduced. "Yeah."

She took him by the hand and led him to her bed, where she pulled the blanket back to the end of the bed, then crawled onto the mattress, resting her head against the headboard and pillows.

He followed but sat at her feet.

"You can get on the bed, too," she said.

"I will. I want to start here." He picked up her foot and massaged the balls of her feet.

She let out a soft moan. "I'll give you an hour to stop doing that."

Since she seemed to enjoy the foot rub, he lingered there for a while, especially since she lightly teased his thighs and erection with her other foot.

Everything about her body was pretty, including her pretty pink-painted toenails. He was in no hurry, and she'd relaxed back on the pillows, her heavy-lidded gaze watching his every movement. When he moved his fingers up over her ankles, then her calves, she shifted up on her elbows.

"You have expert hands," she said.

His lips curved. "That was just a foot rub. You haven't seen anything yet."

She sighed. "I think I'm going to enjoy tonight."

He shifted so he sat beside her hip. "So you're not sorry we missed the movie?"

As he massaged her thighs, then her hips, she cast him

a wickedly sensual smile. "No, I'm right where I want to be. Naked, with your hands on me."

He liked hearing that. "You're beautiful, Josie. Your skin feels like melted butter under my hand. I've been thinking about this for a long time."

She rolled over on her side. "Have you?"

"Yeah."

"So have I. I'm sorry we waited so long." She reached up to run her hand over his face.

He took her hand and kissed her palm. "You know we aren't on a timetable, right?"

She shrugged. "Most men wouldn't have waited around so long."

"I'm not most men."

She inched closer so their bodies touched. "Mmm. So I've noticed."

He'd resisted as long as he could, but now he wrapped his arm around her and tugged her against him, then brought his lips to hers. She met his lips in a kiss that seared him from the inside out.

He wanted to tell her over and over how beautiful she was, how soft her body felt against the hardness of his, how he felt lost in a sea of blue whenever he met her eyes. Instead, all he could do was touch her, kiss her, and fall into the passion of their kiss.

He'd never been the kind of guy to get wrapped up in sex. It had never been an emotional thing for him. It was fun, and that was it. But with Josie, he had all these . . . feelings that he'd held in check for so long, and he didn't know what the hell to do with them other than express them in the only way he'd ever known—physically. So when he kissed her neck and collarbone, and she reacted by arching upward, he took that as a sign of pleasure.

And damn if that was what he wanted for her tonight. He wanted her to feel good, to relax, to release. He moved lower, taking one nipple in his mouth to suck, and she let out a long, low moan.

Josie's sounds undid him. He was hard and aching to be

inside her, to rock this pleasure along with her. But first he wanted her to unwind, to let go. He moved down her body, and as he breathed her in while he kissed her skin, he felt her tense.

That's what he wanted for her, to let go of that tension, to feel her body go lax and fluid.

And he knew just what he needed to do to get her there.

Josie's entire body was taut with need. Zach had her wound up like a knotted rubber band, every nerve ending tuned in to his movements, the feel of his breathing, his scent, and the way he took his time to get to know her body.

She had thought they'd have this wild fling of passion, that it would be over in minutes, both of them sweaty and gratified. And done.

She'd been so wrong, because at the moment he was leisurely kissing her hipbones as he made his way down her body, and she was nearly hyperventilating from his mouth mapping its way across every inch of her skin.

Not that she was complaining. She was just . . . surprised. Oh, so pleasantly surprised.

And when he moved toward her sex, spreading her legs, and put his mouth there, she arched up and cried out, needing this release.

Zach took her there, giving her just what she needed, that oh-so-languorous sweet ride to heaven, with a tease of delicious hell mixed in. She dug her heels into the mattress and fell right into the oblivion of her orgasm, giving him what he'd coaxed out of her, unashamedly chasing the climax he'd brought out of her all too quickly.

She fell back against the mattress gasping and waited for her breathing to return to normal before she opened her eyes and saw that Zach had moved up beside her, his fingers dancing lazy circles around her skin.

"You're very good at this."

He leaned over and kissed her, a soft kiss that left her feeling drunk with desire. When he lifted his mouth from hers, his lips curved. "You make me want to be good at this."

She traced her finger over the fullness of his bottom lip.

"Oh, I don't know. I think you're already an expert. I didn't even have to draw you a road map to all my hot spots."

He rolled over, then circled her nipple with his fingertip. "Guys need road maps?"

"Some of the ones I've known need a GPS to lead them to the promised land."

He laughed. "Hey, if there's someplace you need me to go and I'm not getting there, feel free to tell me."

She felt relaxed and easy with him, and that was nice. "I don't think you'll need a GPS—or me—to tell you anything. Something tells me you already know."

"Hey, thanks. But just in case, I'm happy to be directed."

She cupped the back of his neck and pulled him toward her. "I'll keep that in mind."

All thoughts of direction were forgotten when his body covered hers. He kissed and touched her fully, taking possession of her body. She was so fully immersed in him, so connected to him, she felt melted to the mattress.

She wound her leg around him and lifted, rubbing herself against his erection. Lightning shocks of pleasure surged through her, and all she wanted now was to feel Zach moving inside of her.

When he lifted his lips from hers, she gently pushed on his chest and he raised himself off her. "I'll be right back."

She slid out from under him and made a quick dash to the bathroom. She came back a few seconds later with a box of condoms.

Zach had rolled over onto his back, and Josie heaved an appreciative sigh. Now that was a sight. An amazingly gorgeous man in her bed—with a huge erection.

Not wanting to lose the, uh, momentum, she quickly opened the box and tossed a packet at him. By the time she laid the box on the nightstand and climbed back into bed, he had the condom on and was pulling her toward him.

She rolled over onto her side to face him, flinging her leg over his hip.

In an instant, she was on her back, Zach looming above her.

"What?" she asked. "Enough foreplay for you?" She raked her nails over his shoulders, feeling the tension there.

He picked up one of her legs and bent it at the knee, sliding against her to tease her flesh with his. "I think we've waited long enough for this, don't you?"

She offered up a smile. "I couldn't agree more. So, what are you waiting for?"

She arched against him. He leaned in and kissed her, his kiss accompanied by a growling groan that sparked her passion from flaming to fiery hot. And when he slid inside of her, she gasped against his lips, her body tightening around him.

He lifted up and swept his hand over her forehead, then down the side of her face.

"Feel that?" he asked.

She surged upward, pulling him in deeper, her insides tingling in response. She gasped out her reply. "Oh, I definitely feel it."

"Yeah, the way you wrap around me, Josie. Tight and hot and pulsing. You feel so good."

He focused on her face while sweeping his hand along the side of her body, forcing her to stay in the moment, to stay there with him through every delicious stroke. Her breathing quickened, and she thought she might die from the sensations.

Could someone die from awesome sex? She felt like she couldn't breathe, that at any moment she'd explode from the exquisite pleasure of his hands teasing her nipples, his tongue slowly teasing hers, and his cock taking her on a slow ride to oblivion.

Tension built, and she chased her impending orgasm until she felt dizzy.

Zach increased the pace, giving her that friction she needed to go sailing into her climax. When he shuddered against her and she heard his groans, she dove even deeper into that maelstrom of wild pleasure.

She wasn't sure, but she might have passed out. Or stopped breathing. She could be dead.

That had been intense. Or at least the best sex she'd ever had. It had been perfect. Zach had been perfect, as if he'd been made for just her.

She stilled, looking over at Zach, who had rolled off and laid on his back, breathing heavily.

She stared up at the ceiling, mentally chastising herself for romanticizing the sex. Really awesome, amazing, oh, God, it had felt incredible. But that's all it had been.

Just sex. Nothing more than that.

Zach rolled over and grasped his own throat. "Dying of thirst. Trapped in bedroom. Evil killer cat outside door. Might not make it till morning."

She laughed and shoved at him. "I'll get us some water."

"Or, you know, it's still early. We could still make the movie. Or maybe go out and have some pizza."

Her stomach grumbled at the mention of food. "Oh, pizza. I am kind of hungry."

He got up and swung his legs over the side of the bed. "Let's do it."

She got up and went into the bathroom to clean up. She slid into jeans and her white top, slipped her tennis shoes on, and looked in the mirror in the bathroom to see how badly her makeup had been smudged.

Zach came up behind her and kissed the side of her neck. "Not sure what you're searching for, but you look hot."

She rubbed her finger under her lower lashes where her mascara had smeared. It wasn't perfect, but it would do. "You made me a little messy."

He nuzzled her neck and reached around to cup her breasts. "I like you a little messy. And you taste good."

Just thinking about the ways he'd had his mouth on her made her body heat up, tingles of pleasure shooting straight to her core. She shivered and pressed back against him. "Pizza or sex, Zach."

He straightened, then frowned at her in the mirror. "That's not fair. You can't make me choose between the two."

She laughed, then bumped him back so she could skirt

around him. "I'll make the decision. I'm hungry. We can have sex after pizza."

He let out a dramatic sigh. "Fine. But I'll need a minute because you made me hard."

She looked down at his erection straining against his zipper. Now it was her turn to sigh. If she wasn't so hungry, she'd drag him back to bed right now.

Then again . . .

She slanted a wicked smile at him. "We could have pizza delivered."

He grasped her hands and led her back toward the bed. "Did I ever mention how sexy a smart woman is?"

She laughed, and when they got to the bed, she wrapped her arms around his neck. "No, but once we're naked, we can discuss it in depth."

"Happy to. But one thing."

"Sure."

"Order the pizza first."

She laughed and pulled out her phone.

Chapter 19

BOOK CLUB NIGHT was always so much fun, and Josie looked forward to it, not only for the book discussion, but because it gave her an opportunity to catch up with all her friends.

Now that so many of her friends were married, coupled up, or had kids, it was getting more and more difficult to get everyone together. She was the newest to the group, but with this particular bunch of women, they'd adopted her as one of their own right away, and it was as if she'd been with them forever.

Tonight they were going to discuss Beverly Jenkins's latest historical romance. Josie had devoured the book in two days, and she couldn't wait to get to book club for the discussion. She had loved it so much, she'd called Jillian, and they'd spent an hour on the phone gushing about it. And now they were going to get to talk about it again with all their friends.

So on Thursday night, she gathered up her book bag, said good-bye to Tumbles and Arthur, and drove to Loretta's bookstore, the Open Mind, where they always held book club. Jillian was pulling up right behind her, so Josie waited for her.

"I'm so excited to talk about this book," Jillian said, slinging her bag over her shoulder and then linking arms with Josie.

"Me, too. How was your day?"

"Great. Jeff took me to lunch."

"Really. And how's that going?"

"I don't want to jinx it, but it's going really well. Oh, did I tell you he stayed over Saturday night?"

"You did not."

"He did. We went out to dinner—this awesome seafood restaurant in Tulsa. And then we came back to my place, and we shared a bottle of wine."

Jillian shot her a smile. "That sounds romantic."

"It was. We talked for hours. We always have so much to talk about. His work, my work, our pasts, our future. It's like we fit, you know?"

Josie nodded.

"And then it got late and we had finished off the bottle, and one thing led to another, so he stayed over."

Jillian gave her a happy shrug and a grin. "And by *stayed over*, I mean there was sex."

Josie laughed at her friend's exuberance. "I kind of gathered that. So things are progressing nicely between the two of you."

"Very nicely. He's so incredibly hot, and he has amazing hands. Of course, he's a doctor, so I should have known about the hands."

Josie figured she wouldn't mention that history teacher slash football coach Zach had pretty darn good hands as well. Since her friend was on a roll talking about her sexual escapades, it would be bad form to one-up her BFF.

"Yes, good hands are important." They stopped at the front door to Loretta's bookstore, and Josie rested her hand on the doorknob. "I like seeing you happy like this, Jillian."

Jillian smiled, then let out a contented sigh. "I like being this happy. But it almost feels too good to be true."

"What does?"

"Jeff. How I feel about him. It's happening so fast. He's

almost too perfect. He texts me periodically throughout the day to see how my day is going. We go out to lunch. We see each other all the time. He's kind to me, and the sex is . . ."

Josie waited while Jillian formulated the words to describe what, obviously to her, was something monumental.

"Well, the sex is mind-blowing."

Josie laughed, and they walked inside the bookstore. "Isn't that how it's supposed to be?"

"I guess. Maybe I was imagining a relationship to be more . . . I don't know. Dramatic?"

They waved to Kendra, one of Loretta's employees, as they made their way to the back of the store.

"It doesn't have to be dramatic. You don't want it to be dramatic, do you?"

"No, of course not."

"Good. A relationship can be two people who find each other and have a great time when they're together." She spotted their friends, and they made their way over.

"Hey," Loretta said as she hurried past. "Got a customer, but I'll be there in a sec."

"Okay," Josie said.

"I guess you're right," Jillian continued as they arrived at the spot where they held book club. "But I have all these feelings, Josie. All these emotions I can't contain. I think I'm falling in love."

Josie stilled at Jillian's words and sat in the nearest spot. For some reason she suddenly felt cold. Why was she so cold?

Chelsea had just come out of the restroom and was sliding into one of the soft, comfortable chairs. "Who's falling in love?"

"I might be," Jillian said as she set her bag down and made her way to the coffeemaker by the window.

"Really. With Dr. Armstrong?"

Jillian nodded, then made herself a cup of coffee. "We've been dating."

"Obviously seriously dating if you're talking the *L* word,"

Megan said as she set out a plate of baked goods. "That didn't take long, Jillian."

Jillian sat next to Josie. "Is there a time requirement on love?"

"Not for me there wasn't," Emma said, balancing her cup of coffee on her lap. "You love when you love."

"I agree," Sam said. "I don't even remember when I realized I was in love with Reid, or how much time had passed from the time we got together to the time I fell in love with him. It just . . . happens when it happens."

Des came out of the ladies' room with Molly and took a seat. "Love? You just . . . fall. For all of us, it was at different times. But the one thing I do know is that there's no timeline."

Molly nodded and went over to the bar to grab a cup of coffee. "I fought my attraction to Carter. But there was no denying I fell hard and I fell fast. Sometimes love just slaps you upside the head, and you can't avoid it."

Chelsea laughed. "No matter how hard we resist."

Josie finally found her voice, because it had taken her brain cells a few minutes to catch up. "I don't know that I agree with all of you. I mean, having a relationship with someone is one thing. You know, the dating thing with movies and meals and vacations together and sex and all that. But don't you feel like you should really get to know the ins and outs of someone before you can say you love them? Like . . . years of togetherness?"

Chelsea snorted. "No. I think you can tell within a few weeks if a relationship is going to cut it. Don't you all agree?"

"Definitely," Emma said with a nod.

"I totally agree with that," Megan said. "When I was out there dating, I could tell within the first hour whether I was compatible with a guy. And especially when I wasn't."

"How about with you and Brady?" Emma asked.

Megan inhaled, let it out. "Brady was . . . well, he was something special. It's like there was a slam, pow, wow, you know?"

"But did you know it was love?" Josie asked.

"Love? Not right away. But I knew Brady was something special."

Loretta came over. "Sorry, I had to get a customer lined out with a few hard-to-find books. But the store is getting ready to close, and Kendra can handle that, so I'm free. What did I miss?"

"We're discussing how long it takes to fall in love," Molly said, motioning with her head toward Jillian. "Jillian thinks she's falling in love with Dr. Jeff, and Josie thinks it takes years to figure out love."

"Oh. Well, that's an interesting topic. Let me grab some tea and join in."

"I think you can think you love someone, but it takes some maturity to separate out infatuation from horniness from love."

Everyone looked at Jane, who shrugged. "What? I got divorced. After that, I had some time to think about where it all went wrong. And then I met Will and realized that hot passion and the right guy can go hand in hand. I just started out with the wrong guy. But men of substance aren't exactly a dime a dozen."

They all raised their cups and said, "Truth," in unison.

Chelsea laughed. "I was the queen of dating all the wrong men for a lot of years. And then there was Bash, who I was convinced was the wrong guy. So even when we think we're dating the wrong man, he can often turn out to be the right man."

Josie felt like they were talking in circles. "That's my point exactly. You have to get to know someone before you can truly say you love them. I was in a relationship when I lived in Atlanta, and I was convinced he was the one. The. One. He was smart and sweet and he did nice things for me, and we spent almost all our time with each other. We even moved in together. We were together two years, and I thought I knew everything about this guy."

"So what went wrong?" Des asked.

"I'm going along thinking we're heading toward marriage, you know? And it wasn't like that topic was all in my head, either. He and I had talked about having a future together. Then one day, out of the blue, we were sitting at the kitchen table having breakfast, and he told me he just didn't feel it between us anymore and he was moving out."

Jillian's eyes widened. "What? You never told me this."

"I never told anyone about it. It's not like you broadcast getting dumped."

"Oh, honey, we've all been dumped," Megan said.

Emma nodded. "We could hold a weekend getaway and do nothing but talk about lousy relationships in our past."

"So true," Loretta said.

Josie looked around and saw the sympathetic faces of her friends, and realized she wasn't the only one who'd been through this. So maybe no one would judge her for having made the wrong choice in a guy. "I was shocked, of course, and asked him what was wrong. He gave me the old 'It's not you, it's me' speech and said he needed to find himself or some bullshit like that. I found out later that he had a girlfriend in another city that he'd been seeing for a year."

"Oh, that bastard," Chelsea said with a frown.

"I'm sorry, honey," Des said, offering up a sympathetic look. "Cheaters are the worst."

"I thought I really knew him, you know? And it turned out I knew nothing about this man I thought I would end up marrying. How could I be so utterly clueless?"

Jillian leaned over and laid her hand on Josie's. "It really was him, not you, Josie. You can't take the blame for his failings."

"Jillian's right," Emma said. "That's on him, not you."

Loretta nodded. "Josie, you have to realize not every guy is like your ex-boyfriend."

"Sure, I know that." She knew they were right, but after Dylan, it had been hard for her to trust her own judgment with men. So she'd dated sporadically, but she'd never fallen in love. She'd learned to be adept at putting up a wall, guarding her heart so she never got hurt.

She thought she'd become an expert at that after her mother, but Dylan had somehow gotten through.

Never again.

And now, as she listened to her best friend talk about falling in love after dating Jeff for only a few short weeks? She had to admit she was afraid for Jillian's heart.

The last thing she wanted was for Jillian to get hurt.

Maybe she could talk Zach into doing something couple-y with Jillian and Jeff, so she could watch how Jeff treated Jillian. Then again, what would she even look for? She wasn't exactly the best judge of a guy's romantic intent, was she?

"Are you okay?" Jillian asked later in the evening when they took a break from their book discussion to have a piece of the amazing blueberry streusel Megan had made.

"I'm fine."

"You've been uncharacteristically quiet tonight."

"Have I?"

"Yes. And we'd both gone on and on about this book, yet I'm the only one gushing about how amazing it was."

Maybe she had been thinking about the past and love and trust and all those things that had reared their ugly heads in their earlier discussions instead of focusing on what she should have been focusing on, which was a great book.

"You're right. Sorry. I've just got a lot on my mind."

Jillian rubbed her arm. "What's wrong, Josie? You know you can talk to me about anything."

Anything but this. The last thing she wanted to do was put doubt in Jillian's mind about Jeff. Or about love and relationships. Jillian was euphoric right now, and Josie refused to be the one to burst her bubble of happiness.

At least not right now. Not until she could gather some intel about Jeff.

So she plastered on her happy smile. "Thanks, Jillian. But I'm really okay. It's just school stuff."

"Are you sure it's not your ex-boyfriend that's weighing on you?"

She waved her hand in dismissal. "Oh, God, no. He's so far in the past, I never even think about him anymore."

"But you brought him up tonight, and I feel like that's my fault."

"It's not your fault. Please don't take the blame for something that happened to me several years ago. Trust me when I tell you I'm over it—and over him."

"Are you sure?"

"One hundred percent sure. So sure, in fact, that I'm contemplating another slice of the streusel."

That seemed to appease Jillian, since her focus turned to the dessert. "Ooh. Tempting. I think I'll join you."

In the future, Josie was going to have to leave the past where it belonged. Because nothing good ever happened from dredging up old wounds.

From now on she intended to stay in the present, where she'd focus on having fun. And not falling in love.

So, after book club, she intended to go home, and maybe give Zach a call to see if he wanted to have some fun. She wanted to talk to him anyway, to make sure they were on the same page—the fun page.

The other night with him had been amazing, she thought as she got into her car and drove home. And maybe a little too intense, at least on her part. Which was why she wanted to gauge how he'd felt about it. Though he had called her the next day, she'd had a million errands to run and a to-do list a mile long, so she'd told him she was busy. And then there were planning things to do for school, and she'd been avoiding him all week.

So maybe she'd pushed him away a little.

Or a lot.

Defense mechanism much, Josie?

Okay, fine. So she'd been hiding from Zach. Time to fix that. She could already envision inviting him over. Or maybe she'd surprise him and go over to his place. Either way, they'd get naked and have some sexytimes. That would definitely improve her mood.

But when she pulled into her driveway, a familiar figure was sitting on her front porch, and all her plans for tonight scattered along with the leaves blowing around her front yard.

She got out and walked up the steps to her porch, stopping at the top to see the way-too-thin woman huddled up on her porch swing.

"Was wonderin' when you'd get home, Jo Jo. I've been waitin' here for hours in the cold."

Josie heaved a sigh, her stomach filled with dread. Why couldn't she have a normal life, be excited at the prospect of seeing this woman? Instead, she knew what this meant. And the battle that was coming.

She pushed off the concrete column and headed toward the swing. "Hi, Mom."

Chapter 20

AFTER LOSING LAST night's football game by one lousy point, Zach was in a foul mood. He never took it out on his players, who'd played their hearts out until the final buzzer sounded. In fact, they'd taken the loss worse than he had, so he'd had to pump them up and tell them they'd played better during this loss than they had during all their wins so far this season. He told them stories about his time playing pro football, about how the tough losses hurt and how he'd had to pull himself up, determined to play harder and better the next game. He'd also told them how to grab a takeaway from a loss, how to always make it a learning experience. And as he'd watched their faces, he knew they understood. It would make them all better players.

But it still hurt to lose, and the only person he'd admit that to was himself.

It didn't help that two of his players had ended up benched because of grades, either. One of them had been Paul Fine, who continued to be a problem. Despite Zach's working one-on-one with Paul, Paul's home-life issues were still interfering with his school and athletic life. So today Zach and his assistant coach had a meeting with Paul and his parents.

Or, at least, Paul's mother, who had been the only one to show up. So while he had Paul outside walking the track, he and Larry White, his assistant, sat in the office with Laurel Fine, who looked like she was going to crumple to the ground in a pile of tears any second. She was twisting her fingers together, and her gaze flitted between the two of them.

"My, uh, my husband said to tell you he's really sorry he couldn't make it today," Laurel said. "He, uh, he had to work."

That was a lie, since Zach had contacted Luke to see if he could do a check on Jimmy Fine. He'd finally been picked up for dealing crack last week and was currently sitting in county jail.

"What can we do to help Paul, Mrs. Fine? He's not turning in his assignments, and if he continues to get low grades, he's off the team."

She shuddered in a breath. "He loves to play so much. Please don't do that."

"That's out of our control," Larry said. "He has to do the work."

Laurel swept her hair off her face. "I work two jobs just to pay the rent. Jimmy, he . . . he does what he can, but Paul . . . well, I'm doing the best I can."

Zach saw the tears well in her eyes. He'd always prided himself on knowing what to do. This time, he didn't have a clue. So he got up and dragged a chair over so he could sit face-to-face with Laurel.

"What do you need, Mrs. Fine?"

Tears spilled from her eyes. "Okay, so I lied before. My husband's in jail. Paul's upset. I'm upset. I can't make ends meet by myself. I don't know what I need other than I want my kid to be okay. Out of all of this, I just need my kid to be okay."

He nodded. "All right. Let's get Paul in here and talk to him."

They brought Paul in. He wasn't happy when Zach told him he knew about his dad. At first he was mad at his mom, but Zach and Larry straightened him out in a hurry and told him he needed to step up and quit thinking this was in any way his mother's fault. The only one to blame for what happened was his dad, and now was the time for the two of them to stick together.

After a while, Paul took his mom's hand and told her that his father was an asshole. Zach let that one slide, especially since he tended to agree with the kid.

Zach made some calls to a few charitable organizations, and some food and rent donations were made so Laurel and Paul could have some breathing room to get back on their feet. He gave Laurel some information about getting Jimmy the hell out of her life and away from her and from Paul if that was what she wanted. While Laurel was talking to Larry about all of that, Zach talked to Paul and told him this was his last chance to stay on the football team, and he'd understand completely if football was no longer his priority, considering everything else going on.

Paul looked him in the eye. "Coach, football is the only thing keeping me from losing it right now. I need this."

"Well, you're good at it, so I'd like you to play. But you have to do the schoolwork."

Paul nodded. "I'll get it done." He paused, then said, "I'll try. Some of it's hard."

Zach considered Paul's admission, then said, "How about we arrange for a tutor? There are student tutors who can help you with some of the hard stuff."

Paul frowned. "They'll think I'm stupid."

"Hey. Just because you need some help doesn't mean you're stupid. And none of the tutors we use pass any judgment. They're all good kids. Just like you. Let them help."

"Okay."

Paul went silent, so Zach started to wrap up all the paperwork for Laurel and Paul to take home with them. "Coach?"

"Yeah."

"Thanks for . . . all this. For helping my mom. It means

a lot to me. Nobody has ever cared about me . . .about us like that."

It had to have been tough on the kid, having a parent like his dad who thought only of himself. "I care. All the coaches care. And you're welcome."

"I don't know how to pay you back."

Zach stood and came around his desk. "You pay me back by passing your classes. I need you on my team."

Paul stood and held out his hand. "Consider it done. I won't let you down."

For the first time this school year, Zach believed Paul was telling the truth. More important, that Paul believed he could do it. And that belief in himself would carry him a long way. "I know you won't."

After Laurel and Paul left, Zach headed home to pick up Wilson and then out to run a few errands. Although it was mid-October, the weather was nice today, so he cracked the window, allowing Wilson to breathe in some fresh air. The dog shoved his nose into the corner of the window and snuffled.

"You like that, don't you?" he asked.

Wilson replied by whimpering and put his paws up on the door, lifting his nose even higher. While Zach stopped at the light, a police car pulled up next to them, and suddenly Wilson started barking.

Zach grinned as he realized it was Luke McCormack in his squad car, accompanied, as always, by Boomer, his K9 German shepherd. Luke signaled for him to follow, so when the light turned green, he followed Luke's car to the parking lot of Bert's, one of Zach's favorite places to eat.

Zach parked and went around to lead Wilson out of the car. Luke was already standing on the sidewalk with Boomer. The two dogs did a greeting sniff-off, and Zach was happy that Wilson behaved himself. He shook hands with Luke.

"How's it going?" Zach asked.

"Pretty slow Saturday. Thought I'd stop in for some lunch. You game?"

"Definitely. What about the dogs?"

Luke led Boomer over to a spot away from the door, but still visible through the windows, and attached his leash to a metal hook inserted in the ground. He gave Boomer a command, and the dog sat. "He'll stay there."

Zach looked from Boomer over to Wilson. "Not sure my dog is as well trained as yours."

"You'd be surprised how one dog will mimic another. Come on, give it a try."

Wilson was a good dog, but also very excitable, especially around other dogs. But Zach attached Wilson's leash to the same hook and gave him the sit command. Wilson smiled up at him with an "I don't think so" look.

Zach crouched down. "Don't make me look bad in front of the cop, dude."

Luke laughed.

"Sometimes you have to be stern."

"Stern? Wilson's a cute ball of fluff. How am I supposed to be stern with him?"

"I didn't say mean. Just . . . authoritative. Like this."

Luke walked over and gave Wilson a very firm sit-and-stay command.

Wilson sat like a champion, and Luke started walking toward the front door of the restaurant, so Zach followed.

"It's just that he's intimidated by the badge and all."

Luke slanted a smirk at him. "Uh-huh. And maybe you shouldn't coddle the fluffball so much."

"I'll work on it." Luke was probably right in that Zach felt sorry for Wilson's circumstances, so he wasn't training him properly. He'd have to change that.

As they went inside, they waved to Charlotte and Bert, who were busy working behind the counter.

Anita came over, looking like Anita always looked with her streaked blond-and-brown hair pulled back in a messy bun, a pen stuck behind her ear, and an impatient look on her face. "Take a seat, and I'll be with you soon."

Zach smiled. Anita was one of the first people he'd met when he'd moved to Hope. And Bert's had been one of the first places he'd eaten. He'd come back a lot since then, because of the great food and friendly people who had made him feel welcome.

Luke led them over to a booth near the window, where they had a great view of the dogs. Surprisingly, Wilson had lain down next to Boomer and was sound asleep.

"Your dog is a good influence on my dog," Zach said.

Luke smiled. "You have a good dog without my dog influencing him. You just have to work on your training skills."

"Yeah? You wanna train me to train him?"

"In my spare time when I'm not working with my own dog or the other two dogs at home or taking care of my kid or my house or making sure my wife is happy? Sure."

Zach laughed and put his hands out. "Okay, fine. I get it. You're a little busy."

"Just a little."

He noticed Luke didn't even pick up a menu.

"Cheeseburger?" he asked.

Luke nodded. "Same for you?"

"Yup. They make the best cheeseburgers here. I've never tasted better."

"Same."

Anita came over and pulled her order pad out of her apron and the pen from behind her ear. "Cheeseburgers with the works?"

"Yeah," Luke said. "With fries and a glass of iced tea."

"Same for me," Zach said.

"You got it."

Anita walked away, and Zach settled against the back of the booth. "How are the wife and baby and dogs and house thing going?"

"Couldn't be better. Michael grows and changes every day. He's talking up a storm now, getting into everything— like a toddler does."

"So it's fun? The whole having kids thing?"

Luke looked over at him and gave him a straight look. "It's fun. A lot of responsibility, and some days it's exhausting. But seeing that little kid that's a part of you and a part of the person you love? Man, there's nothing better."

"I can see that."

Anita brought their drinks, so Zach took a sip of his iced tea.

"Why, you thinking about having some?"

Zach slanted a grin at Luke. "Not at the moment. You know, I've never given much thought to having kids. When I first came out of college, it had all been about football. Then I got hurt and had to change my focus, so it all became about teaching—and football, just at the high school level."

Luke grinned. "You're a good teacher. And a great high school football coach."

"Thanks."

"So you're thinking of settling down?"

Zach shrugged. "I don't know. No one has come my way to make me think that."

Until Josie.

"You sure about that? I've seen you with Josie Barnes."

Obviously, he wasn't the only one who'd thought that. He wondered if everyone else had noticed the thing he had going on with Josie. "Yeah, there's Josie."

Anita brought their food, so he didn't have a chance to comment any more than that. And maybe he shouldn't comment at all since he didn't really know what was going on with Josie and him.

They'd had a hot night together last weekend, and then . . . nothing. He'd had to leave her in the middle of the night because of Wilson, but he told her he'd call her the next day, which he had. He thought maybe they could have lunch together.

So he'd called her, and she'd told him something had come up and she couldn't see him that day. Which he thought was no big deal. Stuff happened all the time.

Except when he'd asked her out the next day, she'd told him she was busy. So he told her to let him know when she was free.

He hadn't heard from her all week. He'd seen her at

school and she'd been her normal, polite self, but that was it. So he had no idea what was up, but he figured if she wanted to see him again, she could let him know.

"So, what's up with you and Josie?" Luke asked.

Shit. "Honestly? I don't know. It's like we get close, then she backs off."

Luke grinned over the rim of his glass. "Maybe she doesn't like you."

"Impossible. All women like me."

"Yeah, okay, stud. But seriously. What do you think it is?"

"No idea. I think she's afraid of commitment."

"Huh." Luke studied his drink for a few seconds, then met his gaze. "Isn't that typically the guy's issue?"

Zach laughed. "I guess."

"So, are you?"

"Am I what?"

"Afraid of commitment."

"Oh. No. I mean, yeah, I've enjoyed living the single life."

"But you'd be okay with settling down now. With Josie."

Zach was pretty sure this was the longest conversation he'd ever had with Luke. Punctuated with several probing questions. "What is this? An interrogation?"

Now Luke laughed. "Maybe. Emma and I like Josie. She's good people."

"Yeah, she is. But I'm not the one backing off. Josie is. So let Emma know that."

Luke picked up a French fry and popped it into his mouth. "Ten four."

That conversation with Luke left Zach feeling unsettled. So after they finished eating and said their good-byes, Zach decided to drive over to Josie's house. Her car was in the driveway, which meant she was home. Or at least he hoped she was home. Because he didn't like this feeling, and maybe he just wanted to see Josie.

So he and Wilson would take a detour, and see what happened.

Chapter 21

"COME ON, WILSON," Zach said as he took Wilson out of the car and connected the leash to his harness. "Let's go say hi to Josie."

Wilson hopped up the steps and onto Josie's porch, and Zach rang the doorbell.

Josie answered right away. She had Arthur in her arms, the bunny snuggled up against her chest. "Oh. Hi, Zach. Hey, Wilson. What are you two doing here?"

Her voice was flat, void of emotion. She was wearing black stretchy pants and a T-shirt, and had a blanket wrapped around her shoulders. Her feet were bare, and her eyes were red-rimmed, like she was sick, or maybe she'd been crying.

No matter which, he was concerned. "Hey, are you all right?"

"I'm fine, but I'm not very good company right now."

"I didn't expect good company. I just hadn't talked to you for like a week. I wanted to see you. Are you sick?"

She shook her head. "No. You want to come in?"

"If you're okay with that."

She shrugged and turned around. "Up to you."

She walked away from the door, leaving it open. He shifted his gaze to Wilson, who glanced up at him with a concerned look.

I know, dude, he thought to his dog. *Something's up with Josie. We should go inside and check on her.*

He and Wilson walked inside, and Zach closed the front door. Josie was curled up on the couch, Tumbles wandering back and forth behind her on top of the sofa.

"Okay, buddy," Zach whispered to Wilson. "There's a cat. Not sure what's going to happen, but be ready for anything."

He unhooked Wilson from the leash. Wilson bounded over to Josie and jumped onto the sofa. Zach tensed, waiting for Tumbles to hiss and attack his dog.

Instead, Josie ran her hand over Wilson's back and murmured softly. Tumbles jumped from the top of the sofa and went over to Wilson to sniff him. Wilson wagged his tail, Tumbles lifted his nose in the air in disdain, then flounced on Josie's lap and went to sleep.

That was it? Didn't it figure that the cat would even like his dog instead of him?

He went over and sat next to Josie. The cat's left eye shifted open to stare at him.

"What's going on?" he asked Josie.

She leaned her head back against the sofa, cuddling Arthur closer to her chest. "My mom showed up several days ago, out of the blue, unannounced."

"Okay. Is she here?"

Josie shook her head. "We had a big fight. She thought she could pop in here and ask for money in person, and that I'd hand it over after listening to her sob story about how she'd taken the bus up here from Talihina to Tulsa, then had to use the very last of her money to grab a taxi to my house."

Zach frowned. "Did you know she was coming?"

"Of course not. She's called me twice to ask for money, and I've turned her down both times. So she figured the next-best thing was to show up in person, thinking she could wear me down. When that didn't work, she got mad and stormed out in the middle of the night."

"So you don't know where she is."

"No. She's been gone two days."

He could feel the tension radiating off her, so he knew he had to tread lightly. "Do you want me to go with you to look for her?"

She shook her head, staring down at Tumbles as she petted his fur. "No. For all I know, she was lying about not having money and is already back in Talihina. Or she could still be in Hope, or maybe in Tulsa, trying to score drugs. She could even be prostituting herself to earn drug money."

"Christ, Josie."

Josie shrugged. "It wouldn't be the first time."

Zach couldn't imagine the childhood Josie had, the nightmares she'd experienced. He wanted to drag her into his arms and shield her from any more hurt from the woman who had failed to love and protect her.

But he knew the harsh realities of life. He'd seen it today, in fact, with Paul. He'd seen it a lot in his students. He wouldn't be able to protect Josie. What he could do, though, was to let her know she wasn't alone.

He shifted, giving Tumbles a look that told the cat he wasn't going to fight battles with him today. He pulled Josie against him. Wilson adjusted on her other side, and Tumbles resettled on her lap.

They stayed that way for a while, and Zach listened to the sounds of Tumbles purring. It was a surprisingly relaxing sound. He eventually felt Josie's body go lax.

He thought she might be asleep, but she shifted around to face him. "I know what you're thinking," she said.

"I doubt that." He'd been thinking he might want to take her to bed, undress her, and maybe give her a massage to relax away her tension.

"You're thinking I should go try to find my mom."

Definitely not what he'd been thinking. "Is that what you want to do?"

She shook her head. "I've long ago reconciled myself to

the truth about my mother, Zach. She's a drug addict, and she'll do anything—anything—for a fix. I also learned not to go chasing her down. If I bring her back here, she'll just run off again."

"What about rehab?"

"That will only work if it's her idea, not mine. So far, she hasn't fallen far enough—at least in her mind—that she thinks she needs it. The only reason she wants to be around me is because I have income, and money is a means for her to buy drugs."

He couldn't imagine how frustrating and hurtful that must be for Josie. He lifted her hand and twined his fingers with hers. "I'm sorry."

"I'm used to it."

"How do you get used to having a mother with a drug problem, Josie? I guess that's a stupid question. You don't."

"Actually, you do. You just . . . live with it."

"And what were the times like when she was off the drugs?"

"Kind of surreal. I've known her mostly one way my entire life, so it's like I don't really even know the sober part of her."

"But don't you want to?"

She whirled around, crossing her legs as she faced him. "Of course I do. I want her to get clean and stay that way. But I can't make her do it, and I can't . . ."

"Hope that she'll want to do it for you?"

"She can't want to do it for me, Zach. She has to want to do it for herself."

"Yeah, but she has to love you enough to know how much she's hurting you."

Her eyes welled with tears. "You know an awful lot about addiction."

"My uncle is an alcoholic. It was when I was young, but I overheard a lot of conversations between my parents when they thought I was up in my room asleep."

"I'm sorry. That had to be hard."

"Hard on my dad—it was his brother. And hard on my

aunt and my cousins. Though of course the Powers family swept it all under the rug. No one could know."

"Why not?"

"Because that's just how it was done."

When she frowned, he said, "The Powers family is oil money. Prestigious and powerful connections in Oklahoma."

"Oh, that's right. You were raised in Tulsa."

"Yeah. Anyway, I remember all the hushed talk and making of plans, and how Uncle Maxwell had to 'go away to Europe on family business' for six months, or at least that's how the family spun it."

"Huh. Lucky for your family. All our skeletons were always right out in the open, and considering my mom was always wandering up and down the streets screaming our business, there wasn't a way to hide it anyway."

He smoothed his hand up and down her back. "That couldn't have been easy."

"I took some shit for it from some kids at school who thought I was as weird as my mom. Other people were sympathetic, but they tended to be the adults."

"Kids can be brutal."

"Yeah, but they didn't understand, and were likely afraid of the crazy lady wandering the streets at night."

"Is that her standard MO when she's high?"

Josie raised her knees to her chest and leaned her chin there. "Yeah. For some reason she's always had a war going on with the world, and when she's high, she wants everyone to know what's on her mind."

"Come on, let's go." He stood.

She frowned. "Where?"

"To find your mom. If she's high, then maybe she'll be wandering out where we can find her."

"Oh, Zach, I don't think that's a good idea."

He kneeled in front of her. "You're worried about her. You might not want to admit it, but you are. And you aren't going to rest until you find her."

"She might not even come with me if we do find her."

"Maybe not. But won't you rest better knowing where

she is, that she's okay?" At her look, he added, "Or that she's as okay as she's going to be?"

"Yes. You're right about that. This not knowing is tying me up in knots."

"Then we'll go for a drive and see what we can see. Wilson really likes going for rides, don't you, buddy?"

Wilson stood up on the sofa and wagged his tail.

Josie closed her eyes for a few seconds, then opened them, braced her hands on either side of his face, and brushed her lips across his.

"Thank you. Hold Arthur, and I'll be right back."

She disappeared into the bathroom for a few minutes, so he petted Arthur, who made cute little bunny noises. Meanwhile, the Harbinger of Death regarded him suspiciously.

"Hey, Beelzebub. I care about her, too, so just chill."

The cat inched over toward him and head-butted his hand. So Zach ran his hand over Tumbles's head and back, surprised when he started to purr.

"You're lulling me into a false sense of security. Then you're going to bite me, aren't you?"

But Tumbles continued to purr and rub his head against Zach's hand.

Weirdest thing.

"How can I continue to call you the Prince of Darkness if you're going to be nice to me?"

"Making friends?" Josie asked as she came out of the bedroom. She'd put on a gray sweater and her tennis shoes.

"Apparently."

"Here, let me take Arthur and put him in his crate." She took the bunny, and Tumbles jumped off his lap. Wilson followed the cat, at least until the cat jumped up on the windowsill. Then Wilson barked, and Tumbles flicked his tail.

Zach attached Wilson's leash to his harness, and they headed out to his car. He put Wilson in the back, and Josie climbed into the front seat.

"You know, I realized I've never seen your mother," he said. "So it might be hard for me to help you look. Do you have a recent photo?"

"Oh, right," she said, then pulled out her phone and swiped through her photos. "Here's one she sent me last month."

She handed the phone to him. His mom looked young. So young that she could pass for Josie's sister. She wore her hair longer, in a ponytail. She was smoking in the picture and leaning against a patio table in a backyard. But she was smiling, so that was good. She seemed happy.

Josie definitely had her mom's eyes, only Josie's eyes sparkled with life. There was a disconnect in—

He looked up at Josie. "What's your mom's name?"

"Irene. Rina is what she goes by."

"Pretty name."

"I always thought so."

As he backed down the driveway, he glanced at Josie. Her expression was blank, but he knew she was hoping they'd find her mom.

So was he. And he didn't want to let her down.

JOSIE WAS PRETTY sure that after an hour of driving every street in Hope, she knew her way around better than ever. She knew street names and side streets and shortcuts that she'd never known before.

There was no sign of her mother, at least not in Hope. She'd run off with Josie's hot-pink rain jacket, and providing she was still wearing it, she'd be easy to spot.

Zach had even called Luke McCormack and Will Griffin, since they were a city cop and highway patrol officer, respectively. He'd texted the pic of Josie's mom to them—unofficially, since Josie didn't want to declare her mother a missing person. But they both said that they were out on patrol and they'd look for her.

"Did she take any money when she left?" Zach asked.

Josie shook her head. "Not that I'm aware of. Not any of my money, anyway. Once she showed up, I put my purse in my bedroom closet, knowing money would be what she'd be after. And I don't keep a lot of cash on me, anyway."

"And you checked to make sure? Plus your bank and credit cards. I hate to ask you that."

"Don't apologize. She took off with my wallet once when I was a teen, after I'd gotten my first job. She took my paycheck. I learned my lesson after that. So after she ran off this time, my purse and my bank balance were the first things I checked. Nothing was missing."

He resisted thinking bad thoughts about Josie's mom. But dammit, she'd really hurt Josie. "Okay. So as far as you know, she doesn't have any cash."

She shrugged. "Yes. That was the argument, that she ran out of money and didn't have any cash to get back to Talihina. I offered to either drive her back home or purchase a bus ticket for her and take her to the bus station."

"And?"

"She declined both offers, because she had come here for cash, and she didn't plan on leaving until she guilted me into giving her money."

He glanced at her. "Does that typically work?"

"Her getting cash from me? No. But it doesn't stop her from trying. She's out of money and desperate. So she forgets that I always say no. She always thinks she's smarter than me and that this time her sob stories will work."

"That has to be hard on you."

She looked out the window. "I'm used to it."

"Josie."

She shifted to look at him. "Yes?"

"You don't have to be brave all the time."

"What? I'm not brave."

"Yeah, you are. You blow this all off as something you've gone through since you were a kid. To me that's a nightmare. You should be upset or angry. Or frustrated. It's okay to show me how you feel."

She inhaled a deep breath, then let it out. "Honestly, Zach, I'm just exhausted. I've been through this with my mom for as long as I can remember. She's been a drug addict for as long as I remember."

She thought back to so many years ago, when she'd gotten tired of being alone in the house, hungry and scared.

"One time, I was seven, and she'd been gone for two days. I got tired of being scared, so I put on my shoes and my coat, and I went out one night and searched for her."

He shook his head. "Fuck. You were a little girl."

"Yeah, well, by that time I was the adult and she was the child. I found her behind the Quick Mart, stoned and out of her mind. I walked her home and put her to bed. I also found twenty dollars in her pocket, so the next morning I went to the market and got some food. She was mad about that, too."

"Why?"

"Because I used her drug money to buy food."

"Oh, for—"

"I know. After that, whenever she was passed out, I'd sneak a little money from her wallet and hide it where she couldn't find it. That way when she disappeared on me again, I wouldn't go hungry."

"You do realize that DHS could have taken you into foster care."

"I was more afraid of foster care than I was of her disappearing on me. I did the foster care thing the couple of times my mom went to rehab. I could handle her and her binges. I could even handle a couple of days and nights of being alone whenever she'd disappear. But being taken away and dumped on strangers? Now, that was scary. I didn't like it and never wanted to do it again."

She could still remember strange house smells and stacked-up beds and all those kids she didn't know. Some were okay, but a lot of the kids were mean, and some of them had issues way worse than her mom. She'd had a lot of sleepless nights. Her mother was a known entity. Foster care was scary and unknown. She had always much preferred to stick with the devil she knew.

"I can't imagine. I'm sorry you had to do that."

"So was I."

"What about grandparents? Her parents?"

She snorted out a laugh. "They were über-religious and

wanted nothing to do with my mother and her drug habit or her illegitimate daughter. I might have seen them . . . twice, maybe? No, they didn't want me. Or her."

Zach frowned. "Assholes."

"Pretty much."

He made the turn and entered the highway that headed into Tulsa.

She thought about the number of streets in Tulsa, how many hours it would take to comb them all. She looked over at Zach, at the determination on his face. She so appreciated him doing this for her, but it was a futile endeavor. She reached over and laid her hand on his arm. "Tulsa's a big city, Zach. We'll never find her."

"Will texted me with the locations of a few places she might hang out, so I have some starting points."

She knew what he meant. "Druggie hangout locations."

"Yes."

"Okay. We'll look at some of those, but after that, we're done."

He gave her a quick nod. "Sure."

They made their way to one of the areas. It was downtown, dark, fairly deserted, and Josie wanted to shudder as they drove slowly under the overpass. Shadows flitted here and there, and she knew those shadows were people running from what they likely thought was the police. She strained her eyes searching for the pink slicker, knowing that even in this blackness the hot pink would show.

She didn't see it. More important, she didn't feel her mother's presence. "She's not here."

"How do you know?"

"I just . . . know."

"Okay." He stepped on the gas and drove away. A few miles later, they landed in a dingy area that was much more populated, and where there were a few strip joints, convenience stores and gas stations, and a sprinkling of fast-food restaurants.

Zach drove into one of the strip club lots and parked.

Josie shifted to face him. "Got your dollar bills ready?"

He laughed. "There's a spot behind this building that Will said is frequented by some of the meth crowd. But you can't drive through it."

She grabbed the door handle. "I'll go look."

"And I'll go with you." He turned to Wilson. "Be right back, buddy."

It was a cool night, and Josie was glad she had her sweater.

"Take my hand," he said.

She looked down at the hand he'd held out, then up at his face. "Why?"

"Because I have no idea what kind of element we're going to find back there, and I want to make sure we look like a couple of lovers looking for some . . . privacy."

"Really. You know, just because people take drugs doesn't mean they're all muggers or potential murderers. Mostly they keep to themselves."

"Uh-huh. First, you're too trusting. Second, I'm not taking any chances."

He squeezed her hand as they walked down the hill behind the building. Just as Will had said, a group of about six people was leaning against the building's wall. Josie knew that vacant, stoned look. They all gazed up as Josie and Zach casually walked by. Josie searched the other side of the walkway but didn't see anyone else lurking in the dark corner. They ended up on the main street's sidewalk, and walked around past the strip club toward the parking lot and back to the car.

She masked her disappointment by smiling at Wilson, who was licking the window.

"He probably needs a short walk," Zach said.

"No problem."

Zach took Wilson to the grassy area over by the convenience store while Josie leaned against the car and waited. She watched as he waited for Wilson to do his business, then walked back and forth on the grass with his dog, talking to him the entire time.

For a guy who'd never had a pet, he was doing a great job with Wilson. They were good for each other.

When Zach got back to the car, he came up to her and wrapped his arms around her. "You're cold."

"Am I? I feel fine."

His fingers slid down her back and rested just above her butt. "Yeah, you feel pretty damn fine to me, too."

He dipped his head and took her mouth in a kiss that made her forget about everything except the fire of passion he always seemed to be able to ignite within her. And suddenly she didn't care that they were in a strip club parking lot, or that her mother was missing, or anything but the way his hands restlessly roamed her body, and the need she felt for him.

And maybe this wasn't the best time to be thinking of sex since her mom was missing. And sure, this wasn't the greatest location. But sex was a good distraction, and she needed just a few minutes to not worry about her mother, to worry that something bad had happened. All she wanted was to lose herself in Zach and passion and let her mind go blank. And if there was one thing Zach was exceptionally good at, it was making her lose all focus on everything except touching and kissing and hot, passionate sex.

When he pulled back, she licked her lips. "Ever have a quickie in the car?"

"Yes. But not with you. And the last time I did, I might have been seventeen and had no idea what I was doing."

Her lips curved. "So you're saying you know exactly what you're doing now?"

His gaze was intense. "Hell yes. Get in the car."

He opened the door and she slid inside, her pulse racing while she waited for him to put Wilson in the backseat. He got into the driver's side, locked the door, then pulled something out of his pocket and tossed it on the center console between them.

When she glanced over at it, she saw it was a condom.

She kicked off her tennis shoes, slid out of her pants, and climbed over the center console to straddle him.

"I do like a man who's always ready for action," she said.

He grasped her hips and rolled her back and forth against

his cock, which was already hard and straining against his jeans. "You're beautiful, and hot, and sexy as fuck."

He reached to the side of his seat and pressed a button, moving the seat back. She unzipped his jeans and pulled out his shaft, then reached for the condom, opened the package, and rolled it over his cock, watching his face as she did.

A storm gathered in the deep gray of his eyes, and when she grasped the base of his shaft and positioned herself over him, he dug his fingers into the flesh of her hips.

She eased down, and the pleasure was explosive. She wasn't sure if it was their location, that they could be caught doing this, or because he fit so perfectly inside of her, and she wanted him so badly she was ready to come already.

"Kiss me, Josie," he said, his voice rumbling low and gruff and so damn sexy, her body trembled in response.

She pressed her lips to his and moaned as he gripped her hips. She leaned forward and braced one hand on his chest, the other on the armrest. Then she moved forward, and back, sliding herself along his body, filling herself with every inch of his length.

"That feels so good," she murmured, lost in the feel of him, the way he gripped her and pulled her toward him and arched into her.

"You feel good. God, Josie, the way you look right now."

She searched his face, soaking in the hot intensity of his gaze. She was close, so close to losing it, to giving it all to Zach.

He swept his fingers against her and took her right over the edge. She clenched around him, the spasms of her climax rocketing her into oblivion. She fell forward and kissed him, winding her fingers in his hair as the waves of orgasm continued to make her fly. And when he thrust deeply into her and groaned, she held on to him, wound her tongue against him, and sucked.

"Goddammit," he groaned out against her mouth, finishing with a hard shudder.

She panted and smiled against his lips. "So, was it good for you?"

"I might be having a stroke."

She swept her hand over his jaw. "You seem fine to me. Extremely fine."

He palmed her breasts, cupping one and teasing her nipple. "Yeah, it's too bad we're in the car. In the parking lot. Not naked. I'm ready for round two."

"Dammit. Quit teasing me." She rolled off him and maneuvered her way back into her seat. While he pulled off the condom and righted his clothes, then left the car and disposed of the condom in the Dumpster, Josie climbed back into her clothes and slid into her tennis shoes. She checked the backseat to find Wilson curled up on the blanket, sound asleep. Obviously he found sex boring.

She, however, did not. Her body still sizzled from her scalp to her toes. And, like Zach, she was ready for round two.

Zach came back and slid into the seat. "Well," he said, leaning over to cup her neck and brush his lips across hers. "That was fun."

Her heart rate was still working its way back to normal. "I agree."

He started up the car and headed back onto the street. "So, what do you think? Once a week in the strip club parking lot?"

She laughed. "Oh, sure. The law of averages won't get us caught having sex in public, will it?"

He slanted a wickedly sexy smile at her. "Oh, come on, Josie. Where's your sense of adventure?"

"You just saw it. I'm good for the year."

She thought about it for a second, about how hot it had been, then said, "Or maybe half a year."

"Can I convince you of quarterly?"

She laughed, realizing how relaxed she felt right now. She was so grateful to have had those few moments to let go of some of the tension she'd felt the past couple of days. She slid her hands along Zach's arms and smiled at him. "I'm open to negotiation."

Her phone buzzed and she pulled it from the console, her

heart rate picking back up again, but this time for an entirely different reason. She pushed the button.

"Mom, where are you?"

"I'm at your house, Jo Jo. I rang the bell and knocked, but you didn't answer. Where are you?"

"On my way there now. Are you all right?"

"I'm fine. I'm tired, honey."

Josie sighed, trying not to imagine where her mother had been or what kind of shape she was in. "I'll be there in about twenty minutes, Mom. You just hang tight on the porch. And don't leave, okay?"

"All right. See you soon."

"Bye, Mom."

She clicked off and stared down at her phone, wishing she could just materialize at her house. She didn't trust her mother to stay put, and the last thing she wanted was for her to bolt again.

Zach reached out and squeezed her hand. "I'll get us there as fast as I can."

Josie nodded. "It's okay. Don't break any speed laws or anything."

He continued to drive, but she could see he was hovering just above the speed limit. She wanted to tell him to slow down, but she didn't. If she'd been the one driving, she'd have done the same thing.

She held her breath when he pulled into her driveway. Since she'd turned on the porch light, it was easy to see the figure curled up on the swing. She exhaled in relief.

"She's still there."

"That's good. You want me to stay?"

She unbuckled her seat belt. "No, that's okay." She reached over and grasped his arm. "Thank you for tonight. For helping to look for her. For . . . everything."

"You're welcome. I'm here for you, Josie. Anything you need."

Her heart tumbled in her chest. She wanted to spend more time with him, to ask him to stay over so she could curl up against him in her bed tonight and soak up his warmth.

His strength. She could really use some of Zach's strength right now.

But she had to deal with her mother by herself. She always had, and there was no reason to drag Zach into her nightmare.

She leaned across the seat and pressed her lips to his. "I'll talk to you soon."

He held on to her arm. "If you need me—for anything—you call me. I can come over and help you."

His words were sweet and she knew he meant them, but she wouldn't ask that of him.

"I'm good, but thanks. I'll call you tomorrow."

She slid out of the car and waited for him to back down her driveway. When he'd disappeared around the corner, she turned and walked up the steps and went to wake up her mother.

Chapter 22

ZACH PACED THE house on Sunday, and, despite having football games on to distract him, he found himself staring at his phone, waiting to hear from Josie.

"This is stupid," he mumbled. Staring at the phone wasn't going to make it ring.

He took Wilson for a walk in between games, and they played with the ball out in the backyard. After that, he settled in to watch the next set of games—and also checked his phone.

Still, nothing. He didn't want to call Josie and bother her in case she was in the middle of things with her mom, but damn, he wanted to check on her to make sure she was okay. He wasn't going to, though. He knew she needed her space to be with her mom to figure things out. So he was going to let it be. If she needed him, she'd call or text.

He made himself a sandwich and settled on the sofa with Wilson to watch the late games. Or at least he was watching the games. Wilson curled up next to him and passed out on his back, his feet up in the air.

He was deep in the fourth quarter of a tied game when he got a text message from Josie.

Are you available to talk?

He texted her back right away. Sure. Call me.

His phone rang, and he punched the button. "Hey, how's it going?"

"Actually, pretty good. Mom and I had a long talk last night."

"A good talk?"

"Yes. She couldn't score any drugs after she left my house, and she ended up frustrated and sick and tired and hungry. She slept behind a Dumpster one night, shaking and going through withdrawal. I think that was it for her. She's sick of the need for drugs. She wants to go to rehab again."

"That's a good thing."

"Yes. But she doesn't want to go back to Talihina because all her drug connections are down there. So she wants to stay up here, where she's close to me, but she doesn't know anyone."

"Okay, that's a good sign."

"It is. So, I've made some calls today, and we've got her scheduled for a three-month stay at a rehab facility starting tomorrow."

"That's great, Josie."

"I'm encouraged by her desire to quit. I also know it won't be easy, and she has a tendency to quit things that aren't easy. She's tried rehab before."

"Maybe this time it'll be the one that sticks."

He heard her sigh. "I don't know. It costs too much to hope."

He hated that it had come to that for her—for both of them. But he understood. Family letting you down hurt. He knew that all too well.

"Is there anything I can do for either of you?"

"I appreciate it, but no, thanks. I just wanted to get you up to speed on what's going on and to let you know I've already called in to have a sub fill in for me at school tomorrow while I get all this taken care of and get her settled."

"Okay, thanks. I'd have worried about you if I didn't see you there."

"That's what I figured. And do me a favor and just tell people I'm sick if anyone asks."

"You already know Chelsea and Jane will ask about you."

"I know they will. I'm just not ready to talk about this—talk about her—yet."

"You got it. I'll tell them you got some stomach bug. That usually prevents people from wanting to know details."

She laughed. "That's true. Thanks, Zach."

"No problem. Hey, check in with me tomorrow after you've gotten her settled in, okay?"

"I will. Thanks again for all you did for me yesterday."

"No need to thank me. If you recall, it was an enjoyable experience."

"Yes, it was. I wish we could have built upon that experience. I wanted to bring you back here and get you naked."

Just thinking about it made him hard. "You did, huh?"

"Yes. I wanted you in my bed last night. Or, you know, right now?"

Her talking to him like this was not helping his . . . situation. "Yeah, that sounds good."

"Well, now I guess we're both frustrated."

"Hey, you started it."

She let out a soft laugh. "I did, didn't I? I suppose next time I see you, I'll have to finish it."

"Let's make that soon, okay?"

"Very soon. I'll talk to you later, Zach."

"Bye, Josie."

He clicked off and dropped his phone to the couch, dragged his fingers through his hair, and blew out a frustrated breath.

He saw the football game he'd been watching was going into overtime, but now he was hard and frustrated and needed to work out his frustrations.

He rubbed Wilson's belly. "Come on, buddy, time to go for a run."

Wilson leaped up and dashed off the sofa, his tail whipping back and forth in excitement.

"Okay, little dude, let's do it."

He grabbed Wilson's leash and put on his harness, then, since it was a cloudy and cool day, put on a hoodie.

Wilson pulled at the leash. Despite having only three legs, his dog loved to run.

"I guess my frustration is your gain, huh, Wilson?"

Wilson barked as if to say, *Suck it up, dude. Let's run.*

"Yeah, yeah, let's go."

Chapter 23

"I'M NOT GOING to let you down this time, Jo Jo."

Josie's heart clenched as she pulled into the parking lot of the rehab facility in Tulsa.

She put the car in park and turned to face her mom. "You know you have to do this for yourself, Mom. Not for me or for anyone else."

Her mother nodded. "I know. This time it is for me. I ache inside. It hurts all the time. And then I get better, but it's only for a little while, and then it hurts again. I'm so tired of chasing down my next fix. I'm just . . . so tired, Jo Jo."

She did look tired. That was the first thing Josie had noticed when she'd seen her mom on her porch. Sure, she'd seen her haggard and high and coming down off a bender and rough-looking from no sleep the night before, but she'd never seen her mother look this broken down. It was like she'd finally hit the bottom. Maybe that was a good thing.

Josie brushed her hand over her mother's hair. "I know you are. You'll be able to get some rest here and start building yourself back up again."

Her mother stared down at her lap. "I just feel so worthless."

"You're not worthless, Mom. You have so much talent. Remember how you used to love to paint?"

Josie caught the hint of a smile on her mother's face. "I did like painting. I'd look at the sky or trees or an animal, and I could paint a canvas for hours." Her smile disappeared. "But that was a long time ago."

"That talent still lives in you, Mom. You just have to dig deep and find your passion again. I know you can do it. All you have to do is exorcise those demons first."

Her mother sniffed, then nodded. "I will. This time I really want to, Jo Jo. I want it gone forever."

She'd never heard her mother so determined before. Then again, she'd heard lots of promises before, so she kept her hope to a minimum. There'd been so many times when she'd thought, *This one is it. This will be the last time.*

And she'd always been wrong. She had to take a step back and guard her heart against the hurt.

"It's time to go, Mom."

"Okay. I'm ready."

That was new, too, because usually rehab was something she met with reluctance. This time her mother seemed eager.

They walked inside the facility, and Josie helped her mother fill out the paperwork. When they turned it in and the aide came, her mother turned to Josie and hugged her. "Time for you to go, Jo Jo. I have to walk through those doors by myself."

Josie's eyes welled with tears. "Okay. I love you, Mom."

Her mother's eyes filled, too. "I love you, too, Jo Jo. Now, go. Next time I see you, I'll be whole again."

"All right."

She walked out and got into her car. She turned and looked at the front door of the facility, and for the first time in her life, she felt a sprinkling of joyful hope for her mother. She couldn't help it.

Maybe this time her mother could really do it.

God, she hoped so. She bent her head and sent a prayer

up for her mother, because she was going to need all the strength she had to get through this.

She really wanted her mother back. Whole and healed and healthy and strong and drug free. She wanted that for her mom more than for herself.

Please, God. Give her the strength to get through this. Watch over her and help her.

She gripped the steering wheel and realized her hands were shaking.

Get a grip, Josie. It was time to let it go. She wasn't in control of this, and she knew it.

She put the car in gear and drove off.

Chapter 24

JOSIE DOVE INTO work the following week, which helped to keep her mind busy. She hadn't told anyone other than Jillian about her mom. Of course, there was Zach, but she needed to talk it out with one of her girls, and Jillian was her best friend, so she'd spilled everything one night at Jillian's place. Jill had poured the wine and Josie had talked. And talked some more. And Jillian had listened and commiserated and cried with her while Josie had poured out everything all the way from her childhood until she had dropped her mom at rehab the other day.

Sometimes just talking it out helped. She hadn't had that since . . .

Well, ever. Now she had Zach and Jillian to confide in, and it was making all the difference. But now she had to move on. Since this wasn't her first go-round with her mother in rehab, she knew the best thing to do was to not think about it. It would be a long road for her mom, and there was nothing she could do to help her through it.

Fortunately, she had several things going on in her classes. Her AP English lit class had compositions due, she was giving end-of-quarter tests in her two freshman classes, and she was deep in discussion about some complex narrative elements in another class. All of that meant she was up to her eyeballs in work—just the way she liked it. Busy meant no time to think about anything else. And the week just flew. Before she knew it, it was Friday night and everyone was talking about game night. The Hope Eagles had lost only one game, and they were tied for first place in their division with the team they were playing tonight. Based on conversations she'd been hearing all week, it would appear the entire school was going to be attending the game. Which meant she'd have to go.

Not that she didn't want to go—she did. She was as excited about the prospect of the Eagles taking first place as anyone else. She was also nervous for Zach and wasn't sure she could sit still for four quarters. They'd talked this week, and though he'd played it off as just another game, she knew what this meant to him. If they beat the Round Rock Bears on their home turf, that would leave only one more team that stood between the Eagles and the play-offs. And according to Zach, beating that last team would be easy.

She wanted that for him. She hoped that for him.

She was also waiting for word from Jane, who had an OB appointment today to find out the sex of her baby.

Jane had told Chelsea and her at lunch yesterday that since she already had Ryan and Tabitha, it didn't matter to her what the sex was, but she was kind of hoping it was a boy, so Will would have a son of his own. Then she'd fallen all over herself apologizing because she said Will loved Ryan as his own son and she didn't know why she'd said that, so now she wanted the baby to be a girl.

Chelsea had rolled her eyes and told Jane she was a hormonal mess. And then she wished twins on Jane, who gave her a shocked look and told Chelsea they couldn't be friends anymore.

Chelsea had laughed at Jane and told her she loved her. And then Jane had cried.

Josie had kept her mouth shut, not wanting to say anything to make Jane cry again, but she did hope Jane's baby was healthy, no matter the sex.

She was just full of hope—for everyone lately, it seemed.

She gathered up her books and papers and stuffed the papers in her bag at the end of the day, her head filled with everyone's hopes.

She was in the parking lot on the way to her car when her phone pinged. She shuffled her books to her other arm so she could fish her phone out of her bag. It was a text from Jane.

It's a boy! I cried. Will cried. So happy! Talk soon.

Josie grinned, imagining their elation. She knew that Will didn't care whether it was a boy or a girl. She also knew that he loved both Ryan and Tabitha, and no one could tell him those children weren't his, even if he wasn't their biological father. The new baby was just added joy to his and Jane's lives.

She typed a quick Omg yay! Congrats! text to Jane, then went to tuck her phone back into her purse when the load of books in her arms shifted sideways. She tried to right them, but everything tumbled to the ground.

"Shit," she whispered, since students milled about the parking lot.

She got down and started picking up her books.

"You look like an overwhelmed freshman on her first day of school."

She looked up to see a very hot man grinning at her.

Zach. He crouched down and picked up all the books, and then he stood and held out his hand to haul her to her feet.

"Thanks."

"You're welcome. You planning on a big weekend of grading papers?"

"Something like that. I've got those."

"So do I. I'll walk with you to your car."

They stayed in step as she made her way over to where

she was parked. She pushed the UNLOCK button, and Zach opened the door to the backseat of her car and slid the books onto the seat. He took the bag from her hand and placed that on the seat as well.

Josie dragged her fingers through her hair, tucking her bangs away from her face.

"Thanks, Zach."

He shut the door and leaned against it. "You're welcome. Rough day?"

She shrugged. "Busy day. But it was good. How about you?"

"Same."

"You ready for tonight's game?"

"Yeah. Kids are excited and ready to play. You coming to the game?"

She offered up a smile. "Wouldn't miss it."

"Good."

She thought he'd leave, knew he had a lot to do to prep for the game tonight. Instead, he continued to look at her. So there they stood, the two of them staring at each other, and all she could think about was how much she wanted to reach out and touch his hand, lay her head against his chest, feel the beat of his heart, and align her body close to his.

"I'd really like to kiss you right now," he finally said, his words making her heart rate kick up several beats per minute.

"Ditto. Put a pin in it for later?"

"Yup. It'll give me something to think about for after the game."

She laughed and opened the driver's side door. "Oh, right. I think you'll be thinking about football."

He leaned in and laid his hand on the headrest. "I can think about football and you simultaneously."

After looking around to make sure no students were lurking, she tipped her finger across his jawline. "Focus on the game, Mr. Powers. Fun, later."

"Yes, Ms. Barnes." He winked at her, then straightened. "Good luck tonight."

"Thanks."

He closed her car door and walked off, giving her a fantastic view of his very fine ass encased in his dark jeans. Oh, the man had a sexy walk. Unintentional, but predatory. With purpose, as if he knew exactly where he was going and what he was doing.

How could she be so turned on just watching him walk away from her?

With an appreciative sigh, she backed out of her parking spot. She needed to regather her wits—and her focus— before tonight.

Chapter 25

ZACH ENTERED BASH'S bar, and cheers went up. He waved, soaked in the adulation, then located his friends at their table.

Deacon and Loretta were there, along with Chelsea and Jillian and Jeff. Josie was there, too, talking to Jillian and Megan and Sam. Reid and Brady were up at the bar having a conversation with Bash.

He waved to the table first, then went to the bar.

"There's the man of the night," Bash said, grabbing a beer to slide it over to Zach. "Heard about tonight's game. Sorry I couldn't make it, but, you know, duty calls."

"Yeah, I know how that is." Zach took a long pull of the icy cold beer, letting it slide down his throat. "But you missed a killer game."

"Don't tell me that, man. Tell me it was never close. Tell me everyone was asleep in the bleachers."

"It was intense," Brady said. "Two well-matched teams facing off. You should have been there."

"Yeah," Reid said. "Next time take the night off, Bash."

"Dammit," Bash said. "Not cool, guys."

Zach laughed and took his beer over to the table.

Josie looked up at him. "Would you like to sit next to me?"

"You know I would." He slid into the chair next to hers and leaned close. "You smell good."

"Thank you. You smell victorious."

He grinned at her. "Yeah? And what does that smell like?"

She leaned in and grasped hold of his shirt, inhaled, and offered up a sensual smile. "A little bit woodsy, masculine, and oh-so-hot."

And they'd picked up right where they left off after school today.

He'd managed to push it away into a corner of his brain. He'd had to, so he could concentrate on football. Otherwise, all he would have been able to think about would have been how incredible Josie had looked in her tight black skirt and white silk blouse today, or how the earrings she'd worn had shown off the slender column of her neck. Or how that particular shade of red lipstick she'd worn today had made him think about her mouth. Kissing her mouth and all the other fun things to do with lips.

And before he got hard in front of all these people, he turned and engaged with the group about tonight's game.

"When they kicked that field goal to tie the game with less than two minutes left, I was a little concerned," Chelsea said. "But I knew the Eagles would pull it out."

"That flea flicker on the ten-yard line, though." Josie grabbed for a nacho and let it dangle in her hand. "That was a stroke of genius. Even though my heart was in my throat the entire time."

"It was a game winner, for sure," Deacon said. "You used tried-and-true plays, and then confused the hell out of them with trick plays. Stroke of genius, man."

Zach felt the weight of their praise, but he didn't deserve all the credit. His team did. "I don't know about genius, but I knew we were going up against a seriously good team, so I was going to have to come up with some original offensive plays that were going to confuse a strong defense. And I might have developed the plans, but my guys executed them."

"You sure as hell did that, and so did they," Reid said, coming over to sit down next to his wife, Sam.

"It was a nail-biter of a game," Loretta said. "Hazel enjoyed every second of it."

"Yeah, she enjoyed it so much, she wants to play football now," Deacon said with a wry smile.

"Awesome." Zach cracked a smile. "I hope she does."

"Everyone enjoyed it," Josie said. "The crowd noise was crazy. And we're not even in the play-offs yet."

"But we will be, won't we, Zach?" Josie asked.

"Yeah, we will be." He reached for some of the nachos.

After a few beers and even more food, everyone started to head out.

Zach walked with Josie to her car. She turned to face him.

"So, I'm following you home, right?" she asked.

He hadn't expected her to invite herself over to his place, but he had to admit he was damn happy about it. They'd been leading up to this all day long, and he was more than ready to be alone with her. "Yes, you are."

"Good. I'll see you there."

He had her in his rearview mirror the entire way home. When he pulled into the garage, she was right behind him in the driveway, so he left the garage door open and waited for her, then got to appreciate the way she walked toward him in her low-slung jeans and body-hugging black shirt.

He wasn't sure how a woman wearing bright red tennis shoes could be so sexy, but she was. He was pretty sure she could be wearing bunny slippers right now and he'd still be turned on.

Definitely the woman, not the clothes.

She leaned into him and pressed her body against his. "I've been waiting all night for this."

Then she kissed him, and everything in his world felt right. Her body against his, her mouth touching his mouth, and when he breathed her in, it was as if every tension in his body melted away. Because she belonged here, in his arms—where she was meant to be.

Something major hit him about that kiss, something that felt so perfect in the moment. He shrugged it aside as just a really damn good kiss, because all he wanted right now was to focus on touching and kissing Josie. The other stuff could wait.

But then Wilson barked, and Josie backed away, licking her lips and heaving out a ragged breath. "He probably wants to go out."

Zach nodded, needing to catch his own breath. "Yeah. Let's go inside."

Wilson was by the door, tail wagging furiously.

"I know, buddy. You're ready to go out."

First, of course, Wilson waited to get love from Josie, who crouched down and doled it out with furious rubs and vivacious words.

"Who's a good boy?" she asked. "Who's the pretty boy?"

"You're spoiling him," Zach said as he led a dancing Wilson toward the back door.

"And doesn't he deserve to be spoiled?" Josie slanted a questioning glance toward Zach.

Zach opened the door, and Wilson darted outside. "Okay, he does."

"All right, then." She was leaning against the kitchen island, then turned and saw the batch of muffins. She arched her brow. "You baked?"

"Hardly. That's from the booster club."

"Ah. So you can be had for a dozen"—she lifted the lid off the container—"I'm going to guess banana nut muffins?"

"You would be right on both the muffins and the fact I can be had for baked goods."

She shook her head. "Men are so easy."

"Yup."

She teased her fingertips up and down the front of his shirt. "Making a mental note of that."

"Oh, so you like to bake, huh?"

"I like to do a lot of things." She leaned up against him,

casting a quick glance at the oversized island before lifting her gaze to his. "You know what I'd like to do in this kitchen?"

"What?"

She did a slow visual inventory of his body, starting at his feet, lingering at his zipper, then made her way back up, landing on his face before answering with, "Bake a batch of pumpkin spice cupcakes."

He stared at her for a few long seconds, then blinked. "Wow. That is not where I thought you were going with this."

She laughed. "I know."

"You wanna know what *I'd* like to do in this kitchen?"

"Of course I do. I also know you'd like for me to bake the pumpkin spice cupcakes."

"Hell yeah. But first, this."

He moved the muffins to the counter on the other side, then lifted Josie onto the kitchen island.

She wrapped her legs around him and drew him in for a kiss.

He tasted the hungry passion in that kiss, the desperate need. He'd wanted to play, to tease her a little, but he could tell Josie needed something more. He cupped her butt with his hands and lifted her off the island, walking her upstairs to his bedroom. She had a tight hold on him, laying her head on his shoulder as they made their way upstairs.

When he set her down in front of his bed, she toed off her tennis shoes, shimmied out of her tight jeans, and discarded her shirt, leaving her in some amazingly sexy black underwear.

"Don't just stand there," she said, motioning toward him with her head. "Get those clothes off."

His lips curved. "Yes, ma'am."

He did his own hurried undressing—in fact, he was sure he'd never stripped faster. But then he stood still and gaped at Josie while she teased him by doing a jaw-dropping strip tease with her underwear that left him hard and aching for her.

He came over to her and turned her around so her back was to him. He dropped a soft kiss on her shoulder.

"I like your hair short like this," he said, smoothing his thumbs over the muscles between her neck and shoulders. "You know why?"

"Why?"

"Easy access to your neck." He kissed the back of her neck, breathing in her sweet, sultry scent.

She shuddered. "That feels so good, Zach. I like your mouth on me."

He turned her around. "Where do you like my mouth on you?"

She tilted her head back, her eyes dark pools of desire. "Anywhere. Everywhere."

"I'm going to need you to be more specific in your descriptions, Ms. Barnes."

She offered up a hint of smile. "Here. On my jaw."

He kissed her there.

"And right here, in front of my ear."

He followed her direction.

"On my lips, Zach. Kiss me."

He brushed his lips lightly across hers, then went deeper, taking a full taste of her, enough to make him groan.

He'd wanted to slow things down in order to build up the tension for Josie. He didn't want to just climb on her and give her a quick release. He wanted her relaxed and ready to go off. And with every touch of his lips against her body, he felt her shudder, heard the little moans she made. It made him slightly crazy—and achingly hard—but she was worth it.

He pulled back. "Now where?"

"My . . . my neck."

That's where he could fully breathe her in. He pressed his nose there, took a deep breath, then lightly kissed along the soft column of her throat, letting his tongue rest along the pulse point, feeling it beat faster and faster.

Oh, yeah. The pulse in his cock pounded, too, and he didn't think it was possible to get any harder, but he did, swelling until he felt like he was going to burst. He pushed his erection against her hip, letting her know what she did to him. She reacted by letting out a breath and reached for him, teasing his shaft with her fingers.

"My breasts. Lick my breasts." She was panting out the words.

He knew exactly how she felt. It was like all the air had been sucked out of the room, and he found it hard to breathe. Then again, didn't he always feel like that around Josie?

He maneuvered her toward the bed until the backs of her knees hit the edge of the mattress. Then he pushed her on top of the bed and leaned over her, placing his lips over one of her nipples. It perked up against his tongue like the petals of a flower, soft and delicate. He swirled his tongue around the bud, wrapping his lips around it to give it a gentle suck.

Josie arched her back. "Oh yes. Like that. More."

He gave her more, to both nipples for a while, pleasuring her until she was writhing against his bed. God, how many times had he fantasized about her doing just that?

Sometimes dreams did come true, didn't they?

He kissed under her breasts and lifted his head. "Now where?"

She snaked her fingers over her ribs and down her stomach, cupping her sex, and lifted her head to give him a dazed, sex-fueled look. "Here. Lick me here, Zach."

He gave her a half smile. "Relax. I'll take you there."

She dropped her head to the bed and opened her legs for him. He kneeled down and draped her legs over his shoulders, giving him the perfect view of just how beautiful she was.

Now it was his turn to shudder. Here she was, spread-eagled on his bed, open and vulnerable and so trusting it made his balls quiver.

He put his mouth on her, and she lifted and cried out. She tasted like tart sweetness, so damn good he wanted to slide inside of her and relieve his own ache.

But first, Josie. He went gently at first, getting her used to his mouth and tongue, letting her ease into this. She was relaxed at first and he listened to her sounds, went with how she moved against his mouth to gauge the pressure she needed.

Fortunately, Josie was vocal, telling him how much or how little to give her, and he appreciated that, because he wanted this to be good for her.

And when she tensed and rocked against him, he knew she was close. He gave her more, then used his fingers to heighten her pleasure.

She cried out and shuddered. He held his tongue against her, letting her feel everything as she rode out her orgasm until she fell flat against the mattress.

Then he licked his lips, wiped his mouth, and gently laid her legs down. She raised herself up on her elbows and offered him a lazy smile.

"That was spectacular, and just what I needed."

He crawled on the bed next to her. "You're welcome."

Then she surprised him by pushing him onto his back. "And now it's your turn."

"You don't have to—"

She straddled him, splaying her hands on his chest. "Seriously? Of course I don't have to. I do what I want, Zach."

She leaned over and kissed him, a hot, long, kiss that made his dick pound hard. When she raised her head, she rubbed her breasts across his chest. "You want my mouth on you, don't you?"

She was trying to kill him. He was sure of it. "You're damn straight I do."

"Then lie back and think about how good this is going to be."

He'd lie back and try not to come right away, because he was primed and ready.

She slid down his body, then grasped the base of his shaft in her hand. When she put her lips over the head of his shaft, he lifted his hips, and his breathing quickened.

"Yeah, I like that, babe."

He couldn't resist telling her exactly what he liked, just how much he wanted her to keep doing exactly what she was doing. And when she went fully down on him, the visual coupled with the sensation was almost too much to bear. But he needed to hold on just a little longer, because Josie's mouth was magic.

And her using her hands and mouth on him took him to nirvana. He slid his fingers into her hair and gave himself up to her.

He lost it within minutes, and when it was over, he wasn't sure he still had a brain cell left. It took him some time to be able to form words again, and when he could, all he could say to her was "Damn."

She sat back on her heels and gave him a satisfied smile. He lifted up, wrapped his hand around the base of her neck, and kissed her, deeply. When he pulled back, he stared at her, realizing how utterly lost he'd become in this woman. So lost that the *L* word hovered on his lips.

But he needed to be able to separate "I love you" feelings from "hey, that was a damn good blow job" feelings before he said something he might regret later, so he hopped off the bed.

"I need to let Wilson in," he said. "Plus, I don't know about you, but I'm thirsty. You want something to drink?"

"I'd love a glass of water."

"I'll be right back."

"Okay."

He lingered long enough to watch her get comfortable against his pillows. Totally comfortable naked.

He liked her in his bed. In his house. In his life.

So maybe all these feelings mixing around inside of him weren't all about the blow job.

He went downstairs and let Wilson in, then fixed two glasses of ice water. Wilson got himself a drink, then followed Zach upstairs and made himself comfortable on the dog bed in Zach's room.

Zach handed the glass to Josie.

"Thanks."

He climbed onto the bed and took a sip from his glass, then laid it on the table.

Josie changed positions, moving herself halfway down the bed where he'd raised his knee. She wrapped her arms around his leg.

"This okay?" she asked.

"Of course it is."

"It doesn't hurt?" She looked down at his knee, motioning to the scar from his surgery.

"No. I don't feel it."

"Okay." She smiled at him. "It was a good game tonight, Zach. And next week's team hasn't won a game all season. You've all but sewn up first place in the division."

He hadn't expected a football conversation. Why did she always surprise him?

"Yeah. I never count on a win, so we'll practice hard for next week's game anyway. I don't like looking too far forward."

"If anyone could take those boys to state, it's you," she said. "Though I wasn't here before, from what Jane and Chelsea have told me, they've improved a lot since you took over as their coach."

"Thanks. I'm having more fun coaching these kids than I ever thought I would."

She circled her finger over the scar on his knee, then looked up at him. "More fun than playing football?"

"Nothing's more fun than playing football."

"I imagine that's true if you had it in your head that's what you wanted to spend your whole life doing."

"Yeah. But things change, and you have to adapt."

"You seem to have taken it well."

Zach remembered how well he *hadn't* taken it when he'd been given the news he'd never play football again. "Not so much in the beginning. After the knee injury, I was unpleasant to live with for a good long time."

"I doubt anyone could blame you for that. It was your dream. And losing it had to have crushed you."

"Yeah."

"Did you ever talk to anyone about it?"

He frowned. "About what?"

"How you felt when you lost football."

He thought back to those days. All he remembered was darkness. "No. I was mad for a long time. Then I let it go and moved on."

She slanted him a questioning look. "Can you really move on without talking about your feelings?"

He let out a laugh. "Josie, talking about how I felt about the injury and the end of my football career won't bring it back for me. So it seems kind of pointless."

"Of course. You would know best."

She reached over and grabbed her drink, took a couple of sips, and placed the glass on the nightstand, then leaned against him.

He rolled over and kissed her, trying to get lost in the kiss. But then he raised his head.

"It really sucked."

She pulled back. "What sucked? The kiss?"

"No. When I couldn't play football anymore."

"I can't even imagine what that must have been like for you." She swept her hand across his cheek, the action filled with a tenderness he didn't even realize he'd needed.

He rolled over onto his back and crooked his left arm over his head. Josie sat up next to him.

"For the longest time, I thought my life was over. I felt alone after the injury. When I was playing, I was on top of the world. The team was winning, I felt great, and then, boom. I was injured, I had to have surgery, and my season was over. I learned that I couldn't play football anymore. Suddenly all my friends just . . . disappeared."

She rested her hand on his chest. "What do you mean, 'disappeared'?"

"I mean they left. All my college buddies and my team-mates who would always hang out with me stopped coming by to see how I was doing. They wouldn't return my calls or my text messages. I got ghosted in the worst way."

She raised her hand to her heart. "Oh no. Right when you got injured?"

"No, not right away. They were there in the beginning

when I was in the hospital. At that point, I just thought I'd be out for that season, you know? But then as I started to rehab, it became clear that the doctors weren't going to clear me to play the next season. And the MRI showed an instability in the knee. I kept thinking that was all bullshit because I was young, in great shape, and I could get back out there. But in short order I was released from my contract, and football was over for me."

She rubbed his chest. "That had to be the absolute worst time for you."

"It pretty much sucked. And then slowly, week by week, my friends started dropping off, stopped coming by, stopped calling. They gave me the standard excuses of practice and games and said they'd call me back and come by, but right then they were busy. Until eventually every single one of them ghosted me."

"Oh, God, Zach, that's terrible. Even your best friends?"

"Even my best friends. Or the two guys I thought were my best friends. Guys I'd known since my college days at the University of Oklahoma."

He saw the hurt on her face. He knew the feeling.

"Why did they do that to you?"

He shrugged. "Football players don't like to be reminded how short a player's career can be, ya know? And if you don't have football in common anymore, then what do you have?"

He'd forgotten how much that had hurt. Being abandoned when he'd needed his people the most had gutted him.

She smoothed her hand over his chest. "What about your parents? Were they there for you?"

"For the medical part, yeah. They didn't care about the football. They thought that was stupid."

She blinked. "They thought your football career was stupid?"

"Pretty much. But they're rich snobs, anyway. They told me a career in sports was wasting my life."

"Well, that's ridiculous. What did they expect from you? To become a brain surgeon?"

He laughed. "They wanted me to follow my father into the family oil business."

She wrinkled her nose. "That doesn't sound nearly as fun as playing football. You should be able to do what you love."

"I did. I am."

"How do they feel about you being a high school teacher?"

"I don't know and don't really care. I don't talk to them anymore. After their lack of support about the end of my football career, I was done trying to please them."

"I don't blame you for that." She went quiet for a few seconds, then toyed with his fingertips. "I'm sorry you lost touch with your family. And your friends." She lifted her chin. "I'm mad at all of them. If I had been there when all this happened, I'd have told them all to go suck it."

He smiled at her righteous anger. But at the same time, he liked her standing up for him. He liked that she'd taken up for him, even though she hadn't been there when his parents had looked their noses up at his choice of career and told him how he'd shamed the Powers name. For a while, he'd felt guilty about it. Until he'd gotten hurt and they'd told him maybe he could come to his senses, forget about the whole ridiculous football thing, and enter the family business.

They hadn't cared at all about his feelings, only how they'd looked to their friends and business associates. It was then that he'd walked away from the Powers family and hadn't looked back.

Josie smoothed her hand down his leg. "Families?" She shrugged. "God knows they're hard enough to deal with. But your friends? They should have been there for you, and they weren't. A friend is a friend for life."

He swept his hand along her thigh. "Is that how your friends are?"

She shrugged. "I was speaking theoretically. I never made lifelong friends."

"Why not?"

"When I was younger, I didn't get close to anyone, for

obvious reasons. Most of my high school years were spent dealing with my mom. Then in college, I was either studying or working. That didn't leave much time for developing friendships."

"I'm sorry."

"Me, too."

"But you're making friends now."

She offered him a warm smile. "I am. There are great people in this town. And the women I've made friends with kind of don't let you be standoffish."

He laughed. "So I've noticed. Hope is a good place, Josie. Filled with good people."

"Yes, it is. I hope you've noticed that as well and you know you can count on the people you call friends. They're not going to abandon you when you need them like your former friends did."

He did know that. He'd made friends, people he could depend on. "I guess we both got lucky coming here."

"Yes, we did."

He pulled her next to him so he could kiss her and lose himself in the softness of her lips. When he drew back, he said, "And we got lucky finding each other."

She laid her body fully on top of his. "Speaking of getting lucky, we just finished round one. You ready for round two?"

Just having her naked and on top of him made him hard. "Yeah. And round three, and four, and after that, we could—"

She shut him up by kissing him.

Chapter 26

JOSIE NOTICED EVERYONE was in a bad mood this week, especially at school. Then again, midterm exams were always tough—on both the students and the teachers. But after it was over, everyone could relax. She could relax.

Plus, Zach had told her he wanted to take her on a mini getaway out of town this weekend since the football team didn't have a game Friday night. She was down with that, especially when he didn't tell her where they were going but *did* tell her to make sure to pack a couple of fancy dresses.

She was so excited and yet in the dark about their location and what to wear, she'd immediately gone to Chelsea, who'd happily lent her a couple of dresses—one red and one black. Since Josie's tastes ran more to the vintage side and none of what she owned had any sequins or sparkle, she'd wanted to make sure she was appropriately dressed for whatever Zach had in mind.

Zach had told her he'd pick her up at five on Friday, which gave her plenty of time to get home after school and meet up with Emma to give her a key to her house. Emma had graciously offered to stop by twice a day to feed Arthur and

Tumbles and cuddle them both. As if the vet didn't already have a plate full enough. But she was amazing that way.

"Are you sure this isn't going to be a huge burden?" she asked.

Emma cuddled Arthur in her arms while Tumbles wound around Emma's ankles.

"Of course not. It's on my way to and from work, and I'm off Saturday, so Michael and I can stop in and hang out with your babies."

"You're a saint, Emma. I'm always available for babysitting Michael, you know."

Emma grinned. "I'll take you up on that offer, too."

"Any time."

After Emma left, Josie changed into black yoga pants and a long sweater, then surveyed the contents of her suitcase to make sure she hadn't forgotten anything before she closed it and set it by the front door. She picked up Arthur and gave him several soft cuddles and kisses before placing him in his crated area, and then picked up her cat.

"I'll only be gone for a few days," she said to Tumbles. "And Dr. Emma is going to come by every day to check on you. In the meantime, you have plenty of food and water and your toys. You be a good boy."

The doorbell rang, so she carried Tumbles with her to the door and opened it. Zach smiled at her.

"Hey, gorgeous." He nodded at Tumbles. "Beelzebub."

Josie shook her head and held the door open for him, then realized she'd forgotten her toothbrush.

"Oh, I forgot something." She placed Tumbles in Zach's arms, ignoring his wide-eyed look, and dashed into the bathroom to grab her toothbrush. She noticed her toothpaste wasn't sitting on the counter, so she'd clearly packed that.

"Idiot," she mumbled, then grabbed her toothbrush case from the drawer and slid the brush inside of it. When she came out of the bedroom, Zach was still standing near the front door, having some kind of quiet conversation with Tumbles.

"What are you two talking about?" she asked as she tucked the toothbrush into the front pocket of her suitcase.

"I was bribing him. I told him if he didn't shred my favorite shirt, he'd get a treat."

Josie reached over and scratched Tumbles behind the ears. "Since he's purring against your chest, I think you've struck a deal. Come on into the kitchen."

Zach followed her with the cat still in his arms while Josie reached into the pantry for the treat package. She handed the package to Zach. "There you go."

Zach put Tumbles on the floor. "Well done, Satan." He handed him a treat. The cat nibbled it from his fingers, then walked off.

He handed the treats back to Josie, who tucked the package back inside the pantry. She took one last look around, making sure she hadn't forgotten anything. She'd already let Emma know where the food and treats were for both Tumbles and Arthur, and she'd written everything down and left a note on the counter as well. Plus, Emma was the animals' doc, so Josie knew they would be well cared for. She didn't have anything to worry about. And they'd be gone only a couple of days.

"Okay," she said, looking at Zach. "I'm ready."

Zach looked down at the cat who was currently batting at his shoelace. "What about the Prince of Darkness and Arthur?"

"Emma's going to pop in to care for and play with them."

"Oh. Okay. So you're not boarding them?"

She shook her head. "Tumbles has been through enough trauma in his life, and Arthur is just learning his way around here. A change in environment would be tough on both of them. Even without me here, they're happier staying home."

"Hey, you're the boss. You know what's best for them."

She appreciated that he didn't question her decisions about her babies. "Thanks."

"So we're ready, then?"

"Ready. Are you going to tell me where we're going?"

He slanted a sly smile her way. "Not yet. You look beautiful, by the way."

She had never been impressed by men saying sweet things to her. So what was it about Zach's words that made her all warm inside? "Thank you. You look hot."

Which he did, in dark jeans and a cream-colored henley. Then again, did it really matter what the man wore? He wore *hot* like a brand.

He wrapped an arm around her and tugged her against him long enough to brush his lips against hers. The kiss was brief. A tease, a promise of what was to come. She was so looking forward to spending some extended alone time with him.

She laid her hand against his chest, feeling the fast beat of his heart before he took a step back and said, "We'd better go."

Too bad, because she could have lingered a little longer against his warm body. She grabbed her sweater, and he took her bag outside, so she shut the door behind her and locked it.

It felt weird leaving her house for three days, especially leaving her babies behind. Which reminded her . . .

"Who's watching Wilson?" she asked after they got into Zach's SUV.

"I'm boarding him at Emma's clinic. They all love him there, and he gets tons of attention."

"That's good. You won't have to worry about him there."

"That's what I thought, too."

When they ended up at the airport, her heart skipped a beat. She looked over at him. "We're flying?"

"We are."

But instead of parking in the general parking lot or park and ride, he drove just offsite and pulled up to a gate. He gave his name to the security guard, who motioned him through.

The name of a private aviation company was emblazoned on the building. Josie was filled with questions. Rather than bombarding Zach with them, she decided to wait and see what was going on.

He parked inside a huge building where several aircraft were located. He got out and came over to open her door.

"I have so many questions I want to ask," she said.

"I know you do. Come on."

Some guy had come over to grab their bags.

"Hey, Mr. Powers, how's it going?"

"Pretty good, Mack. How about you?"

"Doing good. Flight has checked out, so we should take off on time."

"Thanks, Mack."

Zach took her hand and led her outside to a small jet. They walked up the stairs and inside. There were four ample, comfortable seats.

"Pick a spot," he said.

She took a seat in the back, and Zach grabbed the other seat across the aisle from her.

The guy who had grabbed their bags climbed into the plane.

"Josie, this is Mack. Mack, this is my friend, Josie Barnes."

Mack tipped the bill of his baseball cap at her. "Ms. Barnes. Pleased to meet you."

"You, too, Mack."

"We'll be taking off shortly, Zach," Mack said. "We're all stocked up, the skies are clear, and we should have a smooth ride all the way to Las Vegas."

Zach smiled. "Great. Thanks, Mack."

After Mack disappeared into the cockpit, Josie turned to face Zach. "We're going to Las Vegas?"

"Yeah. I thought it would be fun to spend a couple of days there and get away from everything for a while."

She was so excited. "I love this idea. Thank you. I've never been to Vegas."

"Oh, yeah? Then we're going to have lots of fun."

"So you know the pilot?"

Zach nodded. "I've chartered flights with Mack's company several times. He has good planes and great staff, and he's always reliable."

"Huh. This is . . . I've only been on a couple of flights before. This must be incredibly expensive, Zach."

"Not as expensive as you might think. And this is the same thing, just smaller planes and no lines."

"I just don't want you to think you have to spend a lot of money on me."

He looked at her, then cupped her face and brushed his lips across hers. "You're unlike any woman I've ever known."

"I'm going to assume you mean that as a compliment."

He smiled. "I do."

"Still, don't spend a lot of money."

"Okay, Ms. Thrifty. But don't worry about it. Despite me cutting ties with my family, I wasn't one of those guys who partied it up on my pro football salary. I was paid well for five years before my injury, and I managed to save almost all of it. Plus, my grandmother Powers left me a sizable sum."

She swiveled around in her seat. "Uh-huh. So you're some kind of multimillionaire disguised as a high school teacher?"

"Something like that."

She'd been joking. Apparently, he wasn't. She blinked, not sure what to make of that. She'd had no idea Zach had money.

"Uh, okay. But just so you know, money means nothing to me. I grew up without it, and all I need is a roof over my head and food on my table. And an occasional nice bottle of wine."

The smile he graced her with was enigmatic. Sexy, yet showed he was deep in thought about something.

"Good to know," he said.

They buckled up, and shortly thereafter, the plane taxied down the runway. It wasn't long before they were in the sky on their way to Las Vegas. Josie tried to tamp down her excitement as she looked out the window at the clouds below them, but she couldn't help herself. She could actually feel her heart beating faster. Part of her wanted to unclip her seat belt and climb onto Zach's lap and express the utter thrill that zinged through her body. But that felt too childish, so she resisted the urge.

"You've never been to Las Vegas?" Zach asked.

She pulled her attention from the puffy clouds back to Zach. "I've never been anywhere."

He frowned. "What do you mean?"

"I've never traveled much. After I left Oklahoma to go to college, I stayed put in Georgia. After college, I got a job teaching there. Other than the occasional road trip to visit some historical sites, I haven't gone anywhere. And then I moved back to Oklahoma to take the teaching job in Hope. That's pretty much the extent of my glorious travel experiences."

They'd leveled off, and the seat belt light went off. Zach got up and went to the front of the plane. "You want something to drink?"

"Sure. Water is good for me."

He grabbed bottled water for both of them from a small fridge, then came back and sat, handing the bottle to her before buckling his seat belt.

"So the lack of travel. Was it fear, lack of interest, or lack of opportunity?"

She'd never thought about it. "To be honest, I don't know. For a while, it was a definite lack of funds. In college, it was all I could do just to make ends meet. After that, I was focused on establishing myself in my job and in getting settled in Atlanta. Dylan—my boyfriend in Atlanta—he was a homebody. All he ever wanted to do was work out and hang out at home."

"Sounds boring."

She'd never thought so before, but she supposed it was his way of keeping her to himself. She'd found it romantic at the time. Until she'd found out about his other girlfriend.

"I guess it was. But when it's all you know, you don't realize what you might be missing."

He leaned over and laid his hand on her arm. "I'm going to show you a really good time, Josie."

"You do realize I don't need the glitz of Las Vegas to have a good time with you."

He crooked a smile. "That means a lot. But as long as we're headed that way, we might as well enjoy it, right?"

She'd been honest with him about Vegas. She didn't need anything fancy. She just wanted to be with him. But as long as they were going, she intended to soak in every second. "I'm looking forward to having some fun."

The flight took only a few hours. Apparently, the magic tiny fridge also held some fancy finger sandwiches and small bottles of wine, too, so they'd had snacks along the way. Josie and Zach talked almost the entire way. She shared stories of her time in Atlanta, and he told her about his childhood.

"You have an older brother?" she asked.

He nodded. "Yeah. He lives in DC with his wife and son."

"Wow. So you're an uncle."

"Yup. It's a great job."

"And this is maybe why your parents felt it was your job to carry on the family biz, huh?"

"Yeah. Phillip, my brother, went into the tech field, so they assumed I'd be the one they could count on. They were utterly disappointed in my choice of football as a career. My uncle is also in the family business, and he has two sons, both of whom are in the Powers business."

"Ah." She'd finished off her sandwich plate, which had also come with a delicious chocolate chip cookie that she'd devoured. She took a sip of her wine. "Family competition must be brutal."

"It is in my family."

"How did they feel when your brother chose a different career?"

"They were okay with it. Of course, since he's older, I think they figured I'd toe the line. I did major in business in college, so they just assumed the whole football thing was for fun, you know? That I'd play football in college, then just . . . get over it and come to work for the family after I graduated."

"But you didn't," she said.

"No, I didn't. I told my father I loved football, and that's where my future was. He didn't understand why I didn't care about the family and the Powers business. But all I'd wanted to do from the time I was a kid was play football."

"It must have been awesome for you to know from such a young age what you were destined to do." She swirled the wine around in her glass. "As for me, I didn't have a clue."

He shrugged. "That's not unusual. Most kids don't."

"I guess."

"When did you know you wanted to be a teacher?"

"My freshman year of college, when I developed this insane crush on my romantic literature professor."

Zach arched a brow. "Really."

Josie laughed. "Yes. And yes, I know. It was terribly childish of me. Fortunately, the professor was utterly professional and totally ignored me. But my crush—and the class—helped me develop a focus for his teaching methods. I learned so much that year, not only about language arts, but the history behind literature. It was that year I realized how much I wanted to be a teacher myself, and continued to foster my love of literature."

"Bet you also got an A in his class."

She waggled her brows. "Hell yes, I did. On merit, of course."

"Of course."

Before she knew it, they were circling the incredible lights of the Las Vegas strip and getting ready to land. The plane taxied to a hangar, and they got out, where a car was waiting for them.

"Thanks, Mack," Zach said. "See you on Sunday."

"You bet."

Josie turned and shook Mack's hand. "It was a great flight. Thank you."

"You're welcome, Ms. Barnes."

Mack handed their bags to the driver, who put them in

the trunk of a sleek black Cadillac, then opened the back
door for them. They climbed inside, and Josie sank against
the soft leather seat and enjoyed the ride. The drive to their
hotel wasn't long, and when they got to the Venetian hotel,
the sun was just going down and the strip was lit up. She
got out of the car and stared in awe at the blinking lights on
every hotel and casino.

Amazing.

Zach led her inside, and the décor was incredible. She'd
felt like she'd just stepped into Renaissance Italy. The stone-
work and sculptures along with the frescoes on the ceiling
took her breath away. And those were just in the registration
area.

She looked at Zach. "Wow. They do it up big here, huh?"

He handed his credit card to the registration attendant.
"Yeah, they do."

She was definitely going to have to take some time to
just . . . gawk. This was pretty incredible. She took out her
phone to snap a few photos.

Zach grabbed the keys to their room and led her through
past a few shops she wouldn't mind stopping in, either. They
had to walk past the casino on their way to the elevators.
The constant ringing of the slot machines was like a siren's
call, incredibly compelling even though she wasn't a gambler at all.

They rode the elevator and headed to their room. When
Zach opened the door, Josie couldn't hold back the gasp.

She entered through a foyer and an elegant dining area,
then walked up a few steps into a luxury bedroom with a
king-sized bed. The doorway led into a massive bathroom
with marble floors, a jetted tub with a separate huge shower,
and a double vanity.

"Wow." This place was impressive.

She walked out of the bedroom and noticed the room
extended down the stairs and into a spacious living room.

She looked over at Zach, who had tossed their keys on
the dining room table. "This room is three times the size of
my first apartment," she said "It's amazing."

"I like a room with some space."

She cocked her head. "This one has space, for sure."

"I have dinner reservations for us at eight at Delmonico here at the hotel."

She reached for her phone to check the time. That was in an hour. "Sounds perfect. I'll unpack and change."

She hung up her clothes, putting the rest in a drawer, then went into the oh-so-amazing bathroom to freshen up. Zach did the same, and it felt so weird to share the bathroom with her. But a good weird. She liked being there with him. It was intimate to share this space. It felt normal. Right.

When she'd been with Dylan, they'd rarely spent the night together. He said it was a weird quirk, that he preferred sleeping alone. She'd told him she understood at the time—everyone had their quirks, after all. As their relationship progressed, she'd asked him again and he got upset about it—like, really upset. He'd apologized to her and said it was just a thing. Since she knew all about having to handle someone with kid gloves, she'd let it go. But after he broke up with her and she found out about the other girlfriend, she figured he'd been leaving her bed to go to the other girlfriend's.

She'd been so stupid.

And he'd been a douche.

She shook her head and forced her ex-boyfriend out of her thoughts. This weekend she'd have fun with a guy who wasn't an asshole. One who actually *wanted* to spend the night with her.

She'd asked Zach about what to wear to dinner tonight and he told her whatever she wanted to, so she chose one of her vintage skirts, a gold one with a lace overlay. She coupled it with a black off-the-shoulder short-sleeved top that clung to her skin. She added a gold chain necklace, a black bracelet, and her black flats, along with her cute black-and-gold chandelier earrings.

Zach was watching television in the living room when she came out. He'd changed into a slate button-down shirt and black jeans and looked utterly delicious, as always.

He stood when she entered the room, his gaze roaming appreciatively over her.

"You look gorgeous," he said.

She warmed under his compliment. "Thank you."

They went downstairs and headed over to where all the restaurants were located, passing by the amazing Grand Canal and oh-my-God so much shopping.

They walked into the restaurant and were seated immediately at a table with white linens and lovely cream and red plates. The restaurant was nicely lit, with a traditional feel. Nothing overly fancy, which Josie appreciated. She felt enough out of her element as it was.

The waiter came over and brought their menus along with a wine list. Zach opened the wine list and read through it, then looked up at Josie.

"How do you feel about a nice bottle of cabernet to go with dinner?"

"I feel pretty good about it."

When the waiter came back, Zach ordered the bottle of wine. Josie opened the menu, her eyes widening as she perused the incredible selections.

"It all looks so good."

"It does," Zach said, scanning the menu. He looked up at her. "We should have appetizers."

"Oh, I don't know. Steak is pretty filling."

"Come on. Splurge a little. We'll take a walk outside after dinner."

"Okay, that sounds like a good idea."

When the waiter came back with their bottle of wine, he took their food order. They ended up ordering oysters for their appetizers to keep it light. Josie ordered the filet, and Zach ordered the rib eye.

She took a sip of the wine. It was smooth, with just a slight bite to it. Perfect.

"Thank you for this," she said.

"The wine?"

"No, this entire thing. I'm so excited for the weekend."

"You're welcome. I know you've had a lot going on, so I thought you could use some fun."

"We can both use some fun, don't you think?"

The look he gave her was purely sensual. "I'm all about having a good time."

She took another swallow of wine, staring at the man she shared a table with. She realized just how much fun she'd had since she'd been with Zach. "You are a good time, Zach."

His lips curved. "Thanks."

The oysters were delicious, the steak even better. By the time they finished dinner, she was full and more than ready to take that walk.

She put on her sweater, and they went outside. Now that it was fully dark, the city lights really stood out. Every hotel and casino was like a beacon, calling to her to come inside and see what they had to offer.

Zach took her hand, and they walked out onto the street. The weather was nice, and it felt good to stretch her legs.

"So, how often do you come here?" she asked him as they made their way along the strip.

"A couple of times a year."

"You like to gamble, huh?"

"I'm not a big gambler. I'll play a little. Sometimes I'll come out for a boxing event or a concert."

She stopped on the sidewalk and turned to stare at him, not saying anything.

"What?" he asked.

"What concerts?"

"I don't know. Concerts."

"Name a few you've been to."

He looked up as he thought. "Uh, Britney Spears. Garth Brooks. Elton John."

Her eyes widened. "Britney—you?"

He immediately looked defensive. "So what?"

"Nothing. I love Britney. And that's quite an eclectic selection."

He shrugged. "I like music. All kinds of music."

She shook her head, and they started walking again. "Every day I learn new, interesting things about you, Zach."

"Hey, I'm a fascinating guy."

"Don't I know it."

He wrapped an arm around her as they walked up to the fountains at Bellagio. It wasn't long before Josie was enraptured by the amazing music, lights, and water show. Who knew water could be so incredibly entertaining? Though what she was actually enticed by was Zach, who held her close the entire time, occasionally looking over at her as if he was checking to see that she was having a good time.

She was definitely having a good time, owing more to the man than to the water show.

When it was over, they went inside. It was opulent in here, and once again, the sounds of the slot machines ringing were strangely compelling. As they walked by, she found herself stopping to see whether anyone was winning money.

"Slots are for suckers," he said.

"Are they?" Still, she lingered.

"You want to play?"

"Oh. No. You said they're for suckers."

"Come on." He moved into the slots area, then put Josie ahead of him. "Pick one that looks fun to you."

She looked back at him. "I couldn't, really."

"Yes, you could." He settled on a dollar machine, then pulled a hundred-dollar bill out of his wallet and handed it to her. "Have a seat and play."

"Zach. No. That's your money."

He sat her at the machine and slid the money into it. "Punch the buttons, Josie."

"No. This is your money."

"I've got plenty of it, and this is my Las Vegas play money. Go for it."

It wasn't play money; it was real money. Josie felt guilty about using it, since it was Zach's. But at the same time, she had to admit she was excited about playing the machine.

She punched the button, and the wheels spun. And she won ten dollars on her first spin.

"I won," she said, smiling at him.

"You did. Punch the button again."

She did, getting into a rhythm with the machine. When she won enough that she'd doubled her money, she pressed the CASH OUT button.

She handed the ticket to Zach.

"You keep it and use it on the next machine."

She felt a little thrill of excitement. "Okay."

They sat side by side at a couple of other machines and played for a while. Josie nearly screamed when she won two hundred dollars on one spin. She cashed out quickly and watched Zach play for a while. He ended up losing fifty bucks, so he cashed out and they moved along.

She did well, surprisingly, racking up money on the machines until she ended up with almost eight hundred dollars. She stopped at the cashier to cash out her ticket and handed the money to Zach.

"No, that's your winnings."

She shook her head. "On your money."

He sighed. "Fine." He took one of the hundreds. "That was my money. The winnings are yours."

She had a hard time agreeing with that, but Zach refused to take the money, so she slid it into her purse. They left the casino and headed back to the Venetian.

"You want a drink?" he asked when they entered the lobby.

She shook her head. "It's been a long day. How about we head up to our ridiculously large room and shed some clothes?"

His lips curved. "And then what?"

She whispered in his ear. "Then we get naked and you can push some of my buttons."

He took her hand, quickening his step as they made their way toward the elevators. "Don't walk so slow."

She laughed, feeling the tension grow as they hit the elevators, which were filled with people. They ended up pressed to the back of the elevator. Zach pulled her against him and wrapped his arm around her. They made several stops, and the ride to their floor took a while.

Josie didn't mind, because her butt was pressed against Zach and he was deliciously hard. His arm tightened around her to draw her closer, and her body flared with heat. The need to get all these people off the elevator and be alone with him was strong.

Fortunately, by the time they got to their floor, they were the only ones left on the elevator. Zach took her hand and practically dragged her off the elevator and down to their room. She was so glad he already had the key out to slide in the door, because her heart was pounding.

He opened the door, and she walked inside. She didn't make it very far inside the dark room before Zach grasped her by the wrist. He closed the door and pressed her against it, his mouth coming down on hers in a rush of heat that stole her breath.

Furious desire overtook her, the passion in his kiss nearly overwhelming in its capacity to make her feel so off kilter. She grabbed hold of his shirt to draw him closer, to feel the heat of his body burning against hers. And when he ground against her, she desperately wanted to be naked with him, to feel that delicious pleasure again, only this time with him inside of her.

"Clothes off," she murmured against his lips.

"Yeah," he said, only he kept kissing her and continued to put his hands on her. She so did not mind that except that now it was a slow tango to the bedroom, neither of them wanting to break contact while at the same time removing their clothes and kicking off shoes. They left a trail of shirts and pants and skirts and underwear in their wake. By the time she fell onto the bed, she had only her panties on. Zach, on the other hand, was completely naked, so he obliged her by removing her underwear, kissing her hipbones and the top of her sex as he did.

And then he put his mouth on her, making her moan and shiver and delight as he proved his talent at licking and sucking her and wringing every ounce of pleasure out of her. He took her to delicious heights until she came with a shuddering cry that left her tingling all over. When he stood, he pulled her to the top of the bed and covered her body with his, kissing her so deeply and for so long that she felt shudderingly drunk with passion. And when he left her to go put on a condom, she felt a chill on her body. She craved his warmth, his presence, and that was a dangerous feeling that she dismissed immediately on his return. Tonight, she was going to think only about pleasure, about hot, sexy passion. Not emotions or feelings.

She stretched her arms over her head and lifted her knees.

"Have I mentioned before how beautiful you are?" Zach asked as he fit himself between her legs.

"Yes. But feel free to never stop telling me."

He slid inside of her, the sensation of the two of them joining never failing to take her breath away. And for a moment, he stilled, swept his hand over her hair, and stared down at her.

"You're beautiful. Inside and out. From your generous heart to your laugh to your sinfully sexy mouth to the welcoming way your body makes me a part of you."

She could barely breathe as his words sank into every part of her. She reached up and caressed his jaw. "And you always know exactly what to say and do to make me feel special, Zach. It's truly a gift."

"No, it's you, Josie. It's how you make me feel."

She didn't know what to say to that. Fortunately, his lips curved, and then he kissed her as he thrust within her. There were no more words after that, just sighs, moans, and the heights of pleasure.

And oh, could he take her higher. The way he surged against her, as if he knew exactly where to go, how to touch her, how to move his body in ways that made her soar.

She tightened around him and flew, her body shaking with her orgasm. He went with her, shuddering and kissing her neck when he came.

After, he held her next to him, and she draped her leg over him.

There were things she wanted to say to him. Eloquent, thankful things. Maybe mixed in with some emotional things, too.

But she was suddenly so tired, and she drifted off.

Chapter 27

ZACH WANTED TO make sure Josie had a good time in Vegas, so he filled Saturday with all kinds of activities.

Since she'd told him she never traveled, he rented a car and took her on a tour of Hoover Dam. On the way over, she'd researched some history of the dam. Zach told her he'd seen it before, but she still had a blast relating the dam's historical details to him. And it made for a fun discussion on the drive.

It had been a fascinating tour, and she was so glad she'd finally been able to see the amazing structure.

After that, they took a desert drive.

"It's really spectacular out here," she said, staring out the window at the rock formations, desert scrubs, and incredible mountains. With every shift of the sun, the landscape took on a different color, from dusty bronze to deep brown to an almost golden color.

"I love it out here," Zach said. "I've taken this drive almost every time I come here. Next time we come, we'll take some tours, get out and explore, and maybe do some rock climbing."

Next time. He mentioned "next time" as if they'd be doing this on a regular basis. She had no idea what to make of that, and she didn't want to delve too deeply into the meaning of it. Not when she was so relaxed and was enjoying herself so much. So instead, she shifted and cast a smile at him. "I'd love to do that. Get out and get more up close and personal with this incredible landscape out here."

"Yeah, it beats the hell out of mostly flat Oklahoma, doesn't it?"

She shifted away from the window to face him. "Oklahoma has its beauty. Hills and valleys and mountain landscapes. It can be absolutely breathtaking. You just have to look for it."

He glanced at her. "Oh, I'm looking right at it." The way he looked at her never failed to spark something elemental and emotional deep within her. It was as if he could see past her surface—the outer shell to the heart of her. And that meant something monumental to Josie.

Or maybe he was just teasing her and telling her that she was hot, and she was making way too much of that look he gave her. She did have a tendency to overthink things.

But it was hard not to when her heart was getting so deeply involved.

So she smiled at him, then turned back to stare out the window.

Zach wanted Josie to have a different experience tonight. When they got back to Las Vegas, it was nearly time for dinner. They got dressed up and he took her to dinner at a nice seafood restaurant; then they had tickets to "O" by Cirque du Soleil.

"I'm so excited to see a show," she said as they got out of their car at Bellagio and headed inside to the theater.

He took her hand. "I hope you enjoy it."

She leaned into him. "I know I will."

She looked incredible tonight in a formfitting black dress and heels that showed off her amazing legs. She wore a silver chain that disappeared into her cleavage, and all he could think about was getting her out of that dress.

One-track mind much, Zach?

Yeah, okay, so he liked seeing her naked, and sleeping with her curled around him last night had felt really damn good. He wanted more of both. A lot more.

In the meantime, he wanted her carefree and having fun, which she'd done a lot of today. She'd smiled all day in the car to and from the dam. He liked seeing her happy.

He hoped tonight's show would continue her happy streak. He'd seen this show before, and it was amazing. So he wanted to watch Josie's reaction to it.

From the moment the lights went down, her eyes went wide. He couldn't blame her. The sights and sounds and performances were incredible. It was a treat for the senses, and he enjoyed every minute of seeing it again through Josie's eyes. Several times she grabbed his hand and squeezed it tightly, or looked over at him as if to make sure he'd seen what she had.

When it was over, she stood and clapped and cheered along with everyone else.

Then she hugged him. "Thank you for that. It was the most amazing experience."

"I'm glad you liked it."

As they walked out, she shook her head. "I'm not even sure I can describe my feelings about it. I was mesmerized by the acrobatics. The pure visual artistry was on a scale of something I've never seen before. I'm typically never at a loss for words, but this was . . . just wow."

He pulled her close. "Glad you had a good time."

"It was wonderful. Thank you."

The valet brought their car, and they drove off. When they returned to the Venetian, instead of going up to their room, Zach headed them toward Tao.

"I've heard of this. It's a club, right?"

"Yeah. I thought you might want to burn off some energy by dancing."

She looked at the line. "It sounds fun, but there's a wait to get in."

"Not for me there isn't."

"You do know people, don't you?"

He laughed. "Some." He went to the front and gave his name. The guy nodded and let them in.

Inside was bouncing, as was typical for a Saturday night. They were led to a seating area toward the left of the DJ, midway to the top.

Perfect.

"Oh, this is amazing," she said. "The seats are nice, and this club is incredible."

"I thought you might like it."

Nancy, one of the bottle service girls, came by and asked what they wanted. "What do you want to drink?" he asked Josie.

"Vodka martini with two olives?"

He ordered bottles of their top-shelf vodka and whiskey. Nancy would mix Josie's drink for her. He'd have his on the rocks.

Nancy fixed their drinks and disappeared. Josie stood and watched the dance floor while sipping her martini. The dance floor was already filled with a good crowd bouncing to a driving beat. He noticed Josie rolling her hips in time to the music.

"Ready to dance yet?" he asked.

She shook her head. "Not yet. I want to watch and have this drink first."

"Sure."

Since it was just the two of them, their seating area had been roped off and split with another party, a group of three couples. One was an older couple in their fifties, along with two couples in their twenties. They were all dressed nicely, and Zach could see a similarity between the older guy and one of the younger guys. Family, maybe?

The older couple leaned across the ropes and introduced themselves as Aaron and Lynn Blume, who were there with their son, Linc, and his fiancée, Maggie, along with Linc's best friend, Travis, and Maggie's best friend, Korinne.

"Linc and Maggie are getting married next month,"

Aaron said, "so we're out here enjoying some fun family-and-friend time before the big day."

"Oh, how exciting for all of you," Josie said. "And congratulations."

"Thank you," Maggie said, smoothing her hands down her skirt. "I'm excited and nervous, and this mini vacation has really been helping to ease the stress."

"Where are you getting married?" Zach asked.

"Redondo Beach," Linc said. "This awesome church that both our families belong to, with the reception at my parents' country club."

Lynn, a lovely woman with beautiful black hair who did not look old enough to be Linc's mother, came over and put her arm around her son. "But we are not here to talk wedding stuff," she said. "We're here to party. Starting with drinks and dancing."

"That's what I'm talking about," Maggie said. "Come on, Korinne. We're hitting the dance floor. You, too, Lynn."

Lynn stood. "As if you could hold me back."

Korinne was tall and built and had a flashy grin. She took a long swallow of her drink, then set it on the table. "I'm in."

"You coming, Josie?" Maggie asked.

Josie looked over at Zach, who grinned. "Go for it."

"Yes," she said, excitement making her eyes glitter like diamonds. "Let's go, ladies."

He watched her head down the stairs and disappear into the crowd on the dance floor. He'd been hoping for this. Not that he wouldn't mind having her all to himself, but making friends and cutting loose a little was just what she needed.

The guys invited him to come over and sit by them, so he grabbed his glass of whiskey and took a seat.

"You played football for Detroit, didn't you?" Aaron asked.

"I can't believe you'd even remember that."

"Well, I consider myself a big fan of the sport. Plus, one of UCLA's best linebackers played for Detroit at the same time you did."

Zach knew exactly who Aaron was talking about. "Fallon O'Hara."

Aaron nodded.

"Great guy," Zach said. "Even better defensive back."

"I think so. And hey, sorry about that knee injury."

"Thanks. Me, too."

"So, what are you doing now?" Linc asked.

"I teach high school history and coach the football team at a small school in Oklahoma."

"No kidding," Travis said, leaning forward with interest. "I teach, too."

"Do you?"

"Yeah. Science."

"Great choice," Zach said.

"Teaching's a fantastic career," Aaron said. "And you get to stay in football with coaching. I'll bet your kids love you."

Zach laughed. "Depends on the day."

"I hear that," Travis said, following up with a short laugh.

The guys talked football for a while, until the women returned. Josie knocked back the rest of her martini.

"That was so fun," she said, grabbing Zach's hand. "Come on. Time to dance."

Lynn took a seat, and so did Korinne. Maggie grabbed Linc. "You, too, buddy."

"Yes, ma'am," Linc said, flashing a grin at his fiancée.

Zach let Josie lead him out onto the dance floor. They were shoved in like overpacked carry-on luggage out there, but he didn't mind, because he got to watch Josie show off her moves. And the woman could definitely move. She swayed her hips, turned, and beckoned to him with her body. He was mesmerized. And when she wrapped her hand around his neck to pull him close, he could do nothing but obey her every command.

As she pressed up close to him, her body shone with a sheen of sweat, and it was the hottest damn thing he'd ever seen or felt. All he could think about was licking her body all over until she begged him to make her come.

He grasped her around the waist and tugged her closer, letting her feel what she did to him. Her expression went hot.

"Clearly you enjoy dancing."

He moved his hips against her. "I enjoy you."

"When we get back to our room, I'll expect you to prove that."

He was hoping she'd want to go back to their room soon. Or now. Now would be good.

But then Korinne showed up with Travis, and Linc and Maggie danced their way over, and a few minutes later Aaron and Lynn joined them on the dance floor. Josie laughed and pulled away from him to mingle with their newfound friends.

She'd really let go tonight. She'd laughed, danced, and drunk—a lot. But she was having a great time, and that was what he wanted for her. It didn't hurt that they'd ended up seated next to a fantastic group of people. Zach had to admit he liked them all, too.

It was three hours later before they made their exit from the club. Josie was draped all over him as they made their way to the elevators.

"Have fun?"

She lifted her gaze to his. "I had a blast. Thank you."

The elevator doors opened, and they walked in. Zach pushed the button to their room.

"My feet are killing me," she said, sliding out of her heels.

He looked at her. "You put away quite a few vodka martinis. Yet you seem stone-cold sober."

She nodded. "Dancing. Sweats all the alcohol out. Plus, I also had Nancy bring me water in between, so I stayed hydrated. I'm not big on getting wasted."

"I understand. You probably saw plenty of that with your mom."

"Plenty. But it doesn't stop me from having a good time. I just know my limits."

"I'm sure you do." The elevator doors opened, and they

made their way out and down the hall toward their room. "How is your mom? Have you talked to her?"

"Right before we left for this trip. She's doing well. She said it's not easy, but she's determined to make it work."

"That's very encouraging."

"It's always encouraging." She leaned against the wall while he fished the key out of his wallet. "She does rehab well, Zach. And this isn't her first rodeo, so she knows what to expect. Plus, when she's away from the temptation of drugs, she'll get clean and clearheaded, and it's all great. It's what happens after that will tell whether it sticks or not."

He could tell she wasn't going to get her hopes up about her mom. Not that he could blame her. She'd probably been disappointed countless times. That had to be hard.

He opened the door, and Josie walked in, flipping on all the lights. She disappeared into the bedroom.

Okay, so no sexy kissing in the dark tonight. Maybe bringing up her mom had been a bad idea. She'd been relaxed and in a great mood, and he'd ruined that. Which was a shame since tonight was their last night in Las Vegas, and he'd wanted to make it memorable for her. For both of them.

Until she peeked her head out of the bedroom with a sexy smile on her face. "I'm sweaty, so I'm stripping down and getting into the shower. Wanna join me?"

It took him less than twenty seconds to get naked.

Chapter 28

JOSIE FELT THE nudge on her shoulder and woke to the sound of Zach's voice.

"Hey, sleepyhead. We've landed in Tulsa."

"We're here already? Wow, I must have really passed out."

Zach unbuckled his seat belt and shot her a grin. "We did stay up kind of late last night."

Josie cast a look at Mack, who still wore his headphones and likely couldn't hear them. She slipped on her tennis shoes, then undid her seat belt and stretched. "Yeah, like all night. You're incredibly demanding."

Zach leaned over her seat and pressed a seriously heated kiss on her. When he pulled back, she was breathing hard.

"I don't recall you complaining at the time, though now that I think about it, there might have been some screaming."

Her body went hot as she recalled just how much sex they'd had last night. And in how many locations of their apartment/suite/hotel room/whatever. And yes, there had definitely been screaming.

She reached up and caressed his jaw. "I'm open to a repeat performance, anytime."

Zach leaned down to kiss her again, but Mack cleared his throat and said, "Hey, guys, we're here."

Josie whipped her attention over to find Mack had turned to open the plane door for them.

They exited the plane, and they both thanked Mack for the trip before climbing into Zach's car and taking off. They stopped at the veterinary clinic, which fortunately was open a few hours on Sunday for boarding pickups so Zach could fetch Wilson, who was extremely happy to see him. After that, he drove Josie home and took her bag to the front door.

When he pulled her against him, she realized she didn't want him to leave. But she knew he needed to get Wilson home, and she needed to see Tumbles and Arthur and spend some serious cuddle time with her babies.

She wrapped her arms around him. "I had fun this weekend. Thank you for this trip."

"I had fun, too." He kissed her and she melted against him, wishing this weekend could go on longer.

But then he stepped back. "So, I'll see you at school tomorrow."

Where they'd have to be polite and civil with each other. "Yes, see you at school."

He started to walk away, and she felt that pang of missing him already. But he'd taken only a few steps before he turned and come back to her, dragged her into his arms, and planted one seriously hot kiss on her, the kind of kiss that made her toes curl inside her tennis shoes. Her hair might have curled on its own, too. And she was certain steam was rising from the pavement. Because, damn. That was a magnificent, panty-dropping, "take me to bed right now" kind of kiss.

And then he pulled back, smiled that devilish smile, and said, "See ya, Josie."

She, on the other hand, had lost the ability to speak. So she just gave him some goofy smile, and she might have waved.

As far as good-bye kisses went, that one was monumental.

She took her bag and went inside.

Chapter 29

"IT MIGHT RAIN tonight."

Josie turned from her closet to Jillian. "Don't say that. Bad enough the temps are going to drop and we're going to freeze our asses off."

"Oh, but there will be beer." Jillian slanted a smile. "Beer will keep us warm."

"Not that warm."

Jillian slanted a look at her. "Come on, Josie. Don't ruin my happy buzz. I'm excited about going to Oktoberfest tonight with you and Zach. And Jeff loves the entire event. It's all he's been talking about."

"Fine. I'm thrilled about it. I'm glad he suggested it to Zach. Even if we are going to freeze."

Jillian was sitting comfortably on the center of Josie's bed, so she pulled her knees up to her chest and regarded Josie with a critical gaze. "Suck it up, girl. Wear your black boots and that super cute gray wool sweater, plus your black leggings. You'll not only look hot, you'll stay warm."

Josie pulled the leggings and her boots out of the closet, then went to the dresser, where her gray sweater was tucked into a drawer. She laid the sweater on top of her dresser, then turned to Jillian. "Good call. What are you wearing?"

"My red sweater and brown leggings, wool socks, and my dark brown boots. I'm taking a coat along, too, because I don't know how cold it's going to get tonight. I want to have it in the car just in case."

Josie slid onto the bed next to Jillian. "And what's the hot doctor wearing?"

"Jeans that fit his amazing ass, no doubt, coupled with a shirt that will mold itself to his sculpted chest and abs."

Josie blinked. "I have no comment for that."

Jillian flung herself down onto her back, then rolled onto her side and leaned her head on her hand. "Oh, come on, Josie. Surely you think about how hot Zach is all the time."

"Not . . . all the time." Just most of the time. Like all this week. After their incredible weekend in Las Vegas, and especially after that smoldering good-bye kiss he'd laid on her when he'd dropped her off, she had to refocus. So she'd buried herself in schoolwork, and so had Zach. But they still found time to see each other every night, either over at her place, over at his, or they'd gone out. And they'd slept together every night, which had made her ridiculously happy. Things were seriously heating up between them, and she had zero complaints about that. They were having a wonderful time together, and she was happier than she'd ever been before.

Jillian's lips curved. "I don't think about Jeff all the time, either. Sometimes I'm asleep."

Josie rolled her eyes. "You've got it so bad."

And that worried Josie. She hoped Jeff was as good a guy as she thought he was, because she'd hate to see her best friend get hurt. Jillian had gotten wrapped up in this relationship with Jeff in a hurry. Fun and games and sex were one thing. Falling in love meant you could be hurt.

She'd see how it went between Jillian and Jeff tonight. Because while she was enjoying her time with Zach, she had tight control over her heart.

She could only hope that Jillian did as well.

So after Jillian left, she ran her afternoon errands, which consisted of grocery shopping and picking up some clothes at the dry cleaner. After that, she fed Tumbles and Arthur and enjoyed some playtime with her babies.

She was so happy with how well Tumbles and Arthur were getting along. Arthur loved to be near Tumbles, and the feeling seemed to be mutual. Josie often found them sleeping together on the floor, cuddled up like two lifelong friends.

Arthur was slowly learning the layout of the house, too, and that was helpful in how he maneuvered through his surroundings. He was getting better and better every day at circumnavigating the living room and kitchen, with Tumbles's expert guidance.

She gave Tumbles extra cuddles for being such an amazing big brother. He nuzzled her chin and purred in appreciation.

When it was time to get ready, she took a shower and did her hair and makeup, then checked the weather. At least the rain had held off—so far. But the forecast still called for the temps to drop tonight. She should be fine with the outfit she'd chosen, but she grabbed her raincoat just in case. It was lined and warm and should protect her against whatever tonight's weather might bring.

She had just put the finishing touches on her lip gloss when the doorbell rang. She opened the door and smiled at Zach.

"Hey."

"Hey, beautiful." He brushed a lingering kiss across her lips, then walked in and shut the door behind him. He went over to the sofa where Tumbles was lounging. He took a seat and smoothed his hand over the cat's back. "What's up, Prince of Darkness?"

Josie laughed. "I'm not sure I've ever heard you say his name."

"We have a mutual love thing going. I pet him and give him treats, but I get to call him the devil."

"Is that right?"

Tumbles rolled over on his back and lightly bit Zach's hand. Zach looked up at Josie and smiled. "See? It's a love thing."

"Oh, I see it." She had noticed how much more comfortable Zach was with Tumbles. Right now, he was tickling Tumbles's belly, and the cat was playing with him. He'd also scooped Arthur up and cuddled him against his chest. It made her heart all squeezy with warmth and love to see Zach bonding with her animals.

She sighed as she watched them, letting that warmth settle over her, imagining a houseful of cats and dogs and bunnies and maybe even a couple of kids, with Zach in the middle of it. He'd make a great dad. He had such a big heart. He could play tough, for sure, but inside he had so much love to give.

Then she realized what she was doing, how she was feeling, the thoughts she was thinking. The cold dread of panic slammed into her.

Oh, hell no.

Not love. Definitely not love. Just happiness, because her animals were her everything. She loved her cat, for sure. And her bunny. Those were her only loves. The animal variety was safe. They gave unconditional love and would never hurt her.

The human kind? Too risky. She slammed the brakes hard on that entire thought process.

"So . . . are you ready, or is there something I need to be doing?"

At Zach's words, she realized she hadn't moved at all since he came in. All she'd done was stare and contemplate her feelings.

Ugh. Feelings. They had always complicated things. She was so much better off not having them.

"Oh, sure. I'll be right back." She pivoted and went into her bedroom, shaking her head the entire time.

This was the problem with having feelings, with falling in—

No, she absolutely wasn't going there, because she wasn't

falling in love with Zach. They were just friends. Friends who happened to be having sex. True, they had grown closer over the past few months, but that meant nothing.

It sure didn't mean love. She could have strong, warm feelings for a guy and not be in love with him. She could have a sexual relationship with a guy and not be in love with him. Eventually that hot flame of passion would burn itself out, and they could go back to being just friends again.

She checked herself in her bathroom mirror.

"Right, Josie?"

Her reflection nodded.

Right, Josie. You've got this. Logical, levelheaded, no emotions involved.

"Good pep talk. Let's go have some fun."

Chapter 30

WAS THERE ANYTHING better than a cold night, a smorgasbord of beer, the best bratwurst in town, and a beautiful woman next to him? Zach didn't think so.

Plus, he was hanging out with Jeff, who loved beer even more than he did. Jeff considered himself an expert on German beers, which made tasting them even more fun because Zach had someone to argue with.

Josie and Jillian had wandered over to the craft booths while Zach and Jeff sat in the beer garden trying out several flavors. Zach was currently enjoying a Köstritzer, which was dark and flavorful, while Jeff had a Santa Fe Oktoberfest.

Zach took a swallow, loving the crispness of the black beer. "Man, this is good. How's yours?"

"Smooth," Jeff said. "I always said if I didn't become a doctor, I was going to brew beer. I still might do that whenever I buy a house."

"You can't live in that apartment forever, dude. You should do the house thing sooner rather than later."

Jeff nodded. "Yeah, I should. I've been kind of busy with

getting the clinic set up. Plus, I figured I'd get married eventually, and the buying-the-house thing would be something I'd do with a wife."

"Maybe no one wants you. You should just buy the house now."

Jeff laughed. "Maybe. I'm not getting any younger."

"What are we talking about?" Jillian asked as she and Josie came over to sit with them.

"Buying a house."

"Oh, you're buying a house?" Josie asked.

"No," Jeff said. "Well, maybe. Zach and I were just talking about beer, and I was saying how I always wanted to brew my own. Which I can't do in my apartment, and the topic got onto me buying a house."

"You should buy a house," Jillian said. "It's a good investment."

Jeff shrugged. "Yeah, I know. I've been meaning to get around to that. But it's such a hassle."

Jillian leaned into him. "It's not a hassle. It's fun."

"Okay, fine. You go with me and help me pick out a house."

Jillian's eyes widened. "Me? You want me to help you pick out your house?"

Jeff's look at Jillian was direct. "Yes. I'd like you to help me pick out my house. The way things are going with us, Jill, chances are you're going to live there, too. Don't you agree?"

"Whoa," Josie whispered, then glanced over at Zach with a wide-eyed look. He gave her the same "I had no idea things were so serious" look in return.

"Uh, yes," Jillian said, grasping Jeff's arm and giving him a warm smile. "I do agree. And I'd love to."

Jeff had this panicked expression on his face. "I mean, it's not an official proposal yet, because I hope I'm a little more romantic than that. Uh, shit. Let's go take a walk."

Jillian laughed. "Sure."

"We'll be back soon," Jeff said.

They got up and walked away together.

Zach took a long swallow of his beer. "That was interesting."

"Very. Don't you think they're rushing things?"

He looked at her. "Rushing things? How?"

"You know they haven't been dating long, and suddenly
they're talking about getting a house together? I worry about
Jillian getting hurt."

Zach laughed. "Are you serious? He practically proposed
to her in front of us. How could that be hurting her?"

"Come on. He blurted without thinking. Blurting isn't
the same as proposing. And now he probably feels embarrassed and obligated, and he'll try to find a way to walk it
back without hurting her feelings."

He couldn't believe these were the thoughts going through
Josie's head right now, when his take on what he'd seen
between Jeff and Jillian was totally different. "Or maybe he's
in love with her and what he wanted to say to her was really
intimate, and he felt kind of bad about blurting that out in
front of you and me."

She sniffed. "Doubtful."

He leaned back in the chair and took a long swallow of
his beer, realizing that maybe he didn't know Josie as well
as he thought he did. "Why do you think that?"

"Because it's too soon. Because it takes a long time to
get to know someone, to figure out if you can trust them
with your heart. Until then, it's all just words."

He was trying hard not to be offended by what she was
saying, but it was damn hard. "And do you have a specific
timeline in mind?"

"No."

"Which begs the question, when you fall in love with
someone, don't you just know? Wouldn't you be able to feel
it, and a calendar shouldn't matter to you?"

She shook her head. "No. It's not like that."

"Then tell me what it is like."

She stared at him. "You're angry."

He leaned forward and took her hands in his. "I'm not.
I'm just trying to understand where your head is about love."

"My head is screwed on perfectly straight. I had a relationship before, Zach. I know what I'm talking about."

"Were you in love with him?"

She opened her mouth to answer right away, then closed it and waited a few seconds before responding. "I thought I was. And it was right away, like Jillian is feeling. I was wrong. He wasn't a good guy."

"So one bad guy breaks your heart, and now you paint us all with the same brush?"

She shook her head and looked down where their hands were connected. "You're misunderstanding me."

He squeezed her hand, forcing her gaze to meet his. "Then help me to understand what you're feeling."

"I don't want Jillian to—"

He cut her off. "Not about Jillian. You know that's not what I'm talking about. About us. Talk to me about how you feel about *us*, Josie."

Her expression went cloudy, showing doubt and none of what he'd really wanted to see when she thought about the two of them. The things he thought when he thought about them, which were clarity, joy. Love. He wanted to know she was in this with him. He'd thought she was.

He might have been wrong.

"I don't know how I feel, Zach. I'm confused and afraid, and I'm not ready for all of this. I just wanted to have some fun with you, you know? Why does it have to get so complicated with talks about love? Why can't we just continue having fun?"

"We can. We can have fun. We've been having fun. But I can't deny how my heart feels. And mine is telling me I'm in love with you, Josie."

She jerked her hands from his, stood, and frowned at him. "Don't."

"Don't what?"

"Don't . . . tell me you love me."

He stood and reached out for her, smoothing his hands down her arms. "I have to be honest with you and tell you how I feel."

She shook her head. "You don't know how you feel, Zach. We've only known each other for a few months."

"It's long enough." He tried to pull her against him, but she took a few steps back.

"No. It's not long enough." She started pacing. "Love is complicated and dangerous and can hurt you."

She stopped and faced him. "I could hurt you."

Yeah, he felt that hurt right now in the pit of his stomach. "Okay, so you don't feel the same way."

She turned away and started pacing a five-foot area in front of him again. "It's not that. It's . . . I don't want to feel this—" She stopped and circled her chest and stomach. "All of what I'm feeling inside."

It was time to slow things down, to sit with Josie and let her explore how she was feeling. He knew where some of her fear was coming from, and he wanted to give her a safe place to talk it out. And he desperately wanted that safe place to be him.

"So tell me what you're feeling inside."

"I'm not explaining myself well, and I never have a problem explaining myself. See? This is what love does to a person. It fills you with confusing emotions and makes you feel raw and exposed and vulnerable and sick to your stomach."

He grimaced. "Well, when you put it that way, it sounds disgusting."

She sighed, came over to him, and laid her hand on his arm. "I appreciate the declaration, Zach, but the bottom line is, I just don't believe in love."

He didn't buy it. Josie was the most genuine, heartfelt, emotional woman he'd ever known. She was warm and caring, and she had feelings that she loved expressing with the people she cared about.

And right now, she was scared to death of putting her heart into this. Into them.

So he had two choices. He could get pissed off and walk away, permanently, or he could back off and give her some space and see if she could come to the—hopefully—right conclusion about the two of them on her own. Because he couldn't force her to love him. She either would or wouldn't.

"Okay. Let me take you home."

She frowned. "Wait. What? So we're done?"

"I'm in love with you, Josie. I want you to love me back, but I can see you're not ready for that. I don't think taking tonight to slam back a bunch of beers and bratwurst is the next step for us, do you?"

He caught the confused frown on her face, and he resisted smiling in reaction.

"I . . . guess not."

Yeah, she thought she could get him to back down from the love thing, and then they could go back to the fun-and-games thing.

But he was dead serious about loving her. And he wanted her to love him in return. He figured she needed some time, and he hoped she could figure out how she felt, but in the meantime, some space was needed.

"I'll text Jeff and let him know we're taking off," he said, whipping out his phone to send the message. "I don't want to interrupt whatever romantic thing he and Jillian have going on."

"Oh, sure, that's fine."

He saw her hesitation as he motioned her through the beer tent and toward the parking area.

Nothing would make him happier than for Josie to change her mind and tell him what he wanted to hear right now.

But he knew Josie. He also knew how she felt. She might not know it yet, but he did.

He was willing to wait.

She didn't say anything on the ride home. He didn't expect her to. He knew she was in her own head, deep in thought.

When he pulled into her driveway, he got out and walked her to her front door.

"You didn't have to walk me to the door," she said.

"Yeah, I did, because I need you to remember something."

She tilted her head back to look at him. "What?"

He cupped the side of her neck and rubbed his thumb over her jawline. "This."

He kissed her, pouring his heart into the kiss. She resisted at first, her body tense. But she didn't pull away, and as he drew her against him, she melted into him, resting her hands on his chest. He opened her mouth and slid his tongue inside, letting her feel all the passion, all the emotion that he'd held in check during their conversation.

He hadn't wanted to overwhelm her earlier. Now he wanted her overwhelmed, wanted her senses to go haywire with this kiss. He wanted this kiss to be the only thing she could think about when she thought about him. He wanted her to remember that no one else would kiss her like this—and no other man would love her as much as he did.

When he pulled back, her eyes were glazed with passion.

He smiled down at her and brushed his lips one last time across hers.

"For me, the sun rises and sets with you, Josephine Barnes. You're it for me, and you're the person I want to plan my future with. I know it might seem fast to you, but when you know it in your heart, then there's no sense in waiting for some magical sign or official waiting period.

"Also? I'm not your ex-boyfriend, and there's no one else in my life but you. So when you're doing all your thinking? Think about me as just me, and no one else but me, okay?"

She sighed. "Okay."

"I'm here when you need me, Josie. And when you're ready to talk, you let me know."

She licked her lips and gave him a quick nod. "Good night, Zach."

"Night."

He walked away and got into his car, then drove off, noticing that she hung outside on her porch watching him.

He'd thought walking away from Josie was going to be easy. But it took everything in him to turn that corner and not pull a U-turn and go back to her.

Staying away from her was going to be even harder. And

he really hoped this wasn't going to be permanent, because as much as he hoped she'd realize she loved him, it could be just as likely that she was too afraid to love him, and she'd tell him she was ending their relationship.

He didn't even want to think about that. So all he could do was hope.

Chapter 31

"SO . . . WAIT. HE told you he loved you, and then he dumped you?"

Josie sat in a booth at their favorite Italian restaurant with Jillian. It had been a week since Zach had left her at her front door, her lips—her entire body, actually—still throbbing from his kiss.

She had spent every day since then thinking about him, missing him, and so damn mad at him she couldn't see straight.

Unfortunately, Jillian had been gone all week at a conference, and Josie didn't want to interrupt her with boyfriend issues, so she waited until Jill had gotten back to town. But now they sat together at Johnny Carino's restaurant in Tulsa, both sipping a glass of merlot and dipping delicious Italian bread into olive oil and balsamic vinegar.

"Yes, he dropped the love ultimatum on me and then promptly left me on my front doorstep."

"Huh." Jillian chose another slice of bread and swirled it around in the olive oil mix. "Surely there was more conversation involved than 'I love you' and 'Good-bye.'"

"Well, yes. Actually, you were kind of the catalyst for the entire thing."

Jillian's eyes widened. "I was? How?"

"You know how Jeff mentioned buying a house when we were at Oktoberfest, then said something to the effect that you might be living in it someday?"

Jillian's lips curved in a warm smile. "I definitely remember that conversation. But what does it have to do with you and Zach?"

"I expressed my concern for you, and Zach jumped all over me. Basically, he said I was being ridiculous."

"Why would you be concerned about me?"

"Because you and Jeff haven't known each other for long, and suddenly he's talking about forever and love and buying a house together."

Jillian gave her a sweet smile. "Yes, he is. Why is that a problem for you?"

Why was it that no one seemed to understand her worries? "You're my friend, and I'm concerned you're not ready for this."

"Ready for what? Being in love? Or is there an issue with Jeff?"

"No. Jeff seems very nice." At least right now he did.

"Then I don't understand what the problem is, Josie. What's your hesitation with Jeff and me?"

"I don't know. I guess I'm afraid you'll be blindsided like I was. That you'll put all your trust in him and he'll hurt you."

"Oh, honey." Jillian reached across the table and touched Josie's hand. "Not every guy is like your ex-boyfriend. Jeff is kind. And more important, he's honest. We've had a couple of very serious discussions about what we both want for our futures. Neither one of us is willing to settle for less than our visions. It just so happens our visions mostly line up."

"Mostly?" She'd hate to think that Jillian would have to compromise on anything.

Jillian's lips tipped up. "Yes. I want a craftsman home, and he's dead set on midcentury modern. We're still deep in negotiation."

Josie smiled, relieved their arguments related to architecture. "I see."

"Do you? I am in love with him, Josie. And we're moving forward, planning a future together. Is it going to be perfect? Probably not. But I trust him and he trusts me, and we trust each other to make it work."

"Okay." She thought for a few seconds, then asked, "But he hasn't proposed yet?"

"No," Jillian said with a laugh. "He felt kind of bad blurting out the house thing in front of you and Zach. He told me he plans to do it the right way. But he made it clear it was in the future. In the near future, because he told me he loved me. And I told him I loved him, too. We both want to start our lives together. It just felt right between us from the beginning. We've talked every day and spent so much time getting to know each other. I've never fallen so fast before. I knew from the very beginning that Jeff was the one for me, Josie. Please be happy for me. And please trust that I know when someone is good for me. Jeff is good for me."

Tears pricked Josie's eyes as she saw the sincerity in her best friend's face. She squeezed Jillian's hand. "Of course I'm happy for you. That's all I want for you."

"Thanks. Now we need to get you to the happy place."

Josie pulled her hand back. "I don't think I can get there."

Jillian took a sip of her wine, then asked, "You sure about that?"

"Yes. I think I've ruined things between Zach and me."

"Oh, I don't know. It seems to me that he left the door wide open. All you have to do is decide to walk through it."

She stared at her wineglass, wishing it held all the answers. Unfortunately, it didn't, so she lifted her gaze to Jillian. "I'm afraid."

"Of course you are. So am I. There aren't any guarantees when you love someone. *Do* you love him?"

"Yes." She realized she hadn't even hesitated. So what was stopping her from taking that step, from telling Zach how she felt?

"Okay, so now what?" Jillian asked.

"I . . . don't know. My life's kind of a mess right now, Jill. My mom and my own trust issues. What if he doesn't want to take that on? What if he realizes it's just too much and he bails?"

Jillian cocked her head to the side. "He already knows about your mom, right?"

"Yes."

"And I think, based on the conversation you had with him, that you've made your trust issues abundantly clear to him."

Josie flattened her gaze at her friend. "Well, thanks."

"Hey, I'm nothing but honest with you, girlfriend. You know that."

"I do, and I appreciate it. But I'm still afraid."

Jillian sighed. "Josie. Sit back and close your eyes and remember your last relationship. As much about how you felt about him as you can. Not when it was bad, but when it was really good between the two of you."

"I don't see how—"

"Just . . . trust me."

"Okay." She closed her eyes and thought back to the first year with Dylan. They'd had fun, gone to festivals, out to eat a lot. And the sex had been decent. But even from the beginning, she'd always felt something was . . . missing.

"What do you remember?" Jillian asked.

"We had fun together. But there had always been a piece missing, like a lost puzzle piece. And now I know that piece was trust. There were always parts of Dylan that he held back from me."

"You mean like the fact he had another girlfriend?"

Josie raised her glass. "Yeah, that was definitely a big part. But he was just never one to open up to me. About anything."

"Okay. Now think about you and Zach."

She and Zach definitely had fun together. He also had loved her animals, had been there for her with the issues with her mom. He listened when she talked. And he talked to her, about his past, his family, his feelings, pretty much everything. He cared about her life. He didn't always agree with her, but he respected her opinion. She laughed so much more when she was with him. And the sex between them was outstanding. She wanted to be with him all the time. She also instinctively knew she could trust him, that she could call him at any time of the night or day and he'd be there for her.

He *had* been there for her when she'd needed him. Even when she'd tried to go it alone.

"And?" Jillian asked.

She opened her eyes. "I love him. He's everything I ever wanted in a man, in a partner, in someone I want to be with forever. He's open and honest with me, and I trust him."

Jillian smiled. "That's good."

Jillian leaned back and finished off her glass of wine, then signaled for their waiter to bring them another round.

Josie finished her glass, then the one after that, the entire time thinking about what she had to do. She'd had so many issues for so long, had feared getting close to someone because the potential to get hurt was so great. She'd put up the great wall and kept herself from falling in love, all in order to protect her heart. Instead, she'd almost walked away from what could be the love of her life.

Why? Because she couldn't trust her mother to love her enough when she was a kid? And because she'd had one bad relationship with a guy she couldn't trust? Zach had never given her a reason not to trust him. And he loved her. God only knew why, because she was so hard to love.

She had to talk to Zach. He'd done all the talking before. Now it was her turn.

Chapter 32

ZACH HAD GOTTEN his boys where he'd wanted to—the play-offs. Now they were playing their first game of the play-off season—at home, fortunately. And he'd never been more nervous in his entire life.

Emerson High had had a kickass season. They had a tough defense and a strong, stable offense. Their quarterback had a wicked arm, and their star running back had racked up an impressive number of yards. Which all set Zach's nerves on edge. If the Eagles won this game, they'd go to the semifinals. His team was just as good as Emerson's players, which was what he'd been telling his kids all week. In fact, he told them they were better than Emerson, and all they had to do was focus and fight.

But he still held his breath when they kicked off to Emerson, and he felt like he wasn't breathing all through the first quarter. Even Wilson seemed nervous, pacing back and forth behind the bench. Usually his dog would find a person to cuddle with, or hang out with the cheerleaders. Tonight he paced.

Zach knew the feeling. He was tense. Until deep into the

second quarter when Robertson threw a long pass to Fine, who ran it into the end zone for seven. Then Zach finally exhaled.

Okay, so they were up by one touchdown. That wasn't going to be enough, but it was a start. Their defense was playing solid, and after a quick three and out by Emerson, Hope High had the ball back.

But on a blitz from Emerson's defense, Robertson fumbled the ball, and Emerson picked it up and scored a touchdown, so now the game was tied, with the clock down to seconds in the first half.

They got the ball back, but only forty seconds remained before halftime. He called a shovel-pass play into Robertson, who tossed it to Adams for a quick run, then let the clock run out. They needed to regroup and come out fighting in the second half.

When he got to the locker room, he could tell his boys were upset and tense.

"Okay, okay," he said, coming into the center of the room. "We already knew it was going to be more intense once we hit the play-offs, so this shouldn't come as a surprise to anyone." He waited a beat before continuing, making sure he had their full attention. "You want to be the best? You want to win state? Then you have to mentally prepare yourselves to face tough competition. None of these games from here on out was going to be easy.

"Which means the wins will taste that much better. So let's go out there in the second half and get one."

They all yelled, and he felt as fired up as his boys.

And they proved it in the second half. After stopping Emerson cold on their first drive, they pushed hard down the field and scored on Adams's twenty-two-yard run. After that, it was all the Hope Eagles, who scored three more times, and the defense shut down Emerson's high-scoring offense.

They won thirty-seven to seven, and the home crowd roared its approval. Zach looked to his assistant coaches and athletic director, who all nodded and smiled.

Zach was looking forward to the semifinals next week. He had a good feeling about this team. He knew they were going to make it to state.

After talking his very excited team down to a reasonable level, he made it clear that hard practices were starting up again on Monday, and they also had to make sure to keep up their grades so that all of them could enjoy this journey. Then he told them he was proud of them because they'd worked their butts off to get where they were.

After they all left, Zach locked up, and he and Wilson headed home. When they got there, he let Wilson into the backyard, then grabbed a beer from the fridge. He leaned against the kitchen island to check his phone. He'd been so busy, he hadn't even checked it after the game. He was slammed with text messages from Bash and Luke and Will and all his friends congratulating him on a great game. Bash said they were all going to the bar to hang out and have some food and drink, and he invited Zach to join them.

They'd all been there at the game. It felt good to have friends who were there for him.

He smiled as he let Wilson inside and headed to the sofa to prop his feet up and scroll through the rest of his messages.

Wilson laid his head on Zach's lap, giving him those cute puppy-dog eyes.

"What do you need, buddy?" he asked.

Wilson blinked.

"Yeah, I miss her, too."

But then he leaned forward when he saw a message from Josie.

Incredible game tonight. If you're not too busy, could we meet after?

He'd totally missed this. He looked at the time stamp on her message and saw she'd sent it an hour ago.

Shit. She was long gone by now, probably out at the bar

with Bash and Chelsea and everyone who'd invited him to join them. He sent a return text.

> Sorry. Missed your message. I'm at home. Want to come over?

He waited and took a couple of deep swallows of beer. When his phone beeped a few minutes later, he grabbed it to look at Josie's reply.

> Be there in a few.

He hadn't heard from her since he'd walked out on her more than a week ago. He wasn't sure how she felt about it, or whether she even cared.

So maybe this was a good sign. Or maybe she wanted to officially end things. Or yell at him for laying down a "love me or else" ultimatum, which, after he'd had some time to think about it, had seemed about as shitty a thing as he could have done.

Because Josie had been right. They'd been having fun, so why mess with the good thing they'd had going on?

So he was glad she wanted to see him, because he needed to talk to her about that. She was probably pissed. And rightly so.

But first, he was going to suck it up and listen to what she had to say.

Chapter 33

JOSIE SAT IN her car outside Zach's house, staring at his well-lit front window, willing herself to turn off the engine and go inside. The problem was, she didn't exactly know what she was going to say once they were face-to-face.

She knew how she felt about him. Feelings were easy. Expressing them and laying herself bare? That was the difficult part.

She'd been thinking all week about how she felt, how they'd left things.

How she'd walked away from someone who loved her.

She'd waited her entire life for someone to love her like Zach did. And what had she done when she found it? She bailed.

Gripping the steering wheel, she stared at Zach's house, where he was no doubt wondering why she hadn't shown up yet. "Stupid, Josie. That was such a stupid move. Why couldn't you just throw your arms around him and say, 'I love you, too'?"

Because she'd loved her mother, and her mother had let her down time and time again. Because she thought she had loved Dylan, and look where that had gotten her. Did she even know what love was? Was she certain what she was feeling was genuine for Zach? Maybe she was so desperate for love, she was grasping onto something that wasn't real.

She closed her eyes and willed her runaway heartbeat to slow down. She was purposely inserting doubt where there shouldn't be any, just like she always did.

"Because you're afraid," she whispered out loud. "Because you always do this."

When Zach's front door opened and he started out toward her car, she quickly turned off the engine. He came over, and she opened the car door.

He crouched down in front of her. "You've been out here for fifteen minutes."

Crap. "You knew that?"

"Wilson barked when you pulled up."

"Oh." This wasn't at all embarrassing.

He got up and held out his hand. "Come on inside, Josie. Whatever hesitations you have, we'll figure them out together."

Tears pricked her eyes, and she blinked them back. "I wasn't hesitating. I was . . ."

You were what? Meditating? Think of something. Why had her mind gone blank?

He arched a brow, and she knew she was fumbling. She took the keys out of the car, grabbed her purse, and took Zach's hand.

He held tight to her hand and led her into the house. Wilson was there to greet her, his tail wagging wildly back and forth. She bent to give him some love.

"Hey there, Wilson. How have you been doing? I've missed you. Have you been having fun?"

Zach closed the front door. "Wilson thinks every day is fun."

She looked up at him and smiled. "I'm sure he does."

She stood, feeling more awkward standing next to Zach than ever before. She wrapped her cardigan around herself like a protective shield.

"Would you like a beer or a glass of wine?" he asked as they moved into the kitchen.

"Wine would be great, thanks."

"Any particular type?"

"No. Whatever you choose would be fine with me."

"Okay. Take a seat in the living room, and I'll be right there."

She pulled up a spot on the sofa. Wilson jumped up next to her, carrying a chew toy. She played tug of war with him while she watched Zach open a bottle and pour the wine into a glass. He looked good. He wore relaxed jeans, a soft gray T-shirt, and no shoes, and all she wanted to do was walk up to him and wrap herself around him so she could breathe him in.

She'd missed his scent and the feel of his skin and the taste of his lips against hers. Lying in bed every night had been agony because her bed felt like an empty cavern without him next to her.

She sighed, feeling that melancholy of loss, even though he was only a few feet away from her. But at the moment those few feet felt like miles.

He pulled a beer from the refrigerator and came into the living room. Wilson perked up, his tail whipping in a frenzy.

"Yeah, I know what you want, buddy." He set their drinks on the coffee table, then threw Wilson's toy all the way toward the front door. Wilson flew off the sofa and dashed after the toy, then dropped it to go chase a ball he'd spotted.

He picked up her drink and handed it to her, then took a seat next to her

"Thanks," she said as she took the glass of wine from him. She took a couple of very long sips, hoping it might bolster her courage. And spark her brain cells.

"You're welcome."

She half turned to face him. "The game tonight was fantastic."

"Yeah, it went our way. I was happy about it."

"So now what? Semifinals, right?"

"Yeah."

"You—and your team—must be so excited."

"The boys are pumped, but I have to rein them in. One game at a time and all."

"Oh. Of course."

She felt lame talking football with him, but at the same time it didn't seem appropriate to launch into the whole relationship thing without a warm-up. Still, their conversation seemed awkward and stilted, and she had never felt that way with Zach before. Their conversations had always flowed naturally, and this really sucked.

"Why were you sitting out in the car so long?"

Leave it to Zach to call it like he saw it. "I was thinking."

"About?"

"About how I messed this up."

He shifted, seemingly relaxed as he placed his long legs on the table in front of him. "Messed what up?"

"Us. I messed us up. Everything was going well."

"Yeah, until I messed things up by throwing down an ultimatum."

She frowned. "Wait. What?"

"I'm the one who messed it up, Josie. I shouldn't have done that. I told you I loved you."

Now she was really confused. "So you *don't* love me?"

He gave her that hot smile that always melted her feet to the floor. "Of course I do. But then I told you that if you didn't feel the same way, we couldn't see each other anymore. What kind of juvenile bullshit was that? It was totally unfair to you."

She wasn't expecting this. She was expecting to come here, to apologize, to tell him she loved him, too, and then beg his forgiveness for running. She hadn't expected him to apologize to her.

"You have nothing to be sorry for, Zach."

He reached over and took her hand. "Yeah, I do. You were right when you said things were good between us. I had to be honest about how I felt. But that didn't mean anything had to change between us."

She laid her wineglass on the table and shifted so she was closer to him. "Oh, Zach. Everything changed when you told me you loved me."

He laughed. "Yeah. You turned pale."

"Okay, maybe my initial reaction wasn't awesome. And I'll be the first to admit that love and I haven't always been the best of friends."

He swept his thumb over her jaw. "I can't think of anyone who deserves love more than you do. But it doesn't excuse the fact that I pushed an ultimatum on you, and then I bailed."

"I'm pretty sure I was the one who bailed."

He shook his head. "No, you wanted things to stay the same between us. I was the one who acted like an asshole and walked because things didn't go my way."

Now it was her turn to laugh. "You do realize we're arguing about love, right?"

His lips curved. "Does that surprise you?"

"Not really. One of the things I love most about you is that you keep me on my toes. My life will never be boring around you."

She realized he was staring at her. "What?"

"You said one of the things you love about me."

"Yes. I love you, Zach. Did I fail to mention that? I love you. I've been in love with you for a while. I loved you back at Oktoberfest when you laid down that dumb ultimatum. But I was afraid. Love hurts, dammit."

He stood and pulled her off the sofa, taking her hands in his. "Love also heals. And makes you stronger. We're a team, Josie. When you laugh, I'll laugh with you. When you cry, I'll lend a shoulder. When you need me, I'll always be there for you. And you'll be there for me for the good and the bad. That's what love's all about."

Her eyes filled with tears. This time she didn't try to stop them. "It's already been that way, and if I hadn't tried so hard to fight it, I would have recognized that you loved me all along." She took a step forward and laid her head on his chest, wrapping her arms around him.

"I love you, Zach. Thank you for being patient enough to wait for me."

"I'll always be patient with you." He tipped her chin back. "And I'll always love you."

And when he kissed her, for the first time in her life, she truly believed in love.

Epilogue

Six months later

JOSIE MADE SURE everything was laid out in Zach's backyard, that the tables were all set and every place setting was perfect. It wasn't every day that they had company over at Zach's place. In fact, this was only the third time they'd had a party here. Progress was slow in some areas of their relationship, but they were getting there.

But tonight was their engagement party, and Josie wanted everything to go off without a hitch. Or, at least, she wanted everyone to have fun.

"You know, at some point you're going to have to decide which house to live in together," Jillian said, coming out of the house to stand on the porch.

Josie shrugged. "We're still in negotiation."

"You're getting married in six months, Josie." Chelsea was already sitting outside in one of the cushioned chairs, cradling her beautiful baby daughter, Audrey, who looked so much like Chelsea, it was uncanny. "Don't you think you two should have decided on that by now? Maybe put one of the houses up for sale?"

"She's stubborn." Zach came outside and put his arm around Josie's shoulder. "She knows she wants to live here."

Josie lifted her chin. "I like my house. It's in a cute neighborhood, and it's right down the street from Chelsea and Bash's house."

"This is true," Chelsea said. "Plus, she's promised to babysit."

"Audrey would love it out here," Zach said. "Wouldn't she, Bash?"

"I'm not getting in the middle of this back-and-forth." Bash scooped his daughter out of Chelsea's arms. "But we're always up for volunteer babysitters, no matter where they live."

The door opened, and Jane and Will and their kids came pouring out. "Hey, it's beautiful out here," she said. "Nice job."

It was a perfect late-spring day, and Josie was so happy to see all her friends arrive. Jane had given birth to her and Will's son, James, only two months ago.

"Where's the baby?" she asked.

"Asleep in his car seat in the living room," Jane said.

"How are you doing?"

"Sleep deprived, but loving every second of having a baby around again. Plus, Tabitha and Ryan are great helpers, and Will is a champion diaper changer. I hardly have to do a thing."

Josie laughed. "I imagine that's not true."

"Okay, I have to do a lot of things, but it's magical having this baby, Josie."

Her heart squeezed. "I'm happy for you."

Before long, all their friends had arrived. They might still be negotiating on where to live, but the one thing she did love about Zach's place was the huge backyard.

Okay, she loved a lot of things about Zach's place, including his magnificent kitchen. She'd wanted to cook up all kinds of things for the engagement party, but Zach had insisted they have it catered. Josie had said it was ridiculous, but he had pressed until she'd given in.

He'd won that battle. She'd won when he'd argued about wanting to have some big fancy engagement party at a restaurant and she'd insisted they make it a backyard barbecue instead so everyone's kids could come.

Jeff and Jillian's engagement party a month ago had been a big country-club event. It had been stylish and fancy and oh so fun. And Jillian had loved it. Mainly because Jillian loved Jeff.

But that kind of thing wasn't Josie's style. It wasn't what Zach wanted, either, even though he thought that was what she might want.

This was her happy place. Relaxed, with everyone dressed down, kids invited, and Zach's dog, Wilson, running around the backyard with Chelsea and Bash's dog, Lou.

It was perfect.

And once she found out that Paul Fine and his mother worked for the catering company Zach had proposed hiring, she was all for having the event catered. Not only had Laurel Fine dumped her husband, Jimmy, but she'd also started working for an amazing catering company in Hope. The difference it had made in Paul had been tremendous. His grades had skyrocketed, and his entire attitude had changed. She'd been so happy for him and for his mother.

And she had to admit she was happy she didn't have to worry about cooking tonight. It was better to be outside visiting with her friends than stuck in the kitchen. Or out at some restaurant where she wouldn't be able to talk to everyone.

This was more comfortable. Plus, she was a big fan of barbecued chicken, and she doubted that would have been on the menu at a fancy restaurant.

She smiled as she saw Lauren unwrapping the food and waved to Paul as he set up tables. She wouldn't interfere with their work, but she wanted to at least say hello.

"Hi, Lauren," Josie said.

"Ms. Barnes. It's very nice to see you."

"Things going well for you?"

"Very well, thanks."

"You look great, Lauren." She wanted to tell her that kicking out her deadbeat husband agreed with her, but that would have been inappropriate. Still, it did totally agree with her. She looked vibrant and young and absolutely happy.

"Thank you." Lauren beamed a bright smile.

Zach was in the middle of a conversation with Paul—about football, no doubt. After going on to win state last year, Zach was even more popular in Hope, especially with the football crowd.

"Hi, Paul," she said as she walked by, not wanting to interrupt their conversation.

"Ms. Barnes." Paul smiled and nodded.

He looked a lot happier than he ever had before, too. Sometimes getting rid of someone who was bad for you made all the difference.

She knew that feeling.

Hours later, the house and backyard were filled with everyone she and Zach cared about. And Josie was thrilled. The food had been delicious, and she was content to have a glass of wine in her hand to make the rounds.

"You know, you could move here."

She leaned back against her mother, who'd put her arms around her. "I could. It's a nice place. But I like my place, too, Mom."

"Sometimes you just have to give in. Plus, this house is big enough to raise some babies in, Josie."

She sighed and turned to face her mother, who looked better than Josie could have ever hoped. Her mom had come through rehab clean and sober and had decided to stay in Hope. She'd gotten a job at Megan's bakery and discovered a love for baked goods, occupying her time with baking instead of hunting down her next fix. She'd put on some weight, found herself an apartment she liked, and had even made a few friends she'd met at the bakery. And she'd started painting again.

She looked lighthearted, and Josie was delighted for her. More important, they had cautiously started to carve out a relationship the past few months. Josie knew it was going to take time to completely trust her mother. Her mom knew that, too. But they had had long talks about taking each day as a new start.

"I could use some grandbabies, you know," her mom said.

"That'll come in time, Mom."

Zach came up and put his arms around both of them. "What are we talking about?"

"Grandchildren, Zach," her mom said. "I need grand-children."

"Hey, I'm ready to start having kids anytime your daughter is."

Josie offered up a smile. "Let's get through the wedding first. Then we'll see about those babies."

"I'm going to go see about getting some more iced tea," her mom said, leaving the two of them alone on the back porch.

"Babies, huh?" he asked.

She sighed and laid her head against his chest. "Yes."

"First you'd have to actually live with me full-time."

She moved away and smacked his arm. "We spend almost every night together."

"Yeah, and it's like a commuter lifestyle. You're either packing an overnight bag to stay here, or Wilson and I are packing up to stay over there. That's not a way to start a life together."

She knew he was right.

"Come on. Tumbles and Arthur will love it here."

She lifted her gaze to his. "What if I asked you to come live with me at my place, even though it's smaller? Would you do that? Seriously."

He looked down at her. "Yes."

She believed him. She knew he loved her and he'd do anything for her. She'd been the one who'd been hesitant about fully committing to moving in with him. He'd been so patient with her all these months.

"I'll put my house up for sale on Monday," she said.

"Only if that's what you want, Josie."

She grasped his shirt and tugged him close. "What I want—what I've always wanted—is you."

He slid his arm around her. "You've got me. Always and forever."

He kissed her and sealed the deal.

READ ON FOR A SPECIAL EXCERPT FROM
THE FIRST BOOK IN JACI BURTON'S NEW
BROTHERHOOD BY FIRE ROMANCE SERIES

Hot to the
Touch

COMING SOON FROM HEADLINE ETERNAL

Prologue

August 2005

THEY'D BEEN LUCKY to find this abandoned piece of junk so they could have a roof over their heads during the storm. Jackson was on lookout tonight, because you never knew who might be prowling for space, or the cops might come and bust them, and the last thing they needed was to be dragged back into some shitty foster home worse than the last one.

Foster homes were a crapshoot. Sometimes you got lucky and they were decent. More often than not you got people who were in it for the money, or the system was so overburdened with kids that you ended up shuffled from one home to another and you couldn't even remember anyone's names. And they sure as hell didn't remember yours. And then you got the mean ones. At fifteen, Jackson could handle himself. Rafe was getting there at thirteen, but Kal was only twelve. As the oldest, it was Jackson's responsibility to look out for the younger ones. His brothers. Not by blood, but they were still his brothers.

No, they were better off on their own, where they had one another's backs and no one could ever hurt them again.

Tonight they'd gotten lucky and had a place to sleep out of the rain. They'd scored a whole pizza some jerkoff had left uneaten on his back porch while he fought with his girlfriend, so they had full bellies. Rafe and Kal were asleep on the floor in another room while Jackson stood watch. He gazed out the living room window of the old beach house, admiring the lightning arcing across the Atlantic Ocean.

He looked away from the water, scanning the street out front to make sure it was still clear. Because of the rain, no one was wandering around, which made him feel more secure.

Not that he could ever feel completely safe. Not when you lived like they did.

He pushed off the wall to walk around. Lots of windows in this place. He'd bet it was killer when the sun was out. But tonight, the rain made it cold, so they'd shut all the windows earlier. His boots creaked on the worn wood floor. As he moved from room to room, he could imagine a family with a couple of kids and maybe a dog running this joint. They'd probably have nice furniture, some cushy-looking couch where they'd all cuddle together and read at night.

Or at least that's how he thought it went with families. In his head, anyway. It had never gone that way with his family—at least not that he'd remembered, so what did he know? Anyway, this was a decent beach house, and maybe someday it would get fixed up. Or maybe torn down. But tonight it was their shelter. Having made a circuit of the first floor, he returned to the living room and sat down in the corner. He leaned back against the wall and settled in.

JACKSON WOKE UP coughing, something burning his lungs so badly, he couldn't breathe. He tried to open his eyes, but when he did, they burned.

He fought to suck in air, found his voice so he could call out for Rafe and Kal. They didn't answer. His stomach tightened as he saw flames lick up the wall across the room.

Oh shit. He didn't want to die. He didn't want his brothers to be dead. Tears pricked his eyes as he tried to see through the thick, black smoke. He pushed himself onto his hands and knees, trying to remember where the door was, what room the boys were sleeping in. Had they been right next to him, or had he moved into another room? His brain was fuzzy, and he couldn't remember.

He coughed, the smoke entering his lungs with every breath he took. He pulled his raggedy T-shirt over his mouth, trying to stifle the smoke. He had to get to Rafe and Kal. He was the oldest. It was his job to save them.

He called out to them, rasping out a cough with every few words. But he kept at it. They had to hear him. If he could hear them, he could get to them. Then they'd figure a way out. Because no way were they dying in this piece-of-shit building today.

Finally, he heard voices. The sound was faint, but he wasn't imagining it. He'd definitely heard it. It was them. It had to be them. Which meant they were alive. He crawled toward the sound, his own voice hoarse as he yelled out in response.

"I'm here! I'm on my way to get you." The smoke grew thicker, and he could feel himself slipping away, but sheer determination kept him conscious. He was their brother. They'd been through so much together, had survived so much together. This fire wasn't going to get them.

When he saw the light and the tall shadow looming over him, he thought maybe it was too late. He was dead, and this was some dark angel come to take him away. But then strong arms scooped him up.

"It's okay, buddy," the dark angel said. "I've got you. You're safe now."

Jackson shook his head and gripped the angel's arm, barely able to stay conscious. "My . . . my brothers."

"They're safe, too. They're outside. Come on. Let's get you out of here."

Jackson sighed in relief and let himself fall into the darkness.

Chapter 1

Present Day

JACKSON DONOVAN WAS having the best dream of his life. It involved his favorite spot on the beach, a spectacular blonde in a barely-there bikini, and hot sex on a Jet Ski. He was just about to maneuver her onto his lap while they were simultaneously bouncing across the waves, because, hey, in a dream anything was possible, when a loud noise sent him jolting off the sofa in the firehouse.

He'd thought it was the firehouse alarm, so he was instantly alert.

"Calm down," Rafe said, not even looking up from the video game he was playing. "Just Richardson dropping shit in the kitchen."

Jackson blinked, that sweet dream vanishing instantly. He rubbed his eyes and stretched. "Oh. Okay."

"So, good dream?" Rafe asked, grinning as he kept his attention on the TV.

Now that he knew he didn't have to gear up, Jackson leaned back in the chair. "None of your business."

Kallan, his other brother, laughed. "That means it was about a girl."

Sometimes, working with his brothers was great. Other times, it was annoying because they knew him too well.

They'd been together for longer than Jackson could remember. Jackson had hit the streets at twelve. He'd hooked up with Rafe when he was thirteen, Rafe being a little under two years younger than he was. They'd picked up Kallan when the kid was ten and he'd been beaten up and kicked out by his stepfather. After that, the three of them had been inseparable. They might not be real brothers, but they had all shared similar circumstances. And all those years they'd lived on the streets, they'd looked out for one another, had one another's backs, and had vowed to never be separated.

Which didn't mean his brothers weren't a constant pain in the ass.

"You three intending to spend this shift sitting on your asses?"

Jackson looked up to see their father, Battalion Chief Josh Donovan, glaring down at them. Off duty he was loving and protective and fun. Everything Jackson had always wanted in a father. Off duty he was Dad. The guy who'd saved their lives that night in the house fire.

And the man who'd adopted them, as had his wife, Laurel. Their mom.

But on shift? On shift he was their battalion chief—demanding and strict. He expected a lot of every firefighter who worked at the station. His own kids got no preferential treatment.

"No, sir," Kallan said, giving their father the respect he was due.

"Good. Because the fridge smells like something died in there. Go investigate."

"Oh, come on, Chief," Kallan said. "Let the probies do that."

Dad shot Kal a look that said there'd be no argument. Kal sighed. "Yes, sir. I'm right on it."

And just at that moment, the alarm went off. It looked

like there'd be no cleaning the fridge—at least not until after the call they were headed out to.

They all ran out to the engine room. Jackson put on his bunker pants and jacket, grabbed the rest of his gear, and climbed into the truck. Despite having been on this engine for the past seven years, he felt a thrill every time he heard the sirens, every time the engine roared out of the house. The sounds and vibrations filled him with a sense of belonging, of knowing that this was right where he was supposed to be.

And all those years he lived on the streets, he never thought he'd feel this way.

The night that firefighter Josh Donovan rescued him and Rafe and Kal from that house fire changed his life. Changed all their lives.

"Dude, you even listening?" Rafe asked.

He blinked. "What?"

"You dreaming about that girl again?"

Jackson shook his head. "No. Just thinking."

"No wonder you looked so pained."

He glared at his brother. "Fuck off."

This was one of those times he was glad both of his brothers weren't on the same truck with him.

They arrived at a strip shopping center near the beach. Smoke poured out of the open door of a tattoo shop named Skin Deep.

"No flames visible," Jackson said as they pulled up in front of the building.

They jumped out and immediately went to work, gearing up with their SCBA and regulators so they could breathe through the smoke. Jackson was first in, calling out to see whether anyone was inside.

They didn't see anyone outside, and the door was open. Hopefully no one was in here.

But then he heard the sound. It was faint, but he heard it.

Coughing. That thick cough that came from breathing in smoke. He knew that sensation all too well. Even though it had been fourteen years, he could still remember what it had felt like to breathe in that smoke, to not be able to take in a breath of fresh air. He remembered the overpowering panic. He never wanted to experience it again. He never wanted anyone else to feel it, either.

"Fire department," he hollered. "Anyone in here?"

No answer, but he heard the coughing again.

"Someone's in here," he said into his mic. "I'm heading farther back in to investigate. Still no sign of flames."

"Right behind you," Kal said.

He knew his brother would have his back. One or both of them always did.

He was about to turn the corner into a room when he was met face-to-face with a short, masked . . . he had no idea. Woman, maybe? Yeah, definitely a woman. He saw a swinging ponytail. She had a bandanna tied around the bottom half of her face, and he wasn't sure whether she was the owner or whether she was looting the place, because she had her arms filled with what looked like tattoo equipment.

"Get out of my way," she said, then erupted into a heavy cough.

He'd figure out the owner-versus-looter question after he got her out of there. "Fire department, ma'am. You need to vacate the premises."

She shook her head and pushed at him to move him out of her way. "I need to get my stuff."

"Your stuff can wait. We have to get you out."

"I'm not"—she stopped, racked by spasms of coughing—"leaving."

He didn't have time to argue with her, so he started to pull her toward the exit. She resisted, turning back toward the storage room. He tried to draw her in the right direction, but it was obvious they were going to play tug-of-war, and the smoke was getting thicker back there.

He didn't have time to argue with her, so he had no choice but to hoist her over his shoulder and carry her out. Everything she'd had in her arms clattered to the floor.

"What the hell are you doing?"

He didn't bother answering her since what he was doing was obvious. He passed Rafe and Zep.

"Found the source of the smoke," Rafe said. "An electrical outlet short. We've got electrical turned off. They're breaking into the wall now to make sure there's no fire in the walls."

Jackson nodded. "I'm getting her out of here. I'll be back."

"Okay."

"Put me the hell down." She was wriggling, which didn't make his job any easier.

He also didn't intend to let her win this battle no matter how much she fought him.

He made it outside and set her down. She started back inside again. He grabbed hold of her arm and dragged her over to the truck. He pulled his mask off and opened the door where the oxygen was located. EMTs should be showing up soon, and then she'd be their problem. Until then, he needed to give her oxygen.

He put the mask on her face. "Breathe."

"I'm fine." But her body betrayed her by coughing, and her voice was raspy from the smoke.

"Breathe."

She took a couple breaths of oxygen, then pushed the mask away. "Okay. I'm good now."

She tried to get up, but his hand on her shoulder kept her on the bumper of the rig. "You're not going in there."

Her face was smudged gray from the smoke, but she had a gorgeous set of blue eyes, currently glaring up at him. "And you can't stop me."

"Actually, I can. What the hell were you thinking not evacuating at the first sign of smoke?"

"I was thinking that everything I own is in there, and I was trying to get as much of it out as I could before the fire broke out. I would have run like hell if I'd seen flames. I didn't see flames."

She let out a series of deep coughs, so he put the mask on her face again.

"Smoke can kill you, too."

She glared up at him. "I'm alive, aren't I?"

He shook his head. She was one hell of a smart-ass. But at least she was right about one thing.

She was alive.

REBECCA "BECKS" BENNING glanced in misery over at her ruined shop. She was glad she didn't own the building. Of course, if she did, it wouldn't have had the faulty wiring, which had led to this massive disaster of a day.

She'd had three appointments for today, and, since it was Saturday and May, it was a beautiful day to be at the beach. Who knew how many walk-ins she would have gotten for tats or piercings? All that beautiful income literally up in smoke. Likely along with a lot of her inventory. She could already imagine how difficult it would be to clean the smoke off her equipment. Her ink was closed tightly in bottles, so maybe it would be okay, but the cleanup was going to be a nightmare.

And since she lived in the small apartment above the shop, chances were everything in there was also covered in smoke.

She'd deal with it. Hadn't she always managed with whatever happened to her? She'd find a way to come out of this. And if worse came to worst, she'd couch surf with some friends until she could get into her apartment again. It was the work that was going to be a problem. And where was she going to store all her stuff? Sleeping on someone's sofa was one thing. Storing her equipment and finding a place to set up shop in the interim? That was going to be the big issue.

Her mind was whirling, and right now she felt a little dizzy. She leaned forward, letting her hands rest on her knees while she breathed in the oxygen from the mask that the EMTs insisted she keep on. She rested in their rig while she watched the firefighters haul out smoke-damaged pieces of her shop. And with every load, she felt her livelihood slipping away more and more.

"You feeling better, miss?"

She gave a thumbs-up to the very nice EMT with the soft voice whose name tag said ACOSTA. His partner was a cute perky blond chick named Smith.

Grumpy Firefighter seemed to be semi in charge of the others because he pointed and gave instructions to the other guys.

She blamed a lot of her woes on him. She'd had nearly all of her tattoo guns and was on her way out of the shop with them when he'd intercepted her. Then he'd had the audacity to pick her up and toss her over his shoulder like she was some damn damsel in distress or something.

She knew what she'd been doing, and she had tied a wet bandanna over her face to keep from breathing in the smoke. Or at least much of the smoke. And okay, maybe she'd been coughing—a lot. But she'd been on her way out the door. She wasn't stupid. She knew breathing in smoke was dangerous.

She sat up and watched Grumpy Firefighter more closely. Hard to tell what anyone looked like under all that gear. He was nothing more than a yellow-and-red blob right now. But earlier, when he'd jerked off his mask, she'd gotten a glimpse of dark hair and extremely intense gray eyes. He had a nice mouth, too.

Not that she was interested in him that way. But he reminded her of someone from way back when. The old days. The bad days.

One of the other firefighters came up to her. "We need to get some information from you, ma'am," he said.

She grabbed the clipboard and filled out the form, then handed it back to him, studying him as she did. This guy looked familiar, too. Hispanic, dark hair, tan skin, soulful brown eyes, and the most amazing thick, long eyelashes. She used to tease Rafael about his eyelashes all the time. She looked at the firefighter's name tag. It said

DONOVAN. So, no, it wasn't Rafe, because Rafe had a different last name.

"Ma'am?"

"Oh. Sorry. I was just thinking you look a lot like someone I used to know."

The firefighter smiled, his teeth bright and even. "Yeah? Who's that?"

"A homeless kid I used to hang out with. I'd tease him about his long eyelashes. You have those same long eyelashes."

He frowned, then looked down at the form and back up at her. "Rebecca. You ever go by Becks?"

Her stomach dropped. "All the time. Your name wouldn't be Rafe, would it?"

"It would. But this can't be. You sure look different. It can't be you, Becks, can it?"

She knew who she was, but this had to be the weirdest coincidence. She and Rafe had been tight—like the closest siblings. She couldn't begin to hope. "But your last name didn't used to be Donovan."

"And yours didn't used to be—" He looked down at the form again before turning his gaze back to her. "Bennington. Damn. It's really you, Becks?"

Tears sprang to her eyes. "It's really me, Rafe."

He pulled her against him, and a hug had never felt so good. It was like she'd just found her long lost family.

"Hey, we don't hug the victims, Rafe."

A tall well-muscled guy had come around the side of the fire truck. Becks looked at him, and damn if he didn't look just as familiar.

"Kal, this is Becks."

Becks studied the guy as he removed his helmet. She saw brown hair and amazing green eyes.

They'd been the same age when they'd hung out. Last time she'd seen him, he'd been a gangly preteen. He'd grown up. Filled out. Damn, he was handsome now.

"Kal."

"Becks? Wow. You grew up."

"So did you." She couldn't believe two guys she'd been so close to had rescued her today.

Rafe threw his arm around her. "Talk about kismet, huh?"

"Rafe, what are you doing?" Another voice interrupted them.

Rafe pulled away. "Jackson, this is Becks. You remember Becks, don't you?"

Becks turned to stare at Grumpy Firefighter. This was Jackson? The one guy who'd made her twelve-year-old heart go pitter-patter?

Wow. So all three of them had stayed together. And now they fought fires together.

Only Grumpy Firefighter's—Jackson's—brows knit in a frown, and he said the words that made her heart sink.

"No, I don't remember her."

Well, damn.

Jaci Burton's Play-by-Play series

... what's not to love?

Irresistible, ripped sports stars – check ✔

Smart, feisty women – check ✔

Off-the-charts chemistry – check ✔

Intimate, emotional romance – check ✔

Available now from

HEADLINE
ETERNAL

HEADLINE
ETERNAL

FIND YOUR HEART'S DESIRE...